Bride of Alvar

The Redemption Saga, Book 1

Silver Reins

Bride of Alvar

DEDICATION

To those who never give up

Bride of Alvar

Bride of Alvar

ACKNOWLEDGMENTS

I'd like to thank my readers on Wattpad who read the first draft of this book and continually encouraged and loved on my work and my characters. Without you, my Wattpad readers, this book would not have made it to where it has. I'd also like to thank my supportive and gracious family and friends who listened to me go on about my worlds, characters, and philosophical musings. Thanks to my mom who is nothing like poor Lucy's mother, encouraged my writing dream from a young age, and assisted me in editing when I was getting the final draft ready.

Bride of Alvar

PROLOGUE

At the vulnerable age of eight, in the basement of my childhood best friend's house on a cold, late December evening, I shared my big secret for the first time.

Emily Hall's family lived in a two-story colonial in an upscale suburb in Elmhurst, Illinois. Compared to the one-bedroom apartment my mother and I shared, it was the ideal place to play in the winter months.

"What's your boy's name?" Emily asked me.

We'd recently gotten our first Ken dolls for Christmas from Emily's parents. My mother discouraged Barbie dolls, but I'd hidden a secret stash of them at Emily's.

"Mine is named Greg. He's a news anchor. Like Amanda's dad," Emily said.

"Mine's name is Alvar," I announced.

"Alvar?" Emily wrinkled her nose at me. "That's a silly name!"

"What are you talking about? It's a great name!" I declared, defensive of Emily's dig at the person my mother had placed on a pedestal for me since I could talk. "It's the name of my future husband and—"

I covered my mouth with one hand.

Oh-my-gosh! I shouldn't have said that!

My mother had instructed me not to tell anyone, and up until that time I'd ensured my secret didn't get out.

Mom would say, *"Lucy, your life here on Earth doesn't matter. And this is good because it means you don't have to worry about anything. When you're old enough, your life will become a real fairy-tale! The magical king, Alvar, will come and sweep you away to live in his castle with him. Can you imagine, Lucy? A castle! Why will he do that for us you ask? You need to marry him, Lucy, so you can create a treaty with his world for us."*

"What are you talking about?" Emily's tone was hushed, and her expression went from teasing to curious as if my secret were exciting to her... as if I were somehow *special*.

Butterflies came alive in me.

Happiness over the fact that poor, awkward, nobody Lucy could be interesting to her cool, popular friend, bubbled through me. Newfound bravery swelled within me. If anyone could hear about it, Emily, my best friend in the whole world should know.

*Maybe she'll even think **I'm** cool!*

I'd never been the cool girl; my secret kept me bound to sitting on the outside looking in.

"Don't tell anyone, it's supposed to be a secret," I said, and glanced around the playroom, checking if Emily's little brother was hiding behind the pool table or if her parents had left the door open on the stairs.

Emily leaned forward and nodded at me, excited and interested, encouraging my transparency. "Okay," she said, "I promise, I won't tell anyone!"

"My mom told me I'm going to save the world someday by marrying a king called Alvar," I whispered to her.

"A king?" she asked, her eyes wide.

"You know like in those fairy tales you read? Well, they're real! Alvar is the king of another, magical world. There's this portal that connects our worlds and Alvar—"

"Lucy, what the *hell* are you talking about?" Emily interrupted me, using a grown-up swear word for emphasis. She frowned, her eyes widened. "You're not serious... are you?"

"Yeah, I mean, not really..." my voice trails and fear gripped me.

This is why Mom told me not to tell anyone.

I'm so stupid for talking about this.

"No, Emily, I was just kidding! It's just a joke," I said and tried to laugh it off, my heart rate steadily rising as every horrible second after my revelation passed.

Too late to take it back.

"But you *were* serious," Emily said pointedly, fear for my sanity in her eyes, she dropped her dolls and scrambled up off the carpet. "That is really, really weird, Lucy, and I hate to tell you this, but your mom... is a *liar*."

Before sharing my big secret, I'd felt separated from all the other kids. But seeing the reaction on my best friend's face, I learned I was an island, separated from the rest of the world by my mother's insanity and my stupidity in believing her.

ONE

Contrary to a large part of the female population, trying on wedding dresses isn't my idea of a good time. I'm one who hates any sort of spotlight.

However, every prospective bride needs a wedding dress, and I'm a bride. So, here I—unfortunately—am at an upscale wedding dress shop located in downtown Chicago.

Why am I not eloping?

While I sit, waiting for my wedding dress consultant, Victoria, to return with a gown, I fidget with the rubber band I perpetually keep on my wrist to stop myself from going down the rabbit hole of my past.

To make matters worse, everywhere around me are brides excited to try on their gowns with their gushing and over-opinionated mothers.

I'm all too aware of why my mother isn't here, and it's not because she's dead, disabled, or abandoned me.

No, all those reasons would be *way* too normal for my life.

If my Mom were here, she'd tell me I'm making the worst decision of my life to marry Michael Jones. She'd also say that my life and the lives of *everyone on Earth* are at stake by doing it.

For a long time, I'd fought her, trying to reason with her delusions, now I've just accepted it: I live in reality, and my mom doesn't.

Rubberband snap. I'm present.

"Hello? Earth to Lucy!" my best friend, Emily, says, waving a hand in front of my eyes.

"Stop it, Em!" I playfully knock her hand from my view. She's the only one here to watch me sift through gowns.

"You look like we're here to choose a casket for your funeral," Emily says, an exasperated expression on her pretty face. "Smile! We're going to get *the* dress today!"

"Yeah, I know," I mumble.

"What is wrong then?"

"My mom," I say without emotion. I don't cry about it anymore to Emily. Now it's only the internal turmoil, the feeling I'm betraying the woman who raised me whenever I do something for myself, that torments my mind. "She wouldn't approve of Mike."

I hate that this is who I am: Raised a freak because of my mother's madness.

"Yeah, but the important thing is *you* approve of Mike," Emily soothes and hugs me. "And you realize she only doesn't approve because she thinks she promised you to the King of Wonderland before you were born."

"King of Underland actually," I remind her under my breath. You'd think Emily would know by now. We'd talked about it enough over the years.

"Lucy, she is unwell, and remember what your therapist told you? Stop feeling guilty about her delusions and remember the years of emotional abuse," Emily rubs my back. "Look! Victoria's back with the dresses."

"Are you okay, dear?" Victoria asks.

"She just misses her mom," Emily covers for my expression. "Lost her mom when she was six."

I don't stop Emily from lying for me about it is because the truth is stranger than fiction.

"I'm so sorry, dear," Victoria says, she takes me gently by the arm and ushers me toward the changing booth. "Come with me, and we'll start trying on these dresses. You are going to look so beautiful."

Minutes later, I walk out of the dressing room and show off the gown in the mirrors to Emily. My hair is ash brown, my eyes are light brown, and my skin is a subtle tan, dark enough that I don't burn in the sun quickly. I'm not beautiful, but I'm grateful for my under-the-radar appearance. I don't like being noticed in a crowd.

Emily has always said I've got a "girl-next-door" thing going for me, but I'm pretty sure that's her nice way of saying "Plain Jane."

"Oh my gosh, you look amazing! You sexy thing! I wish I looked that good in white!" Emily showers me with embarrassing, over-the-top compliments as best friends are supposed to do when you try on wedding dresses with them.

"I think this is the one," I say, my eyes flickering to the EXIT.

I don't care what I'm wearing so long as I marry kind, uncomplicated Mike, and put the past behind me.

"There is no way you're only going to try on one dress!" Emily laughs at me.

I turn back toward the dressing room in time to see Victoria with another dress on her arm in a bag.

"*He* wants you to try this one on," Victoria says while taking the plastic off of it.

"He who?" I give a half laugh at her randomness.

"Alvar," Victoria says.

"C-can you point him out?" I stutter, swallowing hard and feeling the blood drain from my face.

Alvar is not a common name here in the states... *or* anywhere actually.

"He's over there by the reception desk," Victoria says, nodding in that direction. She pulls the dress out of the plastic, and my eyes widen. "Said he wanted Lucy Hammond to try this dress on for him."

"I can't afford that, Victoria. And did you say *Alvar* told you to put this on me?" I laugh nervously. "I don't know anyone named Alvar."

"Of course you don't," Victoria whispers with a giggle. She gives me a "we know a secret" type of smile. "I won't mention it to your friend. And just so we're clear, Alvar said, don't worry about the price. He will buy it for you. You've got a very generous, very gorgeous 'friend'!" She winks at me.

And now she thinks I'm having an affair.

Despite my mortification and embarrassment, I can't help myself. I let her help me into the exquisite gown.

The strapless corset bodice ends in a dropped waist and is embedded and embroidered with sparkling stones.

Real gemstones?

With shaking hands, I run my fingers over them. I know by touch and quality of the fabric, it has to be expensive. The skirt flows out in a sea of white around me.

My heart pounds in my chest as I look up into the dressing room mirror.

I never thought I could look like a princess until now.

Victoria leads me back to Emily.

The gown flounces in a graceful sway as I walk.

Emily doesn't say anything at first. Her eyes get buggy, and her lower jaw drops a little.

"Wha-what do you think?" I break the silence with a stammer.

I still can't believe I put this luxurious gown on considering the circumstances.

I'll admit, this "Alvar" has good taste.

"It's—like—you're a complete goddess!" Emily's voice gets all gushy, and she circles me studying every angle of the dress. "I've never seen anything so beautiful," she breathes. "*I* would marry you in this!"

"I'll just tell all the guys you're taken then," I tease, trying to lighten my anxiety with a joke.

Emily loves guys. Yeah, that's right. Plural.

When Emily was eleven, she'd had her first "boyfriend" and a fake wedding where I was the maid of honor.

Poor, little Timmy Richardson was the first guy out of many to have his heart broken by her.

I tell Emily I'm getting the dress, but I'm lying. I will not get a dress "Alvar" supposedly picked out for me.

My blood chills just thinking about it.

But who would be so cruel as to play a prank like that on me?

I don't have any "enemies" to speak of. My weird upbringing has left me socially incapacitated besides Emily and Mike.

I thought I put the bullies behind me in High School.

After Emily and I part ways, I drive to the grocery store and can't stop thinking about Alvar's name getting dropped.

So sick! Whoever that was, they're a jerk.

Just when I'm trying to put my past behind me living a lovely, quiet, life married to a regular guy, and have his kids in my rebellion to the way I was raised; someone decides to throw a twist in the knife which is my past.

Well, screw them!

Mike, my fiancé, is a promise of a fresh start for me. Mike and I met in college. When he asked me to marry him, of course, I'd said yes. His proposal felt like my ticket out of Looney-town.

I want stability in my life — stability I'd never had as a child. Mike knows ours isn't a passionate love affair; it's a solid friendship. A comfortable arrangement we're both satisfied with.

At that thought, I call him.

Need anchoring. Rubberband snap!

"What's up?" Mike answers after the second ring.

"Hey, babe," I say.

"How did the dress shopping go?" Mike asks.

"I didn't find one. I'm about to get some groceries," I say, keeping it casual, and realizing I'm too embarrassed to talk about my run-in with Alvar.

"Great, I'm starving," Mike says.

"I take it you're coming over for supper?" I ask him with a laugh.

"Definitely, Lucy," Mike says.

"See you at 5:30 then! Love you!" I say, but not sure I'm all for him inviting himself considering my day.

"Love you too!" Mike says.

I enter the grocery store and hold my list up to my nose for a quick recheck.

Okay. Eggs. Milk. Butter—all the usual suspects.

I head to the back of the store to the dairy section. As I am bending to get a carton of milk someone taps my shoulder, so I jolt, dropping the milk on the floor only to see it split open in a wet crash all over someone's expensive black leather shoes.

"I am *so* sorry!" I exclaim, not sure why I am the one apologizing because they'd been the one who'd snuck up on me in the first place.

"No, I'm sorry for scaring you like that," a deep voice comes from the stranger, sending shivers down my spine.

I look up at the owner of the shoes and heat flushes to my face. In addition to his dark, deep, melted-chocolate voice, he's got a powerful presence. So tall his broad chest is at my eye-level, and he's muscular too.

*Oh. He's one of **those** guys.*

At least that's what Emily terms to dark, mysterious, male strangers who make you uncomfortable for reasons you can't explain.

Suddenly, I'm touching my hair and giving a nervous giggle like an idiot.

I'm a freaking engaged woman! What is wrong with me?

"I'll pay for the milk," he says apologetically.

Besides, his general clean masculine exterior, his face throws me. A thick, intrusive scar lines across his right cheekbone and up over his eyebrow, marring an otherwise sinfully handsome face.

That scar almost goes through his eye! Bet there's a nasty story behind it too. Who would mess with this guy though?

"Oh, there is no need! I shouldn't be so jumpy," I try to recover as gracefully as my socially awkward self allows.

"I thought you were someone I knew," the unreasonably beautiful stranger says.

"Oh," I gasp. Why am I unbearably hot right now?

I'm sure he's going to leave and go about his business and I will never see him again.

Thank goodness, too. Men like him should have nothing to do with mousy librarian-types like me.

Since when has any man made me this nervous?

"I'm pleased to see I was correct. Lucy, forgive me for not saying so, but I'm Alvar," he says, his blue eyes are fixed on me as if I were a work of art. He leans down to my height, lips inches from mine. "Forgive me, but your beauty is captivating, may I kiss you, my bride?"

"How dare you! No—no, you may not!" I stutter, backing away, my head spinning. My feet are unsteady, and I practically trip over a produce kiosk.

"Pity, your lips look so soft," he murmurs, his eyes fixed on them so my hand instinctually rises to cover my mouth.

I'm frightfully aware of how this stranger's words are affecting me in a way I've never experienced, even around my own fiancé.

"However, I don't know much about Earth customs and I can see you wish to keep this formal. I shall respect this. See you again soon, lovely Lucy."

He takes my hand and kisses the back of it.

Like he's stepped out of a fairytale, Prince Charming comes to rescue his fair maiden.

I stare at him dumbstruck. How can this be real? Where his lips touched burns into my hand. He rises and goes on his way, turning into an aisle.

For a moment I stand frozen in place, scrambling to gain back control of myself.

Go after him. Tell him off!

I shake myself awake and hurry after him.

I scan the entire store, but the stranger is nowhere to be seen.

Vanished. Like magic.

The memories come flooding in of my strange childhood. I wouldn't wish my childhood on anyone. The years of isolation and anxiety forced on a young girl whose mother made her believe she was going to save the world by marrying a king are not pleasant.

I'd convinced myself to stop believing in her delusions. Emily had helped me get over them and embrace normalcy.

I pull my phone from my pocket and dial Mike up. I'm too polite not to keep him in the loop on my whereabouts.

"Hi—hi, Mike," I stutter. "I—I was wondering if you can cancel dinner plans with me tonight?"

"Sure," he pauses, then, "Is something wrong?"

"No," I rush, almost interrupting him. "I need some time... alone. I think I am obsessing too much about Mom and—and—"

"I understand," Mike interrupts, "don't worry about it, babe. Have a good night."

"You too." I hang up the phone and slip it into my pocket.

Instead of finishing my shopping, I leave the cart where it is and head straight to my car.

I'm going to hate myself for this, but I need to see my mom.

TWO

"What are you doing here, Lucy?" Mom asks, opening the door to her apartment and stepping aside so I can come in.

Upon seeing my mother in the old apartment I'd grown up in, I'm immediately fighting off my guilt for not visiting her more often.

My mom doesn't take care of herself.

I'm not surprised either because I'd always taken care of us.

Our little home had been drab, but tidy when I'd lived with her. Now unread mail covers the dining table, protein bar wrappers litter the dirty shag carpet, and old cereal boxes sit open on the kitchen countertop.

"I came to talk to you about—" I stop myself. It's so hard to say it. "*Alvar*," his name is managed in a whisper.

"I don't want to talk about it." Mom walks over to the window of her apartment gazing away from me at the rain pattering on the glass in glistening droplets.

"But I *met* him today," I blurt out.

Mom's gaze snaps from the rain to me.

"You *met* him?" Mom says, her tone dripping with sarcasm. She may lack in terms of housekeeping, but dramatics are her forte.

"I am pretty sure I did."

"What did he look like?" Mom's voice is hushed with shock, and perhaps she didn't expect me to be serious about seeing Alvar.

"Tall, with dark hair and blue eyes. Looked no more than thirty-five," I mutter. "There was a striking white scar on his face."

"Just like I remember him!" A tear falls from one of Mom's tired grey eyes.

"Just like *you* remember him? How is that possible?" I cross my arms over my chest, a wall to protect myself from slipping back into her delusional world. I snap the rubber band on my wrist a couple of times.

"His world is so different from ours, including aging and time passing," Mom explains. "But we need his world to be at peace with our world or all we know will be lost."

"You're not telling me he's like a fairy or elf. He's human, right?" The words sound like madness as they escape my lips.

Crap. I can't believe I'm starting to believe in Alvar. It's just all too uncanny.

"I wouldn't be surprised if his people spun many of those beliefs into existence," Mom says with brief amusement crossing her face. "But his world is called Axus, and he rules the most powerful country in that world: Underland."

"I know," I say dryly. It's all coming back. All that I'd pushed from thought to preserve my sanity. I remember Axus, Underland, my wedding plans...

"You know? You *know* now, huh?" Mom gets up from her chair, and she crosses and paces in front of me in her living room, slippers crinkling against the plastic wrappers.

"Uh, Mom, let me—pick that up," I say, out of instinct, I kneel and start gathering up the garbage.

"I would keep this place clean if you hadn't left me as you did!" Mom says, back at her old game of blaming me for all her problems.

"Mom," I say, taking a deep breath. I have to say it though. "I'm getting married."

"You certainly *are* getting married, Lucy! You're getting married to Alvar, and from what you're telling me, it's going to be soon." Mom drops to sit on the old blue sofa we've had for as long as I can remember.

I draw in a deep breath and say slowly, "No, Mom, I'm marrying *Mike*."

She glares at me in disbelief.

As if Mike's the man from another world.

"Who the *hell* is Mike?" her tone sharp and accusing.

"Mike is the friend I introduced you to at my graduation party. The one you freaked out about." I drop the trash.

That's it. Mom will never treat me as an adult. I can't keep doing this to myself.

"Does Alvar know?" Mom asks, snorting at the fluttering wrappers.

"Um, I didn't tell him if that's what you're asking," I say pointedly.

"He mustn't find out you are trying to marry another or everyone you know, everyone you love will be in danger." Mom's face dims white as a sheet. She seems haunted with memories of something I do not know, but the idea of a large, intense man like Alvar causing danger to anyone does not surprise me.

"Sit down, Lucy. I think you need your memory refreshed," Mom whispers, patting the sofa.

I do as I'm told, like I always do, despite every part of me wanting to reject her reality as my own.

"Alvar told me he needed an Earth-human bride to keep peace with our world," Mom begins.

Either we're both crazy, or she's telling the truth.

"I made a promise to Alvar that you were to be his." Mom doesn't look me in the eye while saying this. She stares at her hands folded in her lap and sighs. "You were going to die while you were still in the womb and I told him that if he'd save you—"

"So you promised me to this person before I was born? Is he like the God or something? Having powers like that to save a life?" I ask.

"No, his people have abilities we do not have. Abilities to cause healing," Mom's crying as she talks now. "I explained so many times while you were growing up how I had to save your life even if it meant that..." her voice trails.

"I'll be enslaved my entire life to a dangerous king -- who is way older than me -- who requires a human bride to keep peace with our world?" I finish for her and shake my head. My stomach is churning, and I fear I'm going to vomit. "That sounds like a great life to look forward to if you ask me."

"Some of the people of Axus are not friendly toward humans. Alvar does this so his kingdom cannot attack our world and take it for their own," Mom says. "He is saving us by this diplomacy. His powerful kingdom is in treaty with all other countries in Axus, and if he says not to attack, no one will dare attack."

"I can't be his bride. How do I let him know he needs to choose another because I'm taken now? Sorry, buddy, you are too late," I say, jutting my chin forward.

"You can't be *taken*. You have been his chosen bride for many years. The agreement was for you, and only you, to become his queen at his appointed time," Mom states firmly. "To tell him you are not his bride would be more than a horrible insult to him and his people. It would mean war between them and us." She pauses and sucks in a breath. "And I believe they will win."

How does she know that though?

"So what do I do? What do I tell Mike?" I ask, crossing my arms over my chest. "What do I tell my friends?"

"Your friends?" Mom sniffs. "You mean that bitch, Emily?"

"Mom, you've never liked any of my friends because they didn't believe you and encouraged me not to believe you. Don't you realize how crazy you sounded talking about another world needing a bride from here to keep the peace?

21

How backward and medieval that sounded to every friend I've ever had?"

"They turned you against me!" Mom shrieks back, "I understand it sounded crazy, but everything I ever told you is the truth! Now you believe me because you've seen things you can't explain too. You should have always believed me, Lucy. I'm your mother, but you only believe now because you see!"

There she goes making me feel guilty.

I snap my rubber band, so it hurts.

"Alvar told me I could live in Underland to help you prepare for the wedding and then to live with you," Mom informs me with a triumphant smile. "I couldn't have given you up otherwise."

I don't know if that's supposed to sound comforting, but I don't bother arguing with her. Instead, I ask, "When will that be?"

"Since he's visited you like I said before, it will be soon."

"How soon?"

"I'm guessing within the week since your birthday is coming up," Mom says, giving me an annoyed expression. "I'm done talking."

"Okay." I get up from my seat. "Bye, Mom. I'm-I'm sorry again that it's been so long since we've spoken."

"It doesn't cut it, does it?" Mom says, blinking glassy eyes at me rapidly. "I love you, but you hurt me by not believing me." She stops as her voice choked, and the tears begin to fall. "I don't know if I'll ever be able to forgive you, Lucy."

The words and her expression cut me deep.

I leave her and stumble out the door of her apartment fighting to maintain peace of mind, but it's impossible. My life revolves in a toxic circle I can't get out of: Everyone else guilt-tripping me for believing Mom, and Mom guilt-tripping me for thinking her delusional.

And then that all too familiar feeling of "*I am lost, I don't belong here*" creeps in and holds me captive. I don't *want* to be the bride of Alvar. I didn't choose this. Alvar hasn't even asked me to marry him! Doesn't he know you don't just betroth people in this day and age anymore?

Mike calls me while I'm in the car and I sigh with relief. Mike's comfortable, and what's better, he makes *me* comfortable.

"Hey, are you okay, Lucy?" Mike asks. "You sounded weird on the phone earlier, and I just wanted to check in."

I tense my grip on the steering wheel.

"I don't want to talk right now," I say, pushing all of the madness away, fighting to be with Mike where things are comfortable and stable.

"You visited your mom, didn't you?" Mike asks.

"Yeah." *Damn it, he knows me too well.*

"You shouldn't have done that," Mike rebukes. "I keep telling you. You need to move on from her. You should have talked to *me* before going."

Everyone thinks they can tell me what to do.

Emily. Mom. Mike. Alvar. They all have a plan for me. My entire life is mapped out differently by each of them.

I give a disgusted groan and hang up the phone on him.

All conversation has to stop. I need somewhere quiet to brood. I park by a coffee shop and get myself a latte because coffee is life.

Since I don't want to get back into my car, I perch myself on the curb and watch the cold mist of the late autumn float around an old cornfield the coffee shop faces.

I shiver as I sip down the warmth of my latte.

If Alvar is real, and if he is coming for me, I'll have to leave this, Earth, behind.

This world is everything I know. It is where I grew up.

"Underland is a tropical climate. There is no winter in my kingdom. I believe you'll like it in Underland, Lucy." The voice is familiar.

"Alvar," I say, and notice the man I saw in the grocery store is sitting next to me on the curb. "Where did you go off to?" I dryly ask because my life is a shit-show, I might as well make some humor out of it.

Alvar hands me what looks like an old piece of paper. "Here is the agreement," he says.

On that yellowed paper, in bold black ink are these words:

Under oath to Elias, the God of Light, on this day of Earth, October 10, 1993, and this day of Axus, in the twenty-third day of Havath, 2918, an agreement between Hannah Delaney and King Alvar of Underland, that the female child she carries will be betrothed to the King as his future wife and queen to secure a peace treaty between the realms of Earth and the realms of Axus. On a day after this female child has come of age to marry, King Alvar is entitled to return and retrieve Hannah Delaney and her daughter to reside in Underland, after that, having all their material and personal needs provided for by the nation of Underland as well as the protection of the Underland Guard and instruction from the Institute of Underland in the ways and customs of the people.

My mother's name, as well as Alvar's are signed at the bottom.

THREE

I take another sip of my latte and fold the paper that my mother signed away my rights on so I can put it in my pocket.

I set the latte down and rest my palms on the cement of the curb to lean back and inspect Alvar up and down without shame. Now I'm aware of *who* he is, I believe I'm more than entitled to take a closer look.

He wears dark wash jeans that cling to narrow hips and a simple white button-down that fits his muscular frame incredibly. His thick, wavy, black hair, is styled over his scalp, his strong jawline speckled with a five-o-clock shadow, and blue-violet, otherworldly eyes are visually enticing, but that scar...

What causes a scar like *that*?

An accident? Animal claws? No, it's too clean to be from an animal.

However he got it, it gives me the creeps.

"It's quite unsightly, I know." Alvar's right index finger trails over the scar, he seems to sense my scrutiny. "The Bridge is unpredictable. But I knew it would open on your twenty-second year when I met your mother. That makes this time dangerous for everyone here and time is of the essence to close off Earth from Axus."

Whatever that means.

"I don't know why you think I'll make a good bride for you," I begin with a sigh.

"You are the only one," Alvar answers. "We all have to make sacrifices for our people and the greater good. If it makes you feel any better, it is a sacrifice for me too."

That does not make me feel better.

"Why do you care about Earth humans? If your people dislike us, why do you care about keeping the peace?"

"You don't need to know, you just need to trust me that this is necessary," he says, his hand cups my chin and he turns my face toward him. I can't resist.

I am again under his spell, a spell mixed with attraction and fear. There is something not human about him.

"I have a life here," I muster out in a defiant whisper, my throat tightening. "It's nothing special, but it's mine."

*Lie. I'm flailing about for something, even if it's a small something, to be **mine**.*

"What is your life here like?" His voice soothes, and his calmness is catching. "Do you love this life here?"

Alvar's strange eyes are a place of darkness and light mangled together. He's old for his appearance, and I find myself wondering what his sad eyes have witnessed.

"I—I can't love it. There is no certainty about anything. There has never been," I hiss. "My life is in chaos!"

"Chaos?" the word seems to strike an interest in him, he leans forward, his finger traces along my jaw. "For that, I apologize, Lucy. I promise I'll make you *very* comfortable as my queen."

"Comfortable?" I snort. "*You're* the reason I have no certainty and why I can't live my life," I say.

"I believe you will love *me*, Lucy," his tone is sincere but holds frightening darkness to it. It says nothing of his love for *me*. "I will give you more than you could ever dream as my queen!"

"How dare you assume I'll love you?" I yank myself from him, "You don't even know me!"

"You haven't taken him to your bed, have you?" Alvar says as if he can read me like a book.

Nice to know I look like a virgin.

"That's none of your business," I say through gritted teeth, blushing so hard I'm sure my face will burn off.

"Even if you have, I want you to know that it is my duty to marry you and I will honor you and your desires as your husband," Alvar states.

My mouth hangs open, and I gawk at him. He deserves it, talking about us as if we are a duty-bound couple in a medieval fairy-tale.

Mike had put the abstinence rule into place early on in our relationship, and he explained his reasoning was he wanted our first time to be special. His family frowned upon sex before marriage.

I'd liked this *just fine* considering my background, and I'd never felt the urge to break his rule with him.

Before Mike, I hadn't had a single boyfriend in High School because Mom forbade it. She'd hammered down strict precautions from an early age to ensure I remained "pure" because I was "promised to Alvar."

Every talk Mom had given me about sex included Alvar in the picture.

Needless to say, sex and romance have equaled the most uncomfortable topic for me. To this day Emily still teases me about my virgin status.

"I see the fear written on your face, but do not worry. I know you didn't believe I existed until you saw me, Lucy," Alvar says assuredly, patting my hand. "But I must confess I had no idea how beautiful you were going to be." I can sense the warmth of his hand, and it prickles to life a sexual awareness for which I loathe him.

Stop feeling attracted to him, I internally tell my body, *this shouldn't feel like a connection. It should be creepy.*

"In three days, I will come for you. You have till then to tell your friends goodbye."

In a flash of light, his presence leaves me.

I have no idea what is going to happen, but defying someone whom most people don't know exists isn't going to be difficult.

All of Mom's talk of him being powerful and able to destroy humankind doesn't make sense. If that were true wouldn't it be obvious his realm existed? Wouldn't there be records of previous wars with his world?

I get off the curb and head back to my car.

I want a stable, sensible life.

I'd never had that growing up, and Alvar promises nothing of it.

He won't give me a choice.

He doesn't have the right to tell me what to do!

Who does he think he is? He's arrogant, controlling, loathsome, and he doesn't own me!

"I won't marry him," I declare to myself while driving my car back home and add louder in case he somehow can hear me, "I'm not going to be your puppet, Alvar!"

I arrive home and see Mike's car in my apartment's parking lot. I roll my eyes, but I'm also relieved.

Thanks, Mike, for coming to my rescue.

"What are you doing here?" I ask.

Mike is lying back on the couch watching an episode of a crime series and munching on popcorn. His dark blonde hair styled in a tousled look that suits him and he flashes me a huge smile. He's only a couple inches taller than me, and his teeth are crooked, but they add to the awkward charm he possesses.

The face of someone I'm attached to.

"You sounded really down, and I wanted to surprise you," he says, "popcorn?" He holds out a handful toward me.

"No thanks."

Mike bends down next to the couch, and I hear the crinkle of paper.

"What's that?" I ask.

He holds out a bottle of wine. "It's the good stuff, Lucy. I figured you needed it."

"Which is another way of saying, 'not cheap'?" I cock an eyebrow and grin vaguely.

Mike chuckles. "I shouldn't have scolded you about your mom. It's your choice, not mine."

"Thanks, Mike," the urge to sob in relief at his sweetness overwhelms me. This guy has held the position of my buddy since before we even went out. During our time at college he didn't care about my Mom being crazy and the emotional baggage I'd accumulated from it. Like Emily, he'd stuck with me through all the strange.

"You're great. I love you," I murmur, and embrace him close to me.

He pours the wine into two glasses and hands me one.

"To us!" He cheers, tapping glasses with mine.

"Yes!" I drink the glass as quickly as possible.

"Whoa! Slow down, girl!" he warns me. "Wow, today must have been bad! I should have bought some boxed stuff instead of an expensive Pinot if you're going to drink like that!"

"You can say that again," I grumble dryly.

"I'm so sorry, sweetie," he says and pulls me in for a kiss. With his lips pressed to mine, I close my eyes, but then Alvar asking to kiss me starts replaying in my mind. I involuntarily wonder what kissing a man like Alvar would have felt like for me.

No, I don't want to know what kissing Alvar feels like! Why am I thinking such a messed up thought?

I draw back from Mike abruptly, practically pushing him off of me.

"What was that about?" Mike asks, hurt crossing his face.

Too bad he doesn't miss anything.

"Sorry, I'm—uh—just really tired after everything that happened today. Not feeling up to making out." I might as well be honest with him.

The timer beeps from the kitchen.

"The pizza's done!" Mike says.

"I'll get it," I say, trying to escape the awkwardness of the situation. I open the oven door and in my distraction grab the pizza pan without an oven mitt.

"What are you doing?" Mike shouts, making me jump. "You'll burn!"

"Oh!" I let go of the hot pan in surprise, and it drops on top of my oven with a clatter.

Mike hurries over to the sink and turns on the cold water. He grasps my hand and it under the stream.

32

"Let me see," Mike says, concern furrowing his brow.

I splay my fingers and wave my hand in front of his face. "See? Not even a mark," I say with a laugh, "I'm okay."

After dinner, Mike prepares to leave.

"You sure you don't want me sticking around?" Mike pulls me into his arms while we stand at my door. "You know, our wedding is getting really close. I *know* I am marrying you. How 'bout we do something fun tonight? Something we've *never* done before."

He means sex.

At that moment, I stare up at him, wondering what it would be like to actually go through with it with Mike, and I can't picture it. My body isn't responding. My hands splay on his chest, and I kiss his neck.

No fireworks.

I hadn't even touched Alvar, and an electric current had seemingly buzzed between us.

And now, I'm thinking about sex with Alvar. My psychologist would have a field day.

"No, Mike, let's wait," I say, carefully removing myself from his arms with a smile, "We're so close to getting married."

"I never thought *you'd* be the one who'd make us stick with the abstinence thing," Mike mumbles with disappointment.

Why don't I want him as he wants me right now?

We've snuggled on the couch during every movie or football game, and we've had some make-out sessions that ended in Mike—um—losing himself in his pants. So why am I hesitant about going all the way now?

I should defy Alvar by doing this with Mike, but I don't want sex with Mike.

I want to be Mike's friend, not his lover.

Which means I shouldn't be marrying him.

"Okay, goodnight, babe." He leaves me with a peck on the cheek and a confounded expression on his face.

In the silence of my empty apartment, all of it sinks in: My mom wasn't crazy. Alvar is real and coming for me in three days. My young adult life, my education, my job, my relationships…all of them are meaningless here if Alvar is genuinely going to whisk me away to a completely different world. All of my hard work in being a "normal" person has amounted to nothing!

And besides all of that, I shouldn't marry Mike because I have more chemistry with a complete stranger than with Mike.

Oh, my poor Mike, how am I going to tell him that his future with me is impossible even if Alvar hadn't come for me? How will I tell Emily that my mom really isn't crazy and there really is a magical king coming to take me away?

I unfold the agreement Alvar gave me and read it over and over until my frustration over the lack of control in my life bubbles over and I rip the damned thing up and throw it in the garbage.

After that, the rest of that wine Mike brought becomes my friend.

*

"Lucy, Lucy!" someone is saying my name.

"Mmm?" I groan, covering my ears at the painfully shrill sound. My head hurts. It's as if a ton of bricks rests on my forehead.

"Lucy, are you ready for the best bachelorette ever?"

It's Emily?

Come to see me wake up with an embarrassing hangover.

I hear a bunch of giggles.

Correction: not just Emily.

Crap.

I'm still wearing the clothes I'd worn yesterday, and it's times like these that I wonder why I'd ever given Emily a key to my place.

I roll onto my back and focus blearily on the group standing around me.

What time is it anyway? I've never gotten drunk like that before. I'm usually the one glass-of-wine-at-a-party kind of girl.

"What are you doing here?" I moan, rubbing my head to ease the pain.

"Here's some water," one of the girls hands me a glass.

Who even is that? I think I sat by her once in a college class. What is she doing at a party for me?

"I'm not even going to ask why my friend who never drinks has a hangover because we don't have time! We're giving you your bachelorette party!" Emily is grinning from ear to ear. It dawns that all of Emily's friends from college are dressed in skimpy bachelorette party outfits.

"I told you nothing too over the top," I croak instead of speaking the words as I sit up.

"I'm not doing anything over the top, Lucy. No male strippers, no penis decorations—" Emily begins with a huge grin.

"Okay, I get it," I say, my cheeks flush, and I silence her from going on, "My virgin ears can't take it!"

"We're taking you bowling first," one of the girls' chimes with a giggle at my comment about being a virgin.

"Isn't it a little early for bowling?" I ask, not sure if I can stand up, let alone hold a bowling ball.

"It's already 2 p.m., Lucy!" Emily says with a laugh, she grasps my hand and drags me out of bed. "Now, C'mon! Let's get you into something slutty!"

FOUR

The restrictively tight red dress Emily somehow scrounged up for me is quite impractical for bowling. Things get better when Emily takes us to a fancy Italian place where, after a glass of champagne and some friendly encouragement, I loosen up a bit.

All of us head back to my apartment for the rest of the night to open gifts and play silly bachelorette party games.

The presents are quite predictably scandalous and sexual: lingerie, a sexy dice game, and even a pair of pink fuzzy handcuffs.

I try to laugh with them, but even with champagne dulling my senses, it's hard to enjoy it all. Overthinking about my sexual future is enough to send my brain into a panicked frenzy.

"What did you think?" Emily asks after everyone has left.

"I had fun," I say with a forced smile, striving to keep my doomed outlook a secret. Emily isn't the best person to share fantastical stories with as I well know.

"I know you're worried about something. You've seemed kind of lost today. Is it your Mom again? Is it about the gifts?"

"Yeah, Emily, it's about my mom," I lie, "but there isn't anything you can do."

"You have three days to tell Mike and your friends goodbye."

What a nice guy for giving me a whole three days!

"Emily, I am thankful for our friendship." I hold her tight in our hug.

"You're welcome, love you," Emily says. She lets me go and turns to the door. "See you later, Lucy."

See you later.

The door closes behind her and my phone buzzes with Mike calling me.

I can't pick it up, and I watch helplessly as my phone rings out his number, snapping the rubber band on my wrist until there's a red line on my skin.

My door opens, and I jolt.

Thankfully it's just Emily, and not Alvar coming to get me.

"I forgot my scarf." Emily smiles apologetically.

"Oh, here," I mumble and take her into the living room.

"I can't believe how cold it's getting out there," Emily says, she picks up her scarf.

The sound of shattering glass in my bathroom causes both of us to jump and scream. We snap our gazes into the direction of the noise.

Holy crap, someone just broke through my bathroom window!

The lights flicker and shut off. We're surrounded in darkness, and my unadjusted eyes can't see anything.

Heavy footsteps sound from the bathroom.

There is more than one person in my house.

I stumble panicked in the dark toward my front door and fumble for the knob.

"We know you're in here, filthy Earth human," a scratchy male voice calls. "Now don't do anything stupid."

I bring my phone to my face, the phone illuminates the door, and I attempt to dial 911 with shaking hands.

"There you are!" A deep voice exclaims, and I hear Emily scream.

"Let go of me! Lucy! LUCY!" Emily's cry comes from the right of me. I shine my phone light in her direction to see two twisted monster-like creatures grabbing my friend by her arms.

"Shut up and come quietly, bride of Alvar," one of the creatures orders. His pointed teeth glint in the light of my phone as he speaks to Emily.

"*What* are you? What's is hap—?" Emily screams, but her voice abruptly stops when a flash of light illuminates the room. For a fleeting second, I see the three figures more clearly; two large menacing ones and one small, struggling Emily figure. Then it falls dark, and their presence vanishes, much like Alvar had.

"Emily!" I scream and start toward the empty space left behind, grasping at air.

My phone falls from my grasp as I trip over something in the dark.

"Nine-one-one, what is your emergency?" I hear from the phone on the floor.

Someone grabs my hand, and I hit and scream at whoever has caught me.

The monsters must be back for me!

Despite my kicking, I am pulled up from the floor to find myself face to face with Alvar.

"We must go," he says gruffly, his expression intense, worried.

"Emily," I cry, gasping for breath, the shock hitting me and constricting my lungs in panic. "Where's Emily?"

"You must come with me earlier than expected. I apologize if you haven't yet said your goodbyes," Alvar's voice is wooden. His eyes shine a fiery red.

I blink up at him. *What the—?*

Alvar touches my forehead with a glowing white crystal and wraps his arms around me.

My world explodes into white oblivion. A rush of cold makes me cling to Alvar for warmth.

We're suspended in a cold black space, with lights passing us.

"Where are we?" My voice holds no echo to it at all.

This is freaky. The silence of this place makes my spine tingle.

"The Bridge," Alvar whispers, he holds me tighter. "We are about to enter Underland. I need you to keep holding onto me as tight as you can."

I roll my eyes at him. "Isn't that convenient for you?"

"Oh, you think I'd use this as an excuse to hold you close to me?" Alvar asks with a snort of annoyance. "I'm not that desperate or hopeless, Lucy. I only say this because if you are lost in the Bridge, you are lost forever."

"Where is Emily?" I can't stop thinking about her or her screams of horror.

"Emily?"

"Some of your goons took her," I accuse, realizing I'd just used the word "goons" and wondering whom on Earth uses that word except me. Then I start thinking how I'm probably not on Earth anymore, so it doesn't matter.

"I didn't send anyone to take her, so I haven't the faintest idea what you are talking about," Alvar says, giving me a confused, concerned expression.

"You don't know?" I bite my lip and start trembling.

Emily, who took you then?

Wait.

They'd called her a bride, hadn't they?

"Oh my gosh! They thought Emily was me!" I exclaim.

"How do you mean?" Alvar asks.

"They called her bride of Alvar!" I exclaim, "Why would they say that if they hadn't come from your world?"

"Maggort!" Alvar growls, his eyes turn to fiery red glass.

What is up with that?

"What is going on with your eyes?"

"My eyes?" He looks down on me, eyes blazing.

"Your irises are *bright* red?" I say, "They're freaking me out."

Alvar ignores my statement and raises the crystal upward. A circular window appears ahead of us. It's a circle of darkness compared to the white space of the Bridge.

"The planet of Axus is very different from the planet of Earth, but it has enough similarities such as gravity and atmosphere that the transition shouldn't be too difficult for you," Alvar informs cryptically.

We launch into the portal and fall together onto a soft landing of velvety grass.

"Whoa," I say, panting and staring up at the sky.

We're on our backs in a field. Above us, two moons shine brightly in the night. One of the moons is lavender in color and shaped like an oval, and the other is white and the same size and shape of Earth's moon. Stars spatter the clear purple night sky. A warm breeze whisks my disarrayed hair from my eyes.

I struggle to believe I'm no longer on Earth, but on the grounds of Axus, Alvar's world.

"They are beautiful," Alvar says, our hands clasped together as he stares up at the moons wistfully. For some reason, I don't want to let go of his hand. "The lavender moon is named Arlith, and the white is Vesp. After two goddesses of old."

"It's unreal," I murmur, inhaling deeply. The air is lighter than Earth's. A pleasant aroma wafts around us, a mixture of fragrant spices, and early morning dew.

"Welcome to Underland, Lucy, the southernmost country in Axus and my kingdom," Alvar whispers in my ear. "All of this land you will be the mother of as my queen."

"It's different than I expected," I murmur. "So beautiful and strange." My awe is cut short by the horrible memory of Emily's screams. "Who is Maggort and why did he want Emily—uh—me?"

"A gobli lord. He lives in the mountains of Ferar in Goblia. He wants you because he does not wish for peace nor does the queen who sent him," Alvar says.

Alvar drops my hand and sits up, scanning the horizon ahead of us.

I note his eyes are back to blue-violet color, but I'm now too afraid to question him about it.

"Right now, he most likely believes he has the bride," Alvar says, "Sadly, the queen will know otherwise when she sees Emily. Once she learns she doesn't have you; she will kill your friend."

No, no, no! Please, let her live.

"Kill?" I squeak out, and my lip starts to quiver.

"Fear not, Lucy. We can save her if we seal our marriage. Once I marry you, killing Earth humans will be a crime against Underland. Remora does not want war with me," Alvar says. "We must perform the wedding before they discover they have the wrong bride."

"How much time before the ceremony, and how do I know you didn't set this whole thing up to get me to marry you right away?" I say dryly.

"You won't know." Alvar shrugs, not sugar-coating a thing. "But it truly is the only way. Once we marry, I will order Emily's freedom and have her brought to Underland City."

"And if I marry you, and find you to be lying, our marriage is null!" I snap.

"Fair enough," Alvar says with a grin, probably because he knows he's got the more powerful hand in this twisted game life has placed us in.

"When I get her back, can I send her home to her family and friends?" I ask. It would be what Emily wants. I can't imagine Emily outside of her vast social circle.

"She must stay here," Alvar says without emotion. "I will give her a job as one of your attendants if you wish."

"What if I don't marry you, could we get her back if I don't?"

"I'm sorry, but that is unlikely," Alvar says, "Remora knows I don't have a claim to Emily's life, and she despises humans." Alvar motions for me to get up and continues to search around us. "Shasti should be waiting for me."

"Shasti?"

"My mytonir," Alvar explains.

"Your what?"

"They are like your Earth horses, only much faster. You might have trouble riding it in that outfit you're wearing," his gaze turns to me, and he cocks an eyebrow as if noticing my slutty get-up for the first time. "You do look quite enticing, Lucy, but I doubt you were wearing that for *me*... waiting to meet that fiancé of yours?"

Why? You jealous?

"Has anyone ever told you that you're kind of a dick?" I ask.

"I'm a realist," Alvar says with a shrug. "If that makes me a dick, so be it."

"You can jump *dimensions*, but you haven't invented a non-organic form of travel here?" I say, trying to find my own jab.

"As far as I know, your Earth vehicles cause pollution and are ruin your planet's atmosphere, besides, mytonirs are very *fast*," Alvar says with a challenging smirk. He takes a whistle out of his pocket and blows into it.

The mytonir equivalent to a dog whistle?

He extends a hand down to me. "Come. Get up."

"Yes, my king," I say dryly, taking his hand.

Alvar wasn't lying about mytonirs being fast. In the time it takes for him to pull me up from the grass, a creature appears beside us.

The best way to describe a mytonir is to think: horse mixed with a greyhound or cheetah, cloven-hoofed, lithe, long-legged, and deep-chested, with a smooth-coated body.

Shasti's mane and tail are long, and her white coat is covered in black stripes. She trustingly places her long face against Alvar's chest. She is wearing a glossy black leather bridle and saddle. Her ears are elongated, and four horns decorate her forehead in a beautiful curl against her scalp.

"She's beautiful," I murmur, my eyes wide.

Alvar hands me the whistle. "Call your mytonir."

"My mytonir?" I blink at him.

"I give him to you as my wedding gift," Alvar says. "Titan will serve you well."

"Titan?"

"That is his name." Alvar nods, and points to the whistle. "Now call him to you."

I take the small instrument to my lips and blow.

I hear a whinny and turn around to see a mytonir standing behind me. His horns are slightly larger than Shasti's, and his build thicker.

"Hello, Titan," I say, unable to help a smile. *This beautiful, strange creature belongs to me?*

Titan leans his head into my chest just as Shasti had done to Alvar. He wears the same bridle, and saddle Shasti wears over his silky blue-silver body.

Is this even real?

"What do you think? Do you like him?" Alvar asks as if he hopes he's finally given me something positive to hold onto.

"I love him," I impulsively say.

My hand runs over his neck to find his coat is like silk beneath my fingers.

"You ride mytonir's like earth horses, your mother told me that wouldn't be a problem, she gave you lessons," Alvar says.

I nod.

"Now. Let's go home," Alvar says.

Your home, not mine.

I don't know what else to do, so I mount Titan and sit upright in his comfortable saddle.

Alvar mounts Shasti and pats the side of her muscled neck.

"Secure yourself to Titan," he says, pointing to a strap hanging from my saddle. "The speed of a mytonir is much faster than an Earth horse. Only experienced riders can stay on without a harness."

I do as I'm told and place the strap around myself.

"Titan will follow Shasti so do not worry about steering him just yet. Hold on."

"Okay," I say, leaning down on him to brace myself.

"Kom-rak!" Alvar shouts. The word is foreign to me, and I hope beyond hope people speak a language I can understand here.

Before I have time to ask him what that means, my body jolts as Titan goes after Shasti.

We rush over the fields, and I'm sure we're traveling as fast as a car on the interstate. The wind blows my hair in all directions and over my eyes. I fight to breathe.

In the distance, a great wall appears, and by the way it approaches, I am sure we are about to run right into it. However, Shasti and Titan's unnatural halt at the gate entrance is smoother than expected.

Alvar takes the glowing gem he'd used to cross the Bridge and holds it out at the gate. The gate opens, and he motions his hand for me to follow him.

Inside the gate is an organized town with street lamps lit by strange blue lights that cast a blue sheen on everything.

Seeing Underland City for the first time is more than just a shock to my system.

I struggle to believe I'm *here*.

The buildings lining the white cobblestone streets are made of similarly pristine white rock with dark slate roofs. All of them are uniform in appearance. Besides the click of the mytonir's hooves, it's almost eerie how quiet the streets are. Not a soul is out of their home, but I know there must be people residing in them as some of the houses have lights glowing from their circular windows.

"Where is everyone?" I ask him.

"The curfew," Alvar says cryptically.

"Curfew? There's a curfew here?" I ask, confounded by such an idea. "Why would there be a curfew? Are the streets not safe?"

"Well, homes are the safest place late at night like this," Alvar explains, "It's a safety precaution and not law."

"What do you mean, 'safety precaution'?" I ask.

"There is a dark creature that shadows them from the skies. A creature that sees in the night better than we can," Alvar mutters quietly.

"Should I be afraid of it?" My voice has hushed to a whisper as a chill crawls up my back.

"No, you are with me and with me you are safe," Alvar whispers back. "The creature is not apt to hurt anyone anymore. Still, my people are rightfully cautious."

"So why do *you* travel without bodyguards?" I ask him, suddenly curious, "You are the king, right? Doesn't the king need protection?"

Alvar smiles vaguely at this as if he finds my question amusing. "I have no need of bodyguards, Lucy. My guards stay in the palace, and around the gates where they have a better use than by my side."

I'm not getting anywhere with this conversation, even though I find his dodging my questions suspicious.

"You're working hard to make me like you," I say flatly.

"That's odd because I wasn't trying to make you like me," Alvar says with a shrug. "Besides, you're determined not to."

"Why would I like you? Don't you care at least a little about what *you did* to me? If you did it would be easier to like you," I mutter.

"It must have been quite difficult, growing up apart from everyone else," Alvar says quietly. "I apologize for the distress it caused you, but it was all necessary to save this world and yours from devastation. Sometimes, we have to do things we don't want to for the greater good."

I roll my eyes and say nothing because I hate to admit it, but after everything I've endured today, I'm beginning to believe him.

FIVE

As we near the city center, the houses become grander, and at the end of the street is a magnificent gate with giant gold columns on either side. Ornate carvings of angelic figures lit up by huge lamps line the city streets.

"Once we go through the gates you will be introduced to my chief of the house, Fletch," Alvar says formally. "Be polite. He is a gobli, but nothing like the fiends you met at your apartment. Fletch is a dear friend and a person of great power here. He acts as regent whenever I'm away."

We approach two watchtowers on either side of the columns. Alvar signals to one of the guards on duty and a door opens at the base of one of the towers so our mytonir's can trot through.

The mentioned, Fletch, is not what I expected. Short, with long pointy ears, and skin covered in what appear to be warts, it's hard not to do a double-take. I can't make out the actual color of his skin in the blue light of the lanterns, but his frame is stout as much as it is short, and his nose is large and hooks at the end. He wears a smart tunic with a belt.

"Alvar," Fletch says with a grin, exposing dozens of pointy teeth. I try not to lean away from the little gremlin of a person. So often, I'd seen creatures similar in appearance to Fletch portrayed in fiction and movies as the baddies.

I can't quite shake that unfortunate mental stereotype.

Dammit, does this make me an innate racist here?

"Fletch, it is good to see you." Alvar grins back at him. "I trust everything went smoothly while I was away?"

"Yes," Fletch huffs out the word, he gazes up at me with two beady black eyes. "You brought back the earth maiden in one piece I see?"

"Just barely," Alvar says dryly. "Maggort made a plan to abduct her, but he took the wrong woman."

"Maggort?" Fletch growls the name. "I can't believe his gall. Did he think you'd look upon him kindly for such an act? Perhaps you can dethrone Remora for it."

"She'll claim it was Maggort's doing and not under her orders," Alvar mutters. "Sadly, it will be impossible to prove her wrong."

"Aye," Fletch mutters and spits in disgust.

I try to stop gawking at Fletch. He's so different than anything I've seen, and so real at the same time. Despite that realism, I half expect him to unzip himself from a costume.

If this is all a dream, I've quite the imagination.

"Hm, she's quiet," Fletch says about me with a laugh. "Do you have a tongue, Sweetheart?"

"Sweetheart?" I raise my eyebrows.

"So, she does speak!" Fletch says, clapping his hands, laughing more. He steps up next to Titan, extending a clawed hand toward me. His hands and forearms are larger in proportion to his body than human hands. "Come on down off Titan, and I'll take you to your quarters. I am sure his majesty, King Alvar, is tired after such a journey and will need to *recuperate*." He shoots Alvar a secretive-type expression.

Huh?

"Aye," Alvar sighs, closing his eyes and rubbing his temple. "That would be most excellent. Thank you, Fletch. See to it she finds her way and is comfortable."

"Aye, sir." Fletch salutes.

I'm hesitant.

"Sweetheart, get off the pretty pony and let's go," Fletch says, waving his hand for me to get down.

"And, Fletch," Alvar adds.

"Yes, sire?"

"Be nice to her. She's not used to any of this, you know." Alvar winks at me with a smile and dismounts Shasti. The mytonir follows him to the stable.

Of all the—!

I can't believe Alvar is leaving me like this!

I get off of Titan and cling to his bridle; as of now, Titan is the only thing with which I am familiar.

"Don't be afraid of me," Fletch assures. "I may appear wicked to you, but I haven't got a wicked bone in my body. I promise." His voice is gentle, sincere.

"Al-alright," I stammer. "I'm sorry.... sorry."

"Take a deep breath, Sweetheart. Don't worry; you'll get used to it," Fletch says. He walks inside the gate, and I follow him with Titan. The gate closes behind us.

"Alvar mentioned a flying creature that comes out at night here," I say. I know I'm trying to make conversation out of nervousness, but it helps.

"There is," Fletch mutters, his voice mysteriously masking all emotion. "But it won't be out tonight."

"Oh, good," I say awkwardly.

At a loss for words, I step into the courtyard of the palace. A babbling fountain with lights highlighting the water's movement and vibrantly colored fish living under the surface is in the center of the yard. Lush tropical greenery and more angelic statues are but a few of the lovely touches found in this mystical space.

A pale human male dressed in a white tunic walks up to us, bows, and takes Titan from me without a word. I gaze after Titan, but Fletch directs me through the courtyard.

"You will need new clothes. We will have you dressed as a proper Underland beauty soon," Fletch tells me with a cock of his warty eyebrow.

"You must realize how relieved we are that you're finally here," Fletch continues. "Earth is not ours to take now because of you. Once the Bridge was discovered, there were those here who would give anything to leave this world and start a new life in yours. There are many disagreements among our peoples here in Axus. Not as many as there used to be, mind you, but that does not mean things are stable here. Alvar saved Underland and most of Axus, but there are still those who challenge him. They try to rouse up a disorder for the sake of their claims to power. Maggort is among them. He believes in the old ways of Underland during dark times. Built on the backs of slaves. Selfish, ruthless, and immoral like Saul."

"You do realize I have no idea who this Saul-person is," I say, trying to take it all in, hoping this information he's telling me isn't essential for later. I wish I had more time to process everything. All I know is I don't *want* to be involved in some cosmic battle.

Why couldn't some other girl be *the* one promised to Alvar?

"You will have time to learn everything you need to know, but first, you should rest. Going over the Bridge is always exhausting. I hear tell," Fletch chortles.

"Follow me up this stair, and we'll be upon your private quarters in the Underland palace. Alvar studied Earth to try and make you more comfortable here. Your lessons will begin tomorrow," Fletch explains.

"Lessons?" I ask.

Apparently going back to school too.

"Lessons in history, customs, languages, and your duties as Alvar's queen," Fletch explains, and he leads me through a hall lined with artwork.

I think of Emily as we walk. If I'm frightened seeing the "good" side of Underland than how must *she* be faring?

I glance at some of the artwork lining the gallery and am captured by how many different peoples are depicted: Individuals with wings and feathers like birds, deer-like people, gobli, humans, and mermaid-looking people.

Do they all exist here? Are all the fairy-tales I've heard real in some way?

Another significant piece of art shows a fearsome black dragon with red eyes. It's breathing fire savagely at a crowd of people. The people in the painting are fleeing in terror, some of them have caught on fire, and others already burned to death.

"That one was commissioned by Saul. It was meant to strike fear. It's of a Cursed," the gobli grunts in passing.

"Cursed? That looks like a dragon."

"No, a Cursed is unnaturally indestructible, a supernatural being," Fletch explains with a shrug. "Drakon, which is our word for dragon here, are beasts that can be killed. Cursed look like them, but they aren't the same."

"Oh." *Indestructible?*

There goes my rubber band again.

Fletch opens a door at the end of the hall. "Welcome to your chambers, Miss Lucy."

Wow.

SIX

My footsteps against the spotless marble floors echo into the high ceilings of the expansive living area I'm to call home.

The whole room glows a heavenly white and gold. The lighting, the indulgently funded furniture, the embroidered curtains... all of it glitters in the arlite lanterns.

*No expense was spared when he prepared this place for me. My whole apartment could fit into this living room **twice**.*

"Good sylph, Leeza!" Fletch calls into the expanse. "The bride of Alvar has arrived!"

The sound of nails clicking on the floor indicates Leeza doesn't have human feet and also isn't wearing shoes.

The person who enters through a door at the back of my living room is one of the bird-like people I'd seen in the paintings.

A crest of vibrant yellow feathers grows from the bridge of Leeza's human-like nose and up over her forehead. Black feathery hair falls down her shoulders with hints of yellow downy feathers in her tresses. Leeza's feet resemble bird feet more than human feet. However, she's surprisingly not chicken-legged as very human-like calves and thighs make up her legs. She walks on four toes with curved talons at the end of each, and on the back of her heels is one longer toe with another talon. She wears a yellow dress that opens up in the back for the angel-like wings coming from between her shoulder blades. Her wings are the same vibrant yellow as the feathers coming from the crest on her head. Her skin is rich milky chocolate in color.

Leeza bows to me.

Fletch gives my hand a reassuring pat. "I'll leave you to it then, Lucy."

"As the good regent, Fletch said, my name is Leeza, I am a sylph," this bird-human tells me in a voice with a lilted accent after Fletch takes his exit. "I have prepared your room for you. Would you like to sleep?"

"Uh—" I can't get anything else out.

"You are unfamiliar with the sight of me," Leeza says, she extends her wings out. Now I see there is a mixture of purple in her base feathers. It's breathtaking. It makes me think of a tropical bird, like a parrot or bird-of-paradise.

"I'm a sylph," Leeza continues, "Our people rule the skies. We come from the Skylands of the south. When Alvar set our people free from the tyranny of Saul some of us decided not to return home. We stayed to work for the good king."

"I do not mean to stare," I say to her. "I'm sorry. I did the same with Fletch."

"Tis alright. I am to instruct you in our history, peoples, and customs," Leeza explains with a warm smile. "But first… you must be tired, your highness. Come with me I shall prepare you for bed."

She bows her head and motions for me to follow her.

"Your first lessons tomorrow will be on proper etiquette as a queen of Underland," Leeza continues. "I will teach you how you are to behave during the wedding ceremony too. I'm told it's in a few days, which should give us plenty of time."

Leeza walks me down the hall and into an expansive, elaborately decorated bedroom. The bedding and linens are gold and white. A fireplace with a glistening white marble mantel glows warmly, and a large white fur rug lies across the floor. The bed is so massive I figure I'll get lost in my sleep.

"Alvar will join you in here on the wedding night. He directed that you are not to go to his quarters unless summoned or you've requested, and he's approved," Leeza is explaining everything so fast, but that last statement has me afraid.

*But how could he come here on our wedding night? Does he expect me too—after only just **meeting** him?*

My face and hands get cold, and I pull the rubber band on my wrist like crazy.

Nope. Nope. Nope.

I want to scream. I want to cry. I want to—*go back to Earth*!

"I don't know how it is here, but in my country, from where I come from, women have a say in who they sleep with," I blurt out.

"I'm sorry. I had no idea of your feelings on this!" Leeza coos, she's caught in how distressed I am, and now she seems emphatically worried about me. "I'm sorry I said all of that without realizing this! You should talk to the king. He is a compassionate man, and he'll understand your feelings if you wish not to marry."

"I'm not sure what to think anymore," I say. "I just need some time to think about all of this." I can't let Leeza think I won't marry Alvar, mainly because Emily's life depends on it.

My stomach growls, hunger mixed with stress is a terrible combination.

"Is there any food? I'm kind of shaky," I ask.

"There is indeed much food for you to eat!" Leeza assures. "Shall I get you some?"

I nod.

Leeza presses a button on the wall, and promptly a human woman dressed in an everyday black uniform appears with a tray of fragrantly spiced red meat with a side of seared greens.

My mouth is practically watering by the time she sets it on the engraved silver table near the fireplace in my living room.

"I will leave you to eat," Leeza says. She's taken something out of the wardrobe in my room and places it on my bed. "Change into this when you feel ready and leave your clothes at the door so I can pick them up after you're asleep."

She and the maid leave, and I find myself alone.

I comfort myself with the thought that Mom mentioned Alvar would bring her here for the wedding. At this point, I don't care anymore if my mother and I aren't on the same page psychologically because I need *someone* familiar.

The meat and greens they brought me are excellent. The flavor is something I've never tasted on my budget on Earth, a mixture of spicy, tender, and sweet.

After I'm finished eating because I don't know what else to do, I take off my clothes and change into the silky nightwear Leeza laid out for me.

There isn't much to the clothing. The thin fabric hugs all the subtle curves of my body, but I'll begrudgingly admit it is the most comfortable clothes I've worn in my life.

I climb into the bed and find myself floating on its unexplainable softness.

Wow. This—this is nice.

I'm living in the most breathtaking luxury, but it might as well be a prison cell.

I doze off more comfortable than I thought I would be, but dreams fill my sleep. Some of them are flashbacks. Others are of Emily frightened and alone in a gobli cave. My last dream is one of Alvar with his eyes glowing red, staring at me like a cobra waiting to strike.

I awaken to the sound of my door opening. I sit up in my bed and clutch my sheets up to my chest, covering my thin nightgown.

Alvar stands in the doorway. He's wearing Underland clothes now: a black cape buckled onto a chain of gold hanging around his neck, and red trim and gold embroidery are stitched onto the front of his lux black shirt. His pants are a dark grey and hang nicely from a black leather belt off his lean hips. A band of yellow gold crowns his brow with a bright white gem at its center.

Everything about the way Alvar looks commands respect, and I hate to admit I'm even more attracted to him dressed up in this new exotic regalia than his Americanized fashion.

He's hot, and I hope he doesn't know I think he's hot.

"Did they make you sufficiently comfortable, Lucy?" he asks, an unreadable expression on his scarred face.

Oh, am I comfortable? Is that all he's in here to ask me?

"Yes, I'm comfortable, but it's difficult to accept when I know Emily is in danger because of me."

Alvar runs a hand on the back of his neck and sighs.

Is he nervous? How can I make *him* nervous?

"I heard some news about your friend," Alvar begins as if he doesn't want to tell me because it's horrible news.

My heart skips a beat.

"Yes?" I say while trying to remain calm in front of him.

"She's been handed over to the custody of the gobli queen, Remora," Alvar states. "They've caught on that she's not you. The true bride of Alvar."

"What does that mean?" I ask, holding my breath.

"It means we need to get married right now or—Emily will be executed in the morning," Alvar says quickly.

"Executed," I repeat the word with a hushed voice, the iciness of it settles on me. I swallow again, this time my throat balling.

I slide out of my bed and pace the floor with my arms crossed over my chest, trying to breathe. I want to cry for

Emily, but I can't. With everything going on, my emotions aren't working anymore.

"I brought your mother over the Bridge, Lucy," Alvar states, "because the wedding is tonight."

"Tonight?"

No time to think. No time to plan.

I snap my rubber band once on my wrist.

At the sound Alvar flinches and his gaze pins on the action, eyes narrowing at my wrist momentarily before he pulls his gaze back to my face. "Yes, the sooner, the better, or your friend dies in the gobli custom of execution."

"How is that?" I ask.

"They tear their criminals apart on what they call a Star Wheel. Limbs pulled off one at a time before the head," Alvar says these horrifying words without much emotion.

I shudder.

Why had I asked? How hardened is Alvar to violence that talking about this doesn't visibly upset him?

Emily. Oh, Emily. I'm sorry, Emily. What kind of nightmare world is this?

"If we marry, I will be able to declare all Earth humans protected. If they are, it will mean declaring war on *me*," Alvar states.

"I can't believe it," I mutter, shaking my head, "I have no choice? If you hadn't wanted me as *your wife* instead of giving me a choice like a good guy, none of this would have happened to Emily! I didn't even get to say goodbye to Mike."

"I'm not good at saying things like this... so..." He steps toward me and puts a hand on my shoulder. "Look me in the eye, Lucy."

I gaze up at him, searching for sympathy or compassion.

Searching for something human about him.

"I will do everything in my power to save Emily, Lucy. I apologize for springing the wedding on you. I'd hoped we could ease into it. Take our time to get to know one another first. But this-this is the only thing we can do to save your friend."

"Leeza mentioned we needed to consummate our marriage on our wedding night," I say coldly, my gaze going to where he's placed his hand. "I can't do such a thing with a stranger."

Alvar withdraws his hand quickly as if he's upset with himself for comforting me by touching me.

Huh? What's up with him?

"I am forced to marry you tonight like *you* want so I can save my friend," I say, as calmly and authoritatively as I can. "But I'm not having sex with you."

"Of course, I didn't expect us to. We will give the appearance that I am treating you as my wife," Alvar says, not at all perturbed. "I must spend the night with you. As backward as that seems to you, we must adhere to an old law to be taken seriously by the rest of Axus."

"If you have to stay here tonight, I can live with it, but that's it, you're only *sleeping* in here," I say with a sigh. It feels good that he's not trying to force me into anything, though. I almost appreciate him for it. Almost forget he kidnapped me and is the cause of every struggle I've endured up till this point.

Alvar bows to me with a grateful smile, "You say what you want, and I completely respect your desire to find me an honest man as well. I will prove to you I am."

"Alvar, not that I'm starting to like you," I say, "but you're different than I expected."

"Were you expecting a tyrant who saw you as an object?" Alvar asks, his expression sympathetic and pained as if his words strike an awful memory inside himself. "Know this, Lucy, I've committed unspeakable things in my lifetime, but I have never raped. I prefer being with a woman who *wants* me. I find you, especially in that nightdress, maddening, but I would never force myself on you." He nods at my attire.

My nightdress?

Crap.

I'd forgotten I'm still wearing the skimpy nightgown Leeza gave me. And he's just noticed how it hugs *everything.*

I cross my arms over my chest, cough, and take a step away from him. "Y-yeah, sure. Now, just—uh—leave."

And with that, I made an awkward situation even more uncomfortable.

Alvar turns from me without a word, shutting the door behind him.

After he leaves, I don't have time to ponder my mortification over my upcoming wedding ceremony because the doors to my bedroom swing open. It's Leeza, with Mom standing beside her, holding the wedding dress Alvar bought me on Earth.

SEVEN

My Mom is wearing a satiny beige gown embroidered with red flowers. Her shoulders are bare and glow a bronze tan. Her hair is pinned up in elaborate curls.

Quite the contrast to her appearance on Earth... she took a moment to pamper herself before seeing me.

"Mom!" I exclaim, "I'm so glad to see you!" I rush into her arms and hug her like I'm a child again.

Finally, someone familiar!

"Lucy," Mom says, returning my embrace. "Isn't this palace wonderful? See? I told you we'd never want for anything here! Leeza told me you already ate, so let's get you in your wedding gown."

Leeza lays out my gown, the one I tried on in Chicago. "Alvar got this for you. He said he wanted this from Earth to help you feel as if something were familiar for you tonight."

"Everyone in the city is attending," Mom says with a proud smile. "Isn't that great?"

"*Everyone* in the city?" I squeak.

"Let's get you ready, Princess! We've got a lot of work to do," Leeza interrupts as if sensing my mother is making me uncomfortable, and I need a diversion. "So little time!"

Another sylph woman with blue feathers enters the room. She and Leeza brush my hair and fuss with my eyebrows and make-up.

The blue-feathered sylph says something in a thickly accented voice that I don't understand.

"I'm sorry, I don't understand you," I tell her.

"You must undress," Leeza says, translating for her. "It is a tradition that the bride bathes in arlite."

"Undress?" I clutch my nightshirt to me.

I'm a modest girl, even when around other people of the same gender.

"It's okay, Lucy," Mom assures me. "I'm over here," she says as if she's taken me to a doctor's appointment, and I'm five.

I don't want to get naked in front of all these people.

"I think I'll take my bath alone," I say.

"You're so lovely," Mom praises, embarrassing me further as she always has. "You have nothing to be ashamed of, sweetie."

I wish she wouldn't have said that. It only makes my cheeks burn all the more.

"Come back in like five minutes?" I ask, hopefully.

"Very well," Leeza says, bowing her head at me politely. She, the blue sylph, and Mom leave the room.

I make a mental note that modesty must not be a big deal here in Underland as I remove my nightdress and my trusty rubber band, setting them on the edge of the tub.

I get a glance in the mirror after my bath and realize whatever they put in my bathtub makes my skin glow like the arlite power sources and gems I see everywhere here.

Great, I'm radioactive now. That's got to be healthy. I can't help but think sarcastically.

After I'm dressed up in my gown, and they've delicately braided and adorned my hair with pearls and glittering white crystals, I quite literally am a glowing bride.

"You like what you see?" The blue sylph asks in her thickly accented, broken English.

Why do people speak English here?

"I do," I murmur. "It's magical."

"It's arlite on the skin," the blue sylph clucks, referring to my glow.

"Will it wear off?" I ask, to which the blue sylph giggles.

"Yes, just a beauty treatment. It stops shining in a few days," the blue sylph explains.

"You look beautiful, Lucy," Mom gushes. She starts wiping her eyes and sniffling. "Oh, honey, I'm so happy for you. My daughter, *the queen.* You've saved us, Lucy."

I wonder at her for saying it because if I ever had a daughter, I would hate it if she married a man she'd *just* met out of obligation.

We have different priorities, Mom.

I think of Mike while taking one last glance in the mirror. He was the one who was supposed to see me in this dress walking down the aisle.

I hope I can somehow let him know I'm okay.

Tears brim over my eyes and trickle down my cheeks.

I can't believe I'm about to do this. Marry a stranger.

"She's so happy she's crying," Mom says to Leeza. "Get it out now, honey."

I cry harder. Years of pent up emotions are gushing out.

I should have at least told Mike goodbye. I owed him that.

Someone knocks on my quarters' door and interrupts my sob fest.

"Come in," Leeza says.

It's Fletch. He's dressed in gold silk and wearing a holster with what appears to be a gun-like weapon.

I'm still confused about the technology here. Some things are advanced and other things—say, "consummating" marriages to make them legal—stuck in what would be archaic history to the modern American world I come from.

Still, in tears, I throw the veil over my head to cover my face from Fletch.

"The groom awaits," Fletch says with a chuckle, offering an arm to me. As we walk together downstairs and up to a hall to what I assume is where the wedding will take place, he adds, "You know, my friend Alvar is one of the good ones. You're a lucky lady, Lucy, if you don't mind my saying. Please be patient with him."

Fletch's meaning is lost on me, and I don't reply because I don't have the time to engage with him further on it, although his words stay with me.

I hear music, and as we near, I put a hand over my mouth.

It's the music made by hundreds of voices.

Thankfully, I've stopped crying and, instead blessed emotional numbness sets in to protect me.

Mom holds my wedding dress train as Fletch leads me to stairs going into a chapel-like space.

A low rumble vibrates in the air, and I discover the source to be hundreds of people seated while whispering and muttering in wait for the wedding to start.

How did everyone get here so fast? Such short notice, you'd think no one would make it!

It makes me suspicious as to whether Alvar premeditated everything, but I think of Emily and regain my determination to get through it.

This is for you, Em.

The people seated are a variety of human people, the bird people or sylphs, a few gobli, and people that appear like fauns from Greek mythology on two cloven-toed feet, except instead of goat faces their features are more like that of a deer.

Alvar stands as the master of the room at the front of the chapel. He wears a white doublet paired with white slacks and glowing in arlite too.

The voices start a lovely melody, and I am inclined to float off.

Mom and the sylph attendants motion me to walk down the aisle.

The aisle might as well be a mile long.

All eyes are on me, and I try not to think about it. Instead, I focus on my glowing groom.

My throat is tight. I can hardly breathe. This is my wedding.

My wedding.

I sneak a peek at Alvar, and he smiles at me.

Wow. He's got a great smile, straight white teeth, dimples on his sculpted cheeks even... It lights up his face. So genuine, I almost believe it.

A priestly person, a human man, standing above Alvar on a small platform, raises his arms and seems to bless us, then he hands Alvar a gold goblet, and Alvar drinks from it. Then the goblet is put into my hands.

"Drink the rest of it," Alvar whispers.

With no other choice, I take the goblet and drink from it.

The sweet liquid trickles down my throat, and the rich scent fills my nostrils as I tip the cup and empty it.

Tastes like a dessert wine.

I hand the goblet back to the priest who takes it from me with a smile.

He's a good-looking man, the priest, well built, with kind eyes, hair cut short on his scalp, and wearing golden robes.

The priest raises his arms again and shouts something at the wedding guests. They shout another word back at him. The music starts again. He motions for Alvar to take my hands.

Was that it?

Was that all my wedding entails?

I can't believe it.

"In front of everyone gathered here, we ask you to seal your union with a kiss," the priest says.

I want to appear legit to these people in case any of them are spies for Remora, so when Alvar leans in to kiss me softly on the lips, I meet him with it. My eyes close momentarily, and I'm maddened by the desire to linger in bliss over his lips covering mine.

Feels so good, so right.

It can't be right!

Finally, we withdraw to the applause of every witness.

"Now, we will eat together for the first time as man and wife," Alvar whispers in my ear. "They will follow us to the dining hall."

"I'm sorry I must have missed the rehearsal," I whisper back, unsure why I'm smiling at him. "I guess I'll just have to follow your lead, my king."

"I suppose you will," Alvar says, a bemused smile spreading on his face, and I fight my heart fluttering at the sight of it.

We exit through grand doors at the back of the chapel and enter into an immense dining hall. There are tables and chairs set everywhere. At the front of the room is a long gold table. Alvar takes me to sit at the gold table.

Fletch sits next to me. I don't know what to say to him, but apparently, he and my new husband are close friends, so I begin with a question that comes out more awkward than I intend, "Why did Alvar choose me to marry" I immediately regret saying it.

"Because you are the one he chose," Fletch shrugs.

"Excuse me, your majesty, but I must say your brother would be loath to know this day came," Fletch whispers over me toward Alvar. "You've sealed out the fate he predicted."

"My brother is dead," Alvar says, his tone dark and expression warning at Fletch. "This is a wedding feast, friend. Do not bring up talk of the wicked at a wedding feast."

"Yes, your excellency," Fletch says, the words drip with sarcasm.

"Fletch," Alvar grates with a roll of his eyes, but I notice the corners of his mouth twitch in a smile.

Fletch says, smiling brilliantly, "Forgive me, I can't help feeling immensely pleased with our triumph over it all. After everything, finally, we can breathe."

"You're forgiven as always," Alvar mutters, taking a drink from his goblet.

I don't understand what they are referencing, but my curiosity is piqued.

The priest stands.

"My king, shall I bless your wedding feast?"

"Of course, good Father Ryland," Alvar says with a grin. "I am glad you made it tonight."

"Anything for the man who restored peace and light to Axus," Father Ryland replies.

All of the guests bow their heads, and I follow suit. I can't understand the priest's words, but I respectfully keep my hands folded until the prayer ends.

The food is served after he's finished with the prayer, and it's as decadent and delicious as I expected.

"What about Emily?" I whisper across to Alvar as we eat. "Is it public? The law that Earth humans cannot be killed?"

"Yes," Alvar says quietly. His voice is low, and his eyes for a brief moment glimmer that red hue. He coughs. "If you'll excuse me, I must see Fletch about something. I will meet you tonight in your bedchamber."

"Sure," I mumble.

Alvar gets up with a hand over his eyes, motions his head at Fletch, and both of them leave.

Is it just me who finds it odd that Alvar is leaving his wedding feast?

EIGHT

Minute by minute passes. With bated breath, I pace in my bedroom waiting for Alvar to arrive for our "wedding night."

I peek into my mirror at the gold lingerie Leeza helped me into before Mom hugged me goodbye to leave me to my fate.

Here I am offered up as a sacrifice by my mother and everyone here.

My cheeks redden.

And they expect me to perform my duty in consummating the marriage obediently.

The lingerie is crafted from a silky fabric with gold sewn into cups that shape a surprising amount of cleavage from my small breasts.

I'm self-conscious in these clothes as it bares most of my skin to view, but I hadn't refused to wear it over the fear of not seeming Alvar's bride authentically.

Can't believe Alvar will see me in this.

The door to my bedroom opens, and my breath leaves me.

It's him, King Alvar, and I'm to be alone all night with him.

"Good evening, Lucy," Alvar says with a nod in my direction as he closes the door behind him. "If you don't mind, I find these wedding clothes incredibly uncomfortable, may I remove this doublet?"

"Yeah, no problem," I say with a shrug.

He unbuttons the shirt down the front, and as the gap of fabric widens, I note a chiseled line running down his torso.

My breath hitches.

He's gorgeous. He is powerfully built. On earth, I'd never dreamed a man like this would undress in my bedroom.

*Crap! I hope he doesn't notice how red my face is or how I just **visibly stared.***

"Did you enjoy the food?" Alvar asks.

"Y-yes," I stutter.

I hate the disappointment I feel when his gaze doesn't linger on me in an appreciative glance.

Maybe I'm too plain, even in this freaking "goddess-suit" Leeza put on me.

Alvar walks toward the fireplace and shrugs off his shirt from his muscular, broad back and starts to undo his belt.

I decide if it does come to it, and this is all some elaborate trick, I'm not letting him take me without a fight. We had a deal. My fists clench, and I back up against the bed, but I rest myself when I realize Alvar is still looking into the fireplace. He takes his belt off and places it gently on the mantle.

"The fire is beautiful, Lucy," he says. "Would you like to sit with me by it?" He turns to me, and brow pinches as he studies my attire for the first time. "Oh, by Elias, would you please take *that* off?" The muscles in his jaw tense, and his eyes darken.

"What the—I will not take this off!" I begin, appalled.

"You misunderstand me. I swear I won't look while you change. Just put on something different than *that*," he growls.

"Uh—sure," I mumble. "You don't have to be weird about it."

"Did you want me to tear it off of you instead? It's the kind of gown that makes me imagine all the things I could do to you. But I thought you didn't want that with me?" a darker Alvar appears, the kind I find myself imagining throwing me onto the bed and wrapping in his strong arms; however, I catch a sense of humor underneath that darkness.

"You're right; I don't!" I huff at him but practically trip on my way to the wardrobe at the mental image that stirs to life within me. "Leeza put me in it, so look away."

"I suppose I can manage to do that," Alvar says.

I hurry into a simple white gown I find in my wardrobe and slip a matching white robe with purple-blue and silver trim over it.

"Are you finished over there yet?" Alvar asks over his shoulder.

What a thing to say!

"Yeah, I'm finished," I say, walking over to stand before him.

"Now come sit with me by the fire," Alvar beckons with a curl of his finger in my direction. He's sitting on a bench he's pulled up from my window.

"Why not?" I say with a shrug.

"The arlite makes you look radiant," he murmurs, but it's as if he's scripted his words, and I hate it. He went from teasing me to putting on a dignified kind of mask I don't understand. "You look as if you were born to be royalty, Lucy."

"Thanks, I think."

"I am sorry Fletch brought up my brother," Alvar says.

"Were the two of you close?"

"No."

"Do you want to tell me about him?"

"Not really." Alvar leans toward the fireplace, propping his chin up on tented hands.

A blessed silence overcomes us.

I sigh, and Alvar continues to gaze at the flames.

"So, you're not going to touch me?" The words come out as a relief.

"I'm true to my word, my queen," Alvar says. "Lucy, I promised you that I would have you love me, and I would never do anything to make you feel violated."

"You don't know me," I say. "How can you say something like that with such certainty?"

"We could have a wonderful arrangement. I know there are women on Earth who love men like me. I'm rich, I can give you anything you want. I'm also a just ruler and powerful," Alvar says, and adds, "and you're attracted to me, are you not?"

I bite my lip.

Now I hate you again, Alvar. I am not a gold digger!

"I'm not so shallow to only marry a man for money. I mean, look at the man I was going to marry before you stepped in? And there is more to love than attraction," I say. "Besides, you say nothing about having love for *me*. Not interested in a one-sided sort of thing."

"You didn't love Mike, though," Alvar says.

"What do you know of love?" I ask him; now I'm rightfully angry.

"I know much of the loss of love," Alvar says quietly, not gazing at me. "You are not showing the signs of that kind of pain, only mourning over a life you never had but thought you wanted."

"Attraction isn't love either," I say, not sure what my comeback to his statement could be.

"Yes, but attraction can lead to it," Alvar says.

"Okay, I'll admit it, you're incredibly good-looking... and *you* know it too apparently. I doubt there is a woman alive who wouldn't admit to that though," I say.

"With a scarface like this?" Alvar muses, running a finger along the trailing white line.

"Where did you get it?" The question pops out before I can pull it back in.

Alvar wags a scolding finger at me teasingly and tsks, "You're too curious. You might not like the answers."

"You're not going to tell me? Come on, you're my husband now, tell me where the scar came from," I say. A bold question, I know, but I've finally gone mad and might as well lean into it.

"Someone gave it to me when I was seventeen years old. They told me it wasn't fair I had such a handsome face," Alvar says, laughing bitterly. "They wanted my face to reflect my soul."

"Your soul has scars?"

"It does. Many."

"What do you mean?" I ask.

"What is that?" Alvar says, brushing wisps of my hair from my eyes just as he's brushed off the topic. His gaze is focused downward at my lap, and I'm not sure what he means.

"What do you mean?" I ask, shifting in my seat away from him.

Alvar's hand reaches out to grasp my wrist. "This red mark. It's from that device you had around your wrist, isn't it?"

"Uh—yeah, I guess," I say. "The 'device' around my wrist is called a rubber band."

"Why do you punish yourself with it, Lucy?" Alvar's brow furrows, and his gaze fixes on me. "Is that what rubber bands are for? Some barbaric, self-harming, Earth custom?" His thumb brushes over the red line left behind by my constant rubber band use. The warmth of his touch sends a shiver through me.

"No, they're normally used to tie things, but—I don't know—it grounds me to snap it on my wrist," I say, realizing how wrong it sounds as the words fall from my lips. I force myself to yawn and direct the subject elsewhere. "I'm pretty tired. It's been a long day. Do you mind if I go to bed?"

Alvar's expression is thoughtful as if he's still thinking about the mark on my wrist from the rubber band. "Yes, think nothing of it. Get some rest."

"What about you? Are you going to sleep on the floor?"

"I'll be nearby," Alvar says. "Have to make this marriage look official to the people."

"Yeah, if anyone sees the king leave when he's supposed to be getting it on with his queen, it'd be a scandal," I say with a nervous laugh.

I can't believe I said that!

Alvar laughs with me, which I guess means he at least thinks I'm funny. "Very much a scandal," he says, raising an eyebrow. "Instead, the king is sleeping on the floor and merely dreaming of *getting it on*—as you say—with his queen."

My eyes widen, even though I know he's joking too. In an attempt to keep him from noticing my blush, I hurry over to crawl under the covers of the cloud of a bed I now possess and close my eyes.

"Goodnight," I say in finality.

A million unanswered questions flit around in my head, but it seems a moment later, and I open my eyes, knowing I've dozed off.

The room is dark beside the faint glow of the fireplace where I find Alvar, sitting with his back to my bed, gazing into the hearth.

"What are you doing?" I ask him.

"I'm waiting till morning."

"Don't you need to sleep?"

"Truthfully, I cannot sleep. The floor is made of stone, and it reminds me of—it's too cold," he says, but I'm aware he almost said something else.

There is a dark mystery surrounding Alvar and his world, and instead of being afraid of it—like I probably should be— I'm dying to find answers.

I swallow and wring my hands. "Do you want to come up on the bed?" I ask tentatively, unable to believe my own words.

I can't leave him like that.

"Are you sure?" He gazes up at me with his intense blue eyes, and I'm lost in him.

I sigh. "Yes. Now come on up here before I change my mind."

"You're a kind woman, my queen," Alvar says, bowing his head at me. "I like that."

"You like my kindness or the fact that you're going to sleep in my bed tonight?" I ask.

"Both." Alvar gives a boyish grin.

Huh. Strange look on him... he seems so old in his emotional state most of the time.

But it makes me want to like him, and I'm determined not to like him because he planned my life before I was born and took me out of my world without considering my feelings about it.

"Well, this bed is way too big for just one person anyway," I say dryly.

I'm embarrassingly mesmerized as he stands, the lights of the fireplace dance across the muscles in his chest and back, highlighting every mind-numbing ridge and plane.

I embarrass myself further by a noticeable, sharp inhale at the sight.

Gosh, get a grip, Lucy.

I scrunch my eyes closed and settle into the sheets, pretending I'm not affected. Pretending I'll fall back to sleep quickly, but the sensation of another being climbing onto the mattress is something I cannot will away.

"Lucy, don't worry, I'm not going to touch you," Alvar assures in a soft and careful tone. "Don't be afraid, Lucy. I would never hurt you."

I'm not afraid of him breaking our deal; what I am fearful of is the twinge of disappointment I feel. Yes, the fact that a twisted part of me wishes he *would* touch me frightens me very much.

NINE

I wake up with Alvar facing me. His expression is peaceful in sleep, and with his black hair, tousled carelessly over his dark eyebrows, I forget who he is. I never noticed his thick black eyelashes or his sensual mouth with its slight curve at the corners as if he smiles in his sleep. There is an unexplainably heartbreaking kindness to his features.

My attention fixates on his scar while he sleeps.

Someone purposefully did that to him.

I shift in the bed carefully so as not to wake him and sweep the covers aside to step onto the stone floor. I tiptoe to my wardrobe to dress.

"You can just press the caller if you need anything," Alvar's voice makes me nearly jump out of my skin. "Leeza will come."

"Oh!" I whirl around. "Did I wake you?"

"I'm a light sleeper," Alvar stretches his muscled arms above his head and yawns, the covers fall off him giving me a generous view of his bared chest and abdomen.

I willfully avert my gaze to keep a clear head.

Damn. What is it about Alvar that draws me in like a female animal in heat?

"Did you want me to leave now?" Alvar asks, the corner of his mouth twitches; he's noticed me notice *him again*. "We've spent our night together, and as far as any of the old fashioned people in Underland are concerned, we are officially man and wife."

"Phew, I'm glad that's over with," I say, stifling a giggle.

"If we'd had a different sort of night, I'm pretty sure you wouldn't be so glad for this night to be over," Alvar says with a devilish wink.

"Ha-ha, very funny," I say, rolling my eyes at him, but I laugh at myself and cough, realizing I need to change the subject… fast. "So, when will I see—see Emily?"

"You should see her very shortly," Alvar says. "I sent a direct message to Remora. She agreed and will be sending Emily by Sky Wave."

What's a Sky Wave?

"I hope she's okay," I say.

"We shall see." Alvar throws the covers off and moves to get dressed. He picks up his shirt from the floor and shrugs it on. "Go ahead, press the caller for Leeza, it's by the door."

"We should speak again soon, Lucy," Alvar says. He loops his belt inside his pants.

"So, you know how to dress yourself?" I tease. "I thought servants helped you with that."

"I know how to do a great many things on my own, Lucy," Alvar says, his eyes glinting as if he knows something dark and mysterious. Something an Earth human like me couldn't comprehend.

I involuntarily blush and press my hands to the sides of my cheeks to hide it.

"You are very innocent, aren't you?" Alvar sighs and gets a faraway look in his eyes.

"By innocent, you mean stupid," I accuse. I don't know why I'm taking offense.

"I didn't say stupid," Alvar corrects without retaliating. "Don't talk like that of yourself. Innocence is a gift, and don't let anyone tell you otherwise. Now are you going to press the button, or do you want to figure out your clothing options yourself?"

"I probably could do it," I muse, glancing at the wardrobe.

"Do you know what colors to wear after a celebration like a wedding?" Alvar cocks an eyebrow at me. He sits on the edge of my bed and tugs on his boots.

"Where are you going?"

"I have business to attend. I am a king, you know," he says, obviously amused by how easy it is to tease me.

"Oh, yeah," I mutter.

He stands up straight and bows his head at me. "It was my pleasure spending the night in your bed, wife."

Wife.

I reach for my rubber band but my fingers slip over my bare wrist, and I think of how Alvar noticed and *cared.*

Mike never asked me about my odd habit of snapping my wrist... he never seemed concerned like Alvar did.

"Good day, Lucy." Alvar nods at me. He strides from the room.

"Good day, Alvar," I murmur after him. The way his name rolls off my tongue is admittedly wonderful.

You hardly even know him, and you're starting to fall for him like he's a character in a fairy tale? Remember how he kidnapped you from all you've ever known? Stockholm syndrome anyone? Besides, if Mike knew what you were thinking do you realize how hurt he'd be?

I press the glowing white caller set in the wall next to my bedroom door and wait for Leeza to come and help me dress.

"Your majesty," Leeza says, she bows, her crest of feathers nearly touching the ground. "You look well-rested and radiant if I do say so myself."

Everyone thinks Alvar, and I consummated our marriage. Isn't this awkward?

"Thank you, Leeza. Do you know if Emily will be coming today?"

"She should arrive shortly."

"How shortly?"

"I'd say early this afternoon," Leeza says. "What did you need me for, Majesty?"

"I need to pick out clothes to wear. King Alvar said you'd know which is appropriate for a new bride," I say, holding it together enough not to blush.

"You should wear white," Leeza advises with a smile, she bustles over to my wardrobe. Her wings fold over the back of an ornate, royal blue sari she wears. The color combination with the yellow feathers and blue fabric, remind me of a regal blue and yellow macaw.

Leeza pulls a white top and skirt from my wardrobe and lays it out on my bed.

I pick up the shirt and find it's as if I'm trying to capture water in my fingers, the fabric is so, so light and soft.

"What is this?" I ask in bewilderment and awe.

"It's made from the silk of a Telf spider," Leeza says. "The softest, lightest clothes in Axus one can find or buy."

"Spider?" I say.

This beautiful, lux piece was made from spider silk?

Creepy.

"They are farmed in the Trees of Gomen," Leeza explains.

I have no idea where that is, but I don't bother asking.

"The sylphs domesticated and farm them," Leeza says, beaming with apparent pride over it. "Someday you will visit Sylphvr, the sylph capitol city in the Skylands. You are scheduled to go there in a month to meet and greet the sylph people as the new queen of Underland. Then you can gaze upon the majestic Telf spiders."

I'm not sure if I'm excited about "gazing upon" spiders, but visiting the sylphs sounds—for lack of a better word—cool.

"Will I visit all the peoples of this land?" I wonder if that sounded right. I don't know etiquette here. What if I seem racist by mistake? Or is there even racism in this world? That would be awesome if it didn't exist here. It's very different than Earth. I am lost and realize again how alien everything in Underland is to me.

Leeza laughs. "Of course, you will! You are even scheduled to meet the gobli queen, Remora."

The same queen who wanted to kill my best friend on a Star Wheel?

No thanks.

A loud gong goes off, and the shrill sound of screams and shouts from outside interrupt us.

What is going on out there?

Leeza's eyes get huge. She grasps my hand and runs us to the window, but an eardrum-shattering roar causes us both to cower away from it.

"What is that?" I ask, breathlessly, my heart beating a mile a minute.

"The Cursed in the city during the day!" Leeza sounds panicked and surprised. She pulls my window shut and draws the curtains, shutting out the day. "That never happens!"

"Come, we must go to the safe room!" She cries.

"What is going to happen?" I ask, terrified upon remembering the painting of what Fletch called a "Cursed" when I first arrived here.

I'm still only wearing the robe and the rope tying it together slips open.

Of all things!

I fumble to tie it, but Leeza is in too much of a hurry.

"What is a Cursed exactly?" I find myself questioning the danger of this situation, and I don't know why. "Fletch said it's like an immortal dragon."

"It's a creature of darkness," Leeza explains. "Through and through. They are unnatural beings, Cursed Ones. There is no killing it."

"What do you mean?" My spine tingles with fear at the horrified look in Leeza's eyes as it's obvious she's terrified of this thing, and I should probably be too.

We're headed down secret stairs she reveals in my living area under the great bath in my room.

"Cursed are not always as they appear," Leeza explains, "They look like people just like you and me, but they have a darkness inside them at birth that causes a hideous transformation and turns them into a monster. They fool you with the human appearance, but that is what they truly are: Monsters."

"Wait… Transformation? Like a werewolf?"

"What's a werewolf?" Leeza halts once we reach a small room that is lit by faint arlite torches.

"Men that turn into wolves when a full moon is out," I say.

"You have such creatures where you're from?" Leeza's eyebrows raise in alarm.

"We—well, they are a myth in our world," I explain. "We call it an urban legend. They are said to look like normal people except they turn into a wolf when there is a full moon."

"I see," Leeza says thoughtfully. "Cursed are like that, but they are very real, and they look like normal people except for one thing."

"What is that?"

"The tell is that their eyes turn red when they get stressed."

My blood runs icy cold.

Red eyes.

I don't even want to think it, but—

An echoing roar shakes the palace.

TEN

"It hasn't killed for a long time, but many of us know what it was to find a family torn to pieces by it under Saul's command. It flies over the city, its eyes watching us, but it doesn't descend. It used to belong to the evil tyrant, Saul. He used its power to keep us enslaved to his bidding. Any rebellion left you and your family burned inside your home by its fire." Leeza closes her eyes as if remembering something terrible. "Few survived Saul's wrath when he decided you'd offended him. Those who did survive regretted it as Saul was a master at tormenting those who crossed him. Eventually, Saul had enough men backing him at the threat of the Cursed that he had Axus in the palm of his hand."

This information was too much. A Cursed, like Alvar, had been Saul's pet? How had Alvar gotten rid of Saul? Maybe only Cursed could kill Cursed?

"Are you sure it's the same Cursed that Saul controlled?" I know I need to ask this, considering.

"Most think so, but who can be sure? No one wants to get close enough to find out if it's wearing Saul's Fe collar. Some say it hasn't killed anyone since Saul left because it desires it's master's return first. Some say this is an entirely new Cursed flying above us. If the man responsible for possessing the Curse is discovered, he'll be killed in his human form, when they are most vulnerable. But even that takes drastic measures to finish successfully - a magic dagger specifically created to harm a Cursed."

I want to throw up but lean more toward the idea that Alvar destroyed the previous Cursed over him being the one owned by Saul. He just doesn't seem the homicidal type.

The gong sounds again. Leeza breathes a sigh of relief. "It's gone."

"Good," I mutter, but I highly doubt "it" is gone.

We crawl out of the safe room, and Leeza helps me into the spider silk gown. It's too wonderful feeling to question, and I rationalize that silk on Earth is made by tiny little caterpillars so, why not spider silk?

Just as I'm finished dressing and Leeza has styled my hair in an ornate up-do, my mother enters the room.

"Wasn't the Cursed sighting frightening?" Mom asks.

"Yes," I murmur. I can't believe it still. Maybe I'd only imagined Alvar's red eyes. Perhaps he had some other kind of otherworldly condition, and I am jumping to conclusions.

"Emily is here," Mom snorts and crosses her arms. "I can't believe we're stuck with her here. After what she made you think about me."

"Mom," I begin because I don't have the emotional bandwidth to deal with drama like this right now. "Please, try to understand. We can't send her back."

I know I've done wrong by my mother refusing to believe her, but I don't know where to start to have a good relationship with her. I can't deny that my mother's and my problems go deeper than my not believing her.

Leeza bows to me. "I will fetch your friend if you wish, my queen?"

"Yes, please, I imagine she is quite frightened and in need of a familiar face," I say.

Wow, I'm starting to talk like them already.

"Yes, majesty," Leeza says with a smile and leaves Mom and me alone.

"So how did last night go?" Mom gives me a mischievous look.

Oh my gosh, she's seriously going to ask about the wedding night? Again why our problems didn't end with her promising me in marriage to Alvar.

"What are you expecting me to say?" I ask plainly, trying not to let my anger flare up at her lack of boundaries.

"What? I'm curious," Mom says without any hint of sensitivity to my discomfort.

"Mom, it's personal," I groan and roll my eyes at her.

"I know, I know," Mom says, shaking her head. "But I want to make sure he's taking good care of you."

"He took care of me fine," I snap. "And he was perfectly gentlemanly."

Oh, but he's quite possibly some monster too!

If I'm right, he is what his people live in terror of here.

The door opens and Leeza ushers in Emily.

"Oh my—Lucy!" Emily cries upon seeing me. "I was almost afraid they were lying to me when they said you were here too." She rushes to me, throwing her arms around me.

I hold her tight. "I won't leave. I promise." I murmur.

Mom doesn't even look at her. I think she's upset Emily is still in my life.

Emily finally peels off of me. "Lucy, you're *glowing*!" she says with wide eyes.

I almost laugh.

"They give me a special kind of bath before the wedding to make me glow," I say, stepping back so she can get a good look.

"The wedding?" Her eyes get huge. "You mean—?"

"I married Alvar last night in order to free you from the gobli, Em," I mumble the words as if I'm ashamed of myself for not finding another way to save her.

"What! I can't believe it!" Emily's hand goes over her mouth.

"Why?" I blink.

"You married someone you don't even know in order to save me?" Emily's eyes start brimming with tears.

"Yes."

"Wow, Lucy, I—um—thank you. Thank you so much!" She throws her arms around me.

99

"You don't even need to thank me," I say quietly. "I'm just glad you're safe."

Mom crosses her arms over her chest.

"I'll go back to my quarters so you two can catch up," she cuts in. As she leaves, I wonder why I haven't been invited into her "quarters" yet and where they are.

"Lucy," a deep voice says my name from behind us.

We both turn to see Alvar standing in my doorway. Alvar's tall, lean frame rests against my doorframe, and he flashes me a charming smile. "Is your friend alright?"

He's checking in on me?

Emily turns, and I notice her jaw has practically dropped to the floor. "So this is Alvar?" She asks, her voice husky.

Back off, Em, that's my husband you're staring at!

"I am Alvar, King of Underland," Alvar says, stepping toward us and doing a polite bow. "You must be my wife's friend, Emily."

I practically rolled my eyes. Now he's just showing off.

"Y-yes, I am," Emily stutters. Emily is usually so composed. I can't believe she's coming unglued. Emily turns to me her eyes huge. "You married *this* guy to save me?"

"Yep," I say. I realize by her look of surprise that I'm kind of hurt by it. Did Emily never think me capable of marrying a man she could be attracted to?

Oh, but it feels good to shock her like this.

"Lucy, I am glad to see your friend is safe," Alvar's eyes glint as he speaks the words. Oh my. He's looking directly at me, ignoring Emily's fawning.

Oh, dear... I can't take another minute of his gaze without turning red once again.

"Thank you for checking in," as I say the words I can't believe my bravery, "but I need some time with my friend. I will see you tonight?"

"As you wish," Alvar says with a gentle nod, and he turns and leaves us.

"So—your husband... I'm just going to say it: is H-O-T," Emily exclaims.

*Well, she can giggle and notice hot guys so it must not have been **that** difficult on her with the gobli.*

"I know," I admit.

"Did you two have sex last night? I mean... you really married him, right?" Emily asks.

I should have known this question was coming. Emily is always so pressing for details. I wasn't sure how much I should tell her. Maybe I shouldn't tell her anything because last night was supposed to have been legit. Emily likes to talk, what if she talks about it to someone else?

"Em, I don't want to talk about it," I mutter.

"Oh no! He didn't rape you did he? I don't care if he's the king, I'm going to cut off his—"

"Em, he didn't rape me!" I interrupt her quickly.

"Oh." Emily bit her lip, and then a sly smile spreads across her face. "Then did you?" She giggles while making an obscene gesture with her fingers to which I roll my eyes.

She wouldn't stop! "No, Em, we didn't; he's a gentleman and a king."

And maybe even a monster too.

"So you're still a virgin even after spending a night alone with the king of every straight woman's erotic fantasy?" Emily's eyes light up as if she's amused.

"Yeah, I'm still a virgin," I say with a snort. "But you can't tell anyone," I add, hoping I haven't made a colossal mistake telling her.

"Okay," Emily says, waggling her eyebrows suggestively. "But if it had been me marrying him… let me say; I would have made sure I had that sexy king on lock."

"I'm sure you would have," I grumble sarcastically, and decide to change this subject away from how uncomfortable and condescending it's beginning to feel. "What about you? What happened to you?"

"I don't know if I can talk about it," Emily says, her voice dropping in tone and cheeriness. "It was horrible."

"Tell me a little more about them," I say. I am the queen of this country now. I might as well know what I'm dealing with.

"Think 'ant colony' in terms of their social structure, except the workers are both male and female. All of the males are required to mate with the queen goblin to produce the next generation, but the worker females are infertile and unable to have children," Emily explains.

"Anyway, the goblin queen is this ugly thing that gives out the orders to the rest of them, but she, like, has no conscience! The things I saw while with her, and the things she did to those who made her angry… she makes the queen of hearts from Wonderland look like a saint," Emily says, closing her eyes and sighing. "I thought I was dead for sure. Then she got a message in Arlite that I was not to be harmed and sent to the castle via the Sky Wave."

"What's the Sky Wave like?" I ask interestedly.

"It's an—what do they call it?—arlite-powered teleportation device. I found myself here within, like, an hour, although I'm told the capital city is far from the goblin kingdom. How can this be real though? It's like we're in a weird fantasy movie that we can't get out of! I'm just glad you're here, and I'm not alone anymore."

"Me too," I murmur.

"But, girl, I'd love to take your place." Emily's eyes light up. "The king is yummy."

"Why do you have to be such a ho about it? Besides, that's my yummy king you are talking about, go find your own!" I say as I'm trying to hide my building anger and jealousy. Emily needs to stop making eyes at my man—uh what? Did I just think of him as *my man*?

No, he's not even my man. Get ahold of yourself, Lucy.

"You're so innocent, honey, look at you blush," Emily says with a giggle.

Yes, so everyone tells me. I have no real experience whatsoever in the sex department like Emily does, and if I did go there at some point, I wouldn't want to appear a complete idiot. Then I wonder about what Alvar does considering he's married me out of political reasons. For all I know, he could be sleeping with servants or have a mistress on the side right now and not even expect me to sleep with him.

It sucks that I don't know this man who is now my husband.

Then, *I wonder what they use for protection here?*

Emily sits on the end of my bed. She bounces her hips a couple of times. "This bed is amazing. Here you are living in luxury while I was dying in the goblin caves."

"You mean gobli," I finally have to correct her. "And they live in caves?"

"Didn't I tell you? They are subterranean. It's so dark down there. Ugh, I couldn't stand it. Couldn't see much." She shudders.

"Well, you'll never have to go back down there," I assure her.

A knock on my door interrupts us.

"Come in," I answer.

Fletch steps into the room and bows.

Emily shrieks and hides behind me. "A goblin!"

"Gobli," I mumble, and then, "Fletch is a close friend of Alvar," I explain to Emily, taking her hand and pulling her forward. "He's one of the good guys, Em." *At least I think so. I honestly don't know or trust anything here.*

"I most certainly am one of the good guys," Fletch remarks dryly. "I'm here because I've been ordered to take you to your room, Lady Emily," I note Fletch is wearing tinted spectacles. I wonder if since his people are subterranean, he needs them during the day here.

"I can't believe all your mother's ravings were true," Emily murmurs as if she's distant suddenly.

"Ahem," Fletch raises his funny little warty eyebrows. "Would you come with me? I promise I don't bite."

Emily gives me a look, and I nod in reassurance. "He is just going to show you to your room. Get some rest, okay?"

She lets go of my hand and nervously smiles a little. "Okay."

ELEVEN

After eating, I press the caller for Leeza and take a deep breath.

I wonder where Leeza spends her time when she's not waiting on me.

Put a brave face on. This is your new life, whether you like it or not. You can't hide from this strange reality forever.

"What do you need, my queen?" Leeza asks with a bow.

I clear my throat. "I want to speak with Alvar."

"I think he is in the middle of a meeting, but I will tell him you want an audience after it's finished," Leeza says.

"Thank you, that is all," I say.

Maybe I'll even get good at this "queen" thing, I muse.

Leeza bows and leaves.

As I sit alone, my bedroom becomes increasingly and uncomfortably silent. The urge to get up and explore the palace is overwhelming. Hmm... is it allowed for the queen to leave her room without telling anyone?

I'm not a prisoner. Heck, I'm a freaking ruler now, so it is probably fine.

I walk out of my room and into the living area of my quarters, fighting the urge to tiptoe around as if I don't belong here.

This is going to take getting used to.

The architecture, decorations, and furnishings are luxurious and tastefully placed.

My mom, a single mother who never told me who my father was, had worked as a maid at a local hotel. We'd always lived in a one-bedroom apartment.

It wasn't until I'd grown up and gotten a job of my own that I could afford anything for myself, but *never* anything as lovely as this.

How is it that one can live in luxury and feel helpless? I contemplate.

I make up my mind that I want to revisit the paintings of the Cursed I'd passed while walking with Fletch to my chambers.

I start down the hall quietly, with bated breath.

Calm down, Lucy.

It's not like that old Disney movie I'd watched as a kid, Beauty and the Beast, where the Beast told Belle the west wing was "forbidden."

This is *my* palace now too.

Despite myself, I smile at that thought,

"And where do you think you're going?" An unfamiliar male voice says from behind me, making me jolt. "Sneaking out of your room, aye, your majesty?"

I turn and find a human male wearing a black and white guard's uniform standing next to my door. He's tall and broad-shouldered with light blonde hair and a dimple in his chin. His blue-grey eyes are friendly.

"I just wanted to find the art gallery I saw yesterday."

"Well, you're going the wrong way," he says with a playful expression on his handsome face. "Would you like me to take you there?"

"Please," I say with an embarrassed laugh.

"Come with me, your majesty," he says, turning down the hall.

I follow.

"Did you see the Cursed today?" he asks.

"No, I didn't see it."

"Well, the paintings in the gallery do a good job on the likeness of it. I'm sure that's why you're headed there," he says, "I'm Grey by the way. One of your guards."

"I'm Lucy," I say, extending a hand out to him.

"I know, my queen," he says with a chuckle, taking my hand and shaking it. "We all have to get used to having a queen around here again. Triss passed many years ago."

"Triss?" I ask.

"Alvar's first queen. She died during pregnancy."

"Alvar was *married*?" I practically shout these words and immediately blush at the outburst.

He's a widower! Why hasn't anyone told me? Why hasn't Alvar told me?

"He married her after the war ended, and he was appointed the king. Alas, she died within that same year. A tragedy."

I think of my mother and how Alvar had saved me when she was pregnant with me. How come they hadn't been able to save his first wife?

"Why did she die? What kind of complication rose?"

"It was so sad. She and her baby died from preeclampsia complications. King Alvar and the whole kingdom mourned their deaths."

Whoa! Why hasn't Alvar told me about his wife and child dying?

"Here is the gallery," Grey says pointing to the room. "I'll be over here watching out for you. Once you're done looking just let me know, and I'll take you back to your room."

I smile at him. It's pretty awesome to have a personal guard, and I already like Grey. He doesn't look like someone you'd want to mess with.

I study the paintings and images in the gallery. There is much going on in them. Many of them tell of historical events.

I spot a large painting with a Cursed in it. The huge dragon-like beast stares out of the frame; its wings are jagged and spiked. A tail snakes behind it and its head is shaped like a hybrid between a crocodile and viper. The eyes are red, and the body is black as onyx.

Eventually, I grow frustrated with too many questions that I can no longer look at the gallery. "I'm ready to go, Grey," I say.

*

"Lucy, when you tell me you wish an audience, I suggest next time you don't run off while waiting for me," Alvar scolds me as I enter.

I admit he has a point. Not my most well thought out venture.

"I'm sorry," I begin. "I have much to talk to you about, and I needed answers so I went to the gallery to see if I could find them. The Cursed sighting is troubling to me and after it—"

"Grey, I wish to be alone with the queen!" Alvar speaks over me, his eyebrows raised and eyes flash red, widening for a fleeting second.

I'm not sure if I should cower or run to my bedroom and bolt the door. He's pissed.

"Leave us!" Alvar commands Grey, who bows and exits.

I swallow hard. What is he going to do to me? Does he know *I know*? Will he kill me because I know?

Alvar stalks over to my couch, pinning me with his now intimidatingly bright crimson gaze. "You are not to talk about this with anyone."

"Your eyes are red again," I blurt. "Do you think I'm stupid?"

"No," Alvar says, closing the mentioned eyes and breathing in deeply. "I don't think you're stupid, Lucy. As I'm finding out, you're incredibly perceptive. Magically so."

"Then, is everyone here stupid? It's obvious to me that you're one of the Cursed," I say, shocked by my willingness to confront him. If he is what I think he is, he may decide I'm a liability rather than an asset.

"Lucy," Alvar growls. "They are not stupid either, but they don't see what you see."

"What do you mean?" I ask.

"You—you have Cursed blood," Alvar finally says.

I gasp in true mortification.

*No. That's not true. How **can** that be true? I wasn't even born here! Does that mean I'll turn into—?*

"I know what you're thinking," Alvar continues. "But rest assured, you won't turn into a monster as I do. As far as I know, the Cursed blood that runs in your veins only gives you rapid healing compared to most mortals. You had Cursed blood infused into your veins while you were still in your mother's womb. It was the only way to save your life then. Cursed blood can heal a still-developing fetus," Alvar pauses in deep thought, before adding in a whisper, "You ask what makes you special to me? You are the only one who I know

111

with certainty can carry my children without dying. I'm not saying I need you to have children with me, but you were the only compatible choice on Earth to marry for a treaty. It was an accident—your mother happened upon me. She saw I was magical, and she came to me because she needed a miracle. She said she'd give you to me in marriage if I could heal you. It was as if the gods were with me at last in this opportunity she gave. It presented an alliance for me that I desperately needed to forge at the time. Based on how your mother acted, I had no idea it wasn't normal for parents to arrange marriages for their children where you're from."

"Triss died because of you then, didn't she?" I say, not sure if I should feel sorry for him or not. The more I learn about him, the less afraid of him I feel. But then again, I wouldn't be the first woman with a fatal attraction.

"Yes," Alvar murmurs, his eyes grow distant, and he brings himself away from me. "Yes, she did. It was my fault. She didn't have a drop of Cursed blood in her, and I destroyed her by getting her pregnant. I was a fool. I hadn't a clue at the time how Cursed pregnancies worked."

"But you're saying *I* wouldn't die having your children?" I ask and cross my arms over my chest.

"Yes. After doing much research on it and confirming with multiple record keepers, one of those sources being Father Ryland, our greatest keeper of magical secrets in the kingdom, I know this to be true. The thing is... not *all* of my children would be Cursed if I were to have heirs, at least that is the hope," Alvar says.

"You know, a monarchy isn't thought of as the best way of running a government in my world," I point out.

"But it is in mine. Our culture is based on traditions despite our advancements that surpass yours. Honor, respect, and lineage are severely important in Underland. We live longer here than you do on Earth too. It may take some getting used to for you, but that's how it works here. I pray every day I do not give in to my beast like so many Cursed before me did in the past."

"I guess I need to accept everything you tell me? To trust your word?" I question.

"Lucy, for what it's worth, you're going to make an excellent Queen."

"Why do you say that?" I ask, rolling my eyes at the flattery and annoyed with him for not giving me all this information sooner. It would have helped me understand. I'm tired of people not disclosing the *full* truth to me as if I can't handle it.

My mother left out the full truth too. She said that Alvar would only heal me if she gave me to him in marriage... now I realize she led him to believe arranged marriages are a common cultural practice where I'm from.

"Because you test things, you don't just accept it at face value. You are inquisitive and determined not to be taken for a fool."

My hands ball into fists, and I stomp up to Alvar. I'm on tiptoe, trying to look him in the eye as fiercely as possible. "Yeah, well what kind of person did you think I was going to be? A doormat?"

"What's a doormat?" Alvar asks with an amused chuckle.

"How can you be laughing? I know your secret! I know that *you* are what everyone is afraid of the most here. How could you do that to these people? Not only did you kidnap me and determine my choices for me, but you're also a liar. What makes you a better ruler than someone like Saul?"

"Don't say such a thing!" Alvar growls, within a heartbeat I'm pressed against the wall. The power in his body is like a massive electric charge. I can do nothing when he's this close; the strength of him is astounding. He'd moved me without hurting me, but also without any effort. I inhale sharply and can smell him, a mixture of burnt forest and summer wind.

"Did I hit a nerve?" I ask, narrowing my eyes at him and tilting my chin up challengingly.

Mmm, how good his body feels pressed against mine. Wait. What?

"I am *nothing* like Saul, Lucy, and you should pray you never meet that depraved man!" he seethes through clenched teeth.

"Is there a possibility?" I ask.

TWELVE

"Saul was thrown into your world through the Bridge." Alvar sighs and his brow furrows with pain, and he backs away from me. "It was the only means to defeat him. Without arlite, he was unable to return. But if he does return, this world and possibly yours will be lost to him."

"What do you mean? You killed the Cursed he owned, didn't you?"

"Lucy, I *am* the Cursed he used to gain power," Alvar's eyes connect with mine somberly. "Before becoming ruler here, I-I did many unforgivable things."

"You've killed thousands of people?" I begin, but Alvar shakes his head.

"Don't speak of it," he says, great sorrow and shame in his handsome face; it's enough to make my heart break a little. "I can't have you think of me as a monster. Everything I did was outside of my control." He taps his neck. "I still wear the device of my shame — a Fe collar. The one who placed it upon my neck controlled me. I had a noble sylph priestess bless it to appear invisible, but it's still there. Reminding me every day of that I'm enslaved."

"Do you now understand why I needed to make sure none in Underland would dare venture into your world? If Saul were to get his hands on even a shard of arlite, do you know what that would mean?" Alvar pauses and his eyes beam red. "None know of this except myself, Fletch, and the priestess, Sola, I mentioned. I tell you because I see your mind is quick and I wish to have complete honesty between us. We need to get on the same path, as rulers of this kingdom, and as husband and wife."

"I can't imagine," I murmur, clenching my eyes shut and trying not to imagine. To live without your own will governing your body? Everything in this world is impossible in mine and I am overwhelmed with deep pity for my husband despite my doubts in him.

"Am I understood about keeping this a secret?" His lips are quite quickly inches from mine.

I nod, trying not to show my nerves.

"Thank you, Lucy," Alvar says, breathing out a sigh of relief, he steps toward me again, tentatively. "I think I'd love kissing you, Lucy."

I push him away, but my shove is playful, and I'm kicking myself because I think I'd love kissing him too. "You don't own me, don't forget it!"

"On the contrary, it is you who owns me," Alvar says, a grin spreads across his face as his eyes fix on mine. "I am sorry. I got lost in those beautiful eyes of yours. I can't help but be drawn to you."

"Is this your idea of flirting?" I ask, cocking an eyebrow and crossing my arms over my chest. "Because it's not working on me."

"Oh, but I believe it is," Alvar narrows his eye and scrutinizes me. "Your pupils are dilated. Your breath is husky. Everything about your reaction to my question makes me think you want to kiss me too."

"You are quite presumptuous in your words, sir," I defend myself, although it's forced. "I bet you think I'm going to kiss you right here now that I know the truth. No judgment to women who move that fast, but that's not how I roll."

"I like your resolve, Lucy," Alvar says with a grin. "Still, I want you to know that if Earth human blood runs in the royal family here, your world will be safe forever as will ours. If you choose to, I would have a family with you. I believe in a Creator of our worlds, I believe our world belongs to us, and your world belongs to you humans, we *shouldn't* change the course of our worlds employing the Bridge."

Wow. Deep. It makes me wonder about Alvar's beliefs, but I can't think about it without my head spinning because that question would possibly open up an entire religious history in this kingdom that I know nothing about. So, I change the subject, "What did Triss look like?"

"I don't wish to speak of her," Alvar states coldly, such a change in direction from where we were headed. I'm disappointed.

"Did you love her?"

"Yes, Lucy, I loved her very much," Alvar's voice is far away. I am sure his mind is in the past. "She and Fletch made my reign possible. She helped me throw Saul over the Bridge. She was my sun."

The words are so sincere I can't think of anything to say in reply. I bite my lip.

Am I disappointed or jealous to hear this?

"I don't believe you'll ever love me, Lucy," Alvar says wistfully. He casts his gaze away from me.

"But you told me while on Earth that you'd have me love you," I remind him, wishing he wouldn't give up even if he doesn't believe it. "Why are you giving up on that promise?"

"Now that you know what I am... that I'm Cursed. Loving me is impossible. I know it is. Even Triss couldn't love me truly, but she felt pity for me. I think she mistook her pity for love."

His words hit and resonate with a shock. This conversation is spiraling into places I'd rather not go. I think of Mike. Why is it so easy to forget about him here? I'm a horrid human being to lose track of all he was to me.

Or all I wanted him to be to me...

"You've given me plenty to ponder. I need some time alone," I find myself whispering, and my throat tightens. "Will you please leave me?"

"As you wish," He says and takes my hand and kisses it. Then he adds darkly, "What you know about me has the power to tear this kingdom down and put everything at risk."

"That's what you keep telling me," I say with a sigh. "But don't worry, I won't speak of it to anyone."

"Thank you," he says again.

The pieces of Alvar's puzzle are coming together in unexpected ways. I don't know where to start in how I feel about him.

Alvar leaves me alone in my room.

I've never felt this trapped or conflicted about anything in my life. Everything Alvar has said so far has turned out to be true. Alvar hasn't treated me ill, hasn't forced himself on me, or made me feel uncomfortable, save taking me here in the first place. He been a gentleman and he's a damaged person.

More damaged than me: the girl that no one wanted to do with who was brought up by a crazy woman

Well, no one except Mike and Emily and those who didn't know about my childhood.

I wish I could close the door to thoughts of guilt over Mike. I wish I would have listened to my Mom and never gotten involved with a man on Earth. Now I knew most certainly that I'd viewed Mike as security and as a friend. There hadn't been chemistry, just comfort. Desire had never been a factor in our relationship because I thought it didn't matter. It isn't the only thing marriage is built on; many people have told me so, but maybe it is more important than I'd initially thought.

"My queen, the King has ordered I take you on a tour of the palace," Grey's voice interrupts my mental whipping.

"Uh, yes," I stutter. "Please do."

THIRTEEN

Six days later, I'm beginning to get into the swing of things at the palace:

Breakfast in my room with my fortunately question-less mother, lunches to either be had with Emily or my mother or to join Alvar with a visiting human lord I never quite caught his name. Dinners are always with Alvar. Besides his asking my welfare, we don't talk much. He is too busy with diplomatic meetings involving his marriage to a woman from Earth to make a long conversation with me. Still, I catch his gaze on me from time to time and wonder what he is thinking. Does he think I'm beautiful? Is he comparing me to Triss? I don't know why, but I hope not.

After one of my lunches with Emily, she tells me she's decided that we need to have a sleepover to talk about men and sex. I'm in apparent need of education in those areas. Still, she bails last minute because she meets a hot guy who says he wants to fool around with her in her room. With Emily, this kind of thing is just part of her being Emily. It's a common occurrence in our friendship even in the past. I don't judge and am not offended.

Let her have her fun if it makes her happy, but I kind of wish I could have some fun of my own.

Leeza woke me up this morning and told me Grey was going to take me on tour and explain some things about Underland history.

"This palace has stood for ages, through wars and famine. Of course, there have been improvements made over time here and there, and renovations were done on some of the more ancient places, but most of it is original," Grey says as he begins on his tour. "It wasn't until the power of Arlite was discovered that this place was remodeled completely."

"What exactly is Arlite?" I ask. I've heard the word over and over again. I don't know if it's just what they call their magical rocks or if it, in reality, makes scientific sense. Maybe they think the way we use electricity is magic.

I half-smile at the thought.

"It's a power source, a very clean and efficient power source, but extremely potent. Do you have phones in your world? Phones, television, the internet?"

I blink. How would Grey know about that?

"Yes, we have all of that," I reply.

"Well, we had forms of that here as well at one point. We, however, have shut down anything as vast as what your Internet is," Grey says. "It is too dangerous of a thing. There is no way of policing it. It also isn't healthy to live inside a digital world rather than the natural world. Our histories tell of a cyber war, which caused technology bans to form. Unfortunately, our people fell a bit back in time after many of the technology bans and some backward customs were taken up again. Arlite was discovered and changed the way we viewed the world entirely. Instead of taking forever to get anywhere, we use sky waves. Person to person contact is easy and clean, no need for screens; you want to see someone you can find them. Yes, your digital world may be vast, but it lacks soul. You can forget about souls if you stare too long at lifeless content and persons masked by screens."

I enjoy his explanations, but I am a bit indignant as I feel he is insulting Earth's ways in the process.

"This is the great hall; it is where we had your wedding reception if you'll remember," Grey says, nodding toward it.

We continue, and Grey tells me so much about different columns and rooms I fear the information will make my head explode. There is no way I'll remember everything.

"Where is Alvar's room?" I ask Grey out of the blue.

"The King's living quarters are in the East Wing. You are in the West Wing."

"Oh," I say. "So we're on opposite sides of this palace, huh?"

"Yes, my queen," Gray says. "It isn't customary for the king and queen to live in the same area of the palace, only to copulate do they sleep in the same room with each other. Safety precautions."

Copulate? I try not to laugh. And he'd said it with a straight face too.

"Would you like me to take you to his quarters?" Grey surprises me by asking.

"I thought it wasn't allowed," I say. Really?

See Alvar's inner sanctum?

I've gotten used to Underland city and living in the palace, and I'm feeling a bit braver every day. I'd love to see where my usually stoic husband lives.

"Alvar told me that if you wished to see him in his quarters to allow it; he changed his mind for some reason a few days ago and informed us," Grey explains.

Hmm, I wonder if it has anything to do with my learning about him being Cursed?

Or maybe he's just hoping I'll make a move on him to get this whole "producing an heir" thing started.

"I would like to see his quarters then."

Grey takes me from the great hall and down a gallery hall. There are many paintings and pictures hung on the walls as we walk.

"I need to let the King know you're headed to his quarters," Grey says.

He holds up a glowing slate and slides his index finger in a half-circle, and the slate reacts to his fingers. Glowing marks trail behind his fingertips. It's as if he's writing something on a touch screen.

"He says that it will be alright and that he's sending Leeza to prepare you for the night in his chambers," Grey says.

Wait, I'm staying the entire night there? I try to keep the fear from creeping onto my features; they're all supposed to think Alvar and I have already been intimate. But this hadn't been my intention! I'd only wanted to see where the man lived, not make him think I was coming on to him.

*

Two guards open the double doors into the East Wing where Alvar's quarters are. The place is dark and rich. I'm struck by its appearance so different than my light marble-and-pastel silks style quarters. "Dungeon Elegance" is what I'd label the furnishings and aura of this room. Why does he keep it so dark in here?

Grey bows to me. "Leeza will be here shortly." Then he leaves.

The double doors shut behind me.

Alvar's eating area is large enough to entertain guests. I realize he must like the color red as the drapes are red, the furniture is red, and the accents in the room are red. A black and slate grey tile floor extends throughout the rooms, and the walls and columns supporting the ceiling are the same greys. I open the door to his bedroom and gasp. There isn't a bed in here; but why? There is however an ornate fur rug on the floor and a fireplace is glowing with bright red flickering. The only thing worth resting on in this room is a luxurious red lounge chair that is about the size of a couch.

There is a knock on his bedroom door. "My Queen, you need to come out here for me to attend to you. I am not allowed in his chambers." It's Leeza.

I open the door and note Leeza is shielding her eyes with her beautiful yellow wings. I close the door behind me. "It's alright, you can look," I say.

Her wings swing back from her face and extend out. I'd always assumed she could fly with them, but since I've never seen her use them to fly I wonder if they are more of a decoration than a tool for flight.

"Alvar said to give you this," Leeza says blushing. Is she blushing? Oh dear, what is it?

I take it from her and am surprised at how little fabric the red piece is made of.

"He must have the wrong idea. I only came here to see what his quarters looked like," I say with a giggle.

Leeza cocks an eyebrow and then a vague smile splashes across her face. "My dear, I was under the impression…" her voice trials.

"It's alright," I say, straightening my shoulders and clearing my throat. "I'll handle it. Thank you, Leeza."

"As you wish, your majesty," Leeza says, bowing before leaving me alone.

I sigh and hold out the skimpy garment, getting a good look at the lack of coverage it would give me with a shake of my head.

Alvar's and my cultural clash is getting the best of us. I'm not going to be offended though. If we are going to have any relationship, we'll need to learn how to communicate with each other better.

I place the lingerie on a vanity in the corner of his room.

Something catches my eye on the vanity top: a large red pendant, the size of a golf ball. I curl my fingers around its smooth surface and lift it to get a closer look. It's carved in the shape of a dragon, and the weight of it is heavy in my hands.

Wearing something like this around your neck would be cumbersome, I wonder, *what is it for?*

My fingers brush against the heavy dark red gem, but at the touch, a shock goes through my body, and I fall back on the floor. My vision starts to blur, my head is spinning, and then a black mist surrounds me.

When it clears I realize I'm somewhere and *someone else* entirely.

FOURTEEN

Fletch was a gobli drone who worked in the Ferardian mines as a slave. He was a little grunt of a gobli, scrawny, shorter than a collie, hairless, with long bat-like ears, grey-green skin, and a pug-nosed face.

There wasn't any threat in Fletch, and that's why King Saul had chosen him specifically.

Alvar spotted him under the dim lights of the mines pounding at a chunk of rock.

"I suppose you've come to take me to the over-world." The creature looked up at him with orange eyes and growled.

"Aye," Alvar said, resting his solid, muscular frame against the dingy walls of the mines. "Word is you are the best lock picker of any gobli in the mines."

"If I was, you think I'd still be in chains?" Fletch grumbled and turned back to pounding the rock. Despite his efforts, the rock was barely chipped.

"You aren't much use in the mines are you?" Alvar grinned. He liked the little person already. Gobli were irritable and impatient by nature, but this one had a sense of humor.

"But I hate the over-world more," Fletch said.

"Why?" Alvar cocked his head.

"I hate sunlight. Don't you know anything about gobli?"

"As a matter of fact," Alvar said and laughed as he reached into his pocket for the pair of shaded specs he'd been given. "You won't have to squint wearing these, little one."

"Little one?" Fletch narrowed his eyes at the jab. "I already hate you."

"You can call me, Scarbrow." He didn't bother to extend a hand. Gobli didn't shake hands and hated physical contact with humans. "I have a feeling you've already picked your chain's lock."

"Master Scarbrow? You aren't as stupid as the slave masters. I'll give you that," Fletch said and yanked at the chain around his ankle, which immediately came off.

"Why haven't you run?" Alvar asked. If one had a chance at freedom, one must at all costs take it, in his opinion.

Fletch shrugged. "I have my reasons, but they aren't any of your business."

"Very well." Alvar turned to begin his upward climb back into the light with relief. Not that the tunnels bothered him. He was used to hiding in the dark.

"Hand me those specs first, gutter rat," Fletch said and extended a calloused and warty four-fingered hand.

"As you wish," Alvar tossed them at him. Fletch caught it with the accuracy of a jungle cat snatching a bird mid-air.

They walked out of the mines and into the sunlit barren pit the tunnels were dug into. A slave master passed them on their way but didn't even acknowledge Fletch or Alvar.

"Whose lock am I going to be working on?" Fletch asked, adjusting the spectacles against his ugly little face, now even more hideous in the burning light of the sun.

"The lock of a high-security temple," Alvar answered. "But I do not wish to discuss details in public."

"Look at you, all important and unable to discuss details," Fletch snorted. "You consider yourself a great asset to the king too; I'll bet."

"If you don't want to be beheaded by the king, I suggest you show me some respect," Alvar mumbled.

"Aye, and why is that?" Fletch asked. "The king wouldn't send his son down into the mines. No, I've already figured out what you are, Scarbrow."

"And what is that?" Alvar shot his gaze down at Fletch, wondering if he wasn't as dumb as he was ugly.

"You're wearing an elaborate collar around your neck, but not because you are royalty, that's a slave's collar, and a special one at that," Fletch said.

Alvar's fingers brushed the cold metal that never left his neck. "What of it?" His mind swore at him for not wearing more concealing clothes.

"You are the king's very own pet. I'll warrant, the Cursed one who's given him this kingdom."

"There you are wrong," Alvar snapped. "I'm no pet."

"Aye?" Fletch chuckled and shook his head. "Aren't we all the king's pets now in Ferar and all across Axus?"

"Just shut up, and we'll talk more when we've reached the palace," Alvar noted the sky. The sun was sinking in the horizon, and if he didn't get back fast enough, he'd be late for the conference with the king.

"Now *I* have to shut up?" Fletch asked innocently. The wicked creature knew his words were hitting a nerve.

Alvar didn't bother answering. The sooner they reached the conference, the faster they could finish this blasted mission.

*

Alvar stood in the doorway of the conference room with Fletch waiting for the gesture to approach.

King Saul had grown fat and ugly. With a red, bulbous nose and greasy black bean-colored beard, the man held not a cent's worth of royal countenance. Alvar remembered a day when Saul held a handsome appearance, but now the elaborate clothes he wore, a purple and gold tunic, white and gold turban, and gold shoes were too elegant for him. In short, Alvar thought the man was like dung covered in gold. A tawny-haired slave girl wearing only a thin piece of fabric wrapped around her waist popped food in the king's mouth while he sat at the enormous conference room table. The only women Alvar saw were the king's women. This one wasn't new to his sight. Alvar had observed her serving King Saul for the past month. He strived to keep his gaze in check. Gawking at the king's women when they were uncovered was forbidden. Her lighter colored hair indicated her to be from the north. She was most likely one of the barbarian captives.

"Go away," King Saul told the girl giving one of her lovely apple-sized bare breasts a squeeze with his greasy hand and ending with pinching the nipple. The girl gave a gasp of pain, and her nose wrinkled as she turned from the king carrying the bowl of food with her. Her dark blue eyes flickered toward Alvar, and he turned his face from her even though her gaze aroused a part of him he wasn't allowed to express. The silver chains on her ankles clinked as she walked out of the room.

Fletch snarled and glared his spectacle clad eyes up at Alvar. "I have no patience with a man who uses a female of his kind that way," he whispered.

"Hush," Alvar hissed.

King Saul sucked the food noisily off his fingers one by one and motioned with his other hand for them to sit. Alvar pulled out a chair for Fletch. The gobli struggled to climb atop it. After they sat and the king finished licking his fingers, another man hooded in red entered the room. A priest of Hedomas, the god Saul worshiped.

"Now that we're all here," King Saul began. "I must first say this mission is highly classified and must remain so." His dark eyes went to the gobli first.

"So Scarbrow has already told me," Fletch said dryly.

Alvar would have kicked him under the table, but Fletch's little knobby feet barely reached over the edge.

"You shall not speak unless I ask you to, gobli," the King barked.

Fletch mumbled something in his own tongue Alvar assumed were curse words and crossed his arms before becoming silent.

Alvar looked to the man hooded in red. The priests were everywhere in the palace and served the king's god, Hedomas. Alvar hated them. They were wicked and made up half their prophecies to satisfy their lust for wealth and power.

"I have brought you together to obtain a possession for me," King Saul smiled, his browning teeth showed. "The good priest, Hyphus, will explain the rest."

Hyphus' shadowed face broke into a crooked grin. Something about him was familiar to Alvar, yet since he was heavily clothed, Alvar couldn't figure out how he knew him. "There are rumors a great Memori has been found in the north by the Sylphs. The king wishes for us to attack the temple and obtain the Memori and bring it back to him." The voice of the man was smooth as glass.

"Don't you think Scarbrow and I could make the trip ourselves?" Fletch asked. He glared at the priest with a suspicious gaze. Alvar knew Fletch had no idea what a Memori meant or why the king needed to send a priest.

In truth, Alvar wished he were like Fletch, an ordinary slave who didn't know anything.

"I have my reasons for going," Hyphus answered, "I represent the king's best wishes, and I will make sure those wishes are carried out."

"See that you do and your reward will be great," King Saul said as he handed Hyphus a key with a ruby stone embedded in its handle. The priest's eyes glinted at the honor of such power in his hands. Alvar, however, winced.

"The Memori is kept in a Sylph temple," Hyphus continued. "It will be guarded extensively. Since we do not want this theft to be seen as a reason for an attack on Ferar, we have chosen the gobli to be framed for the deed."

"So my people will get the blame?" Fletch rolled his eyes. "That sounds more than fair."

Alvar was shocked the gobli hadn't been thrown out of the conference room for his impudence yet.

King Saul laughed, "You are quite entertaining. I shall have to have you brought to entertain at my dinners, gobli."

"I would believe my ugliness would ruin your appetite, majesty, but I fear you are far *uglier* than I," Fletch growled.

"He speaks the truth!" King Saul couldn't stop laughing now, and he wiped tears from his eyes.

He waved a hand at Fletch, Alvar, and Hyphus. "Insure Fletch is given a bedchamber so he can be well-rested. Scarbrow you are to go to your hole."

"Give me a stone floor. Much more comfortable than your smothering pillows and sheets," Fletch grunted at Hyphus as they followed the red-clad man from the conference room.

"I know how to find my room," Alvar told Hyphus as he turned from them. A hand on his shoulder made a fire burn in his throat. He wished to be alone. He always wished to be alone. The moments in the "hole" were the best of his life. "What is it?" he asked Hyphus.

"I am your master now, Cursed," Hyphus whispered in his ear, out of earshot from the gobli. "This will be more than enjoyable. The one blessed to be Cursed blood now the lesser of us."

Now he knew why the priest was familiar. In another life, they'd been family.

"You will never be my master, Ashtar."

"You insult me by addressing me by that name, slave." Hyphus' grip on Alvar's arm tightened until his nails, kept long as a priest of Hedomas, dug into the muscled flesh painfully. "They left me to tend the goats and be beaten for *your* shortcomings? *I* have not forgotten. Mother burned for you even though she loved me and not you."

*

The young woman was dressed in a lingerie piece leaving little to the imagination. The gold-encrusted in the bodice and brassiere twinkled in the flicker of candlelight. She stood like a dream by the door to his cell, and he recognized her as the same slave-girl he'd seen attending the king. Her eyes, the only visible part of her beside her hands, gave her away.

"Scarbrow," she whispered.

"What are you doing here, woman?" Alvar glanced behind him to make sure Hyphus hadn't decided to follow for a visit to the cell. "Do you have a death wish?" he snarled.

"Yes, I do," she said, her lashes hooded her eyes as she looked down. "Will you devour me?"

"Why would you want that?" Alavar asked. His voice went hoarse at the end. If he were caught consorting with one of the king's pleasure slaves, he'd be beaten and possibly worse. Alvar cringed.

"The king wishes for my virginity tonight," the girl stated.

Alvar closed his eyes. He didn't want to picture what she'd told him, but the images taunted his mind.

"You looked at me when you weren't supposed to," the girl said. "I *know* you want to eat me. I want to give you what you want."

"The king would flog me if he knew I'd eaten his virgin." They thought he ate humans. Of course, they did. To everyone who knew what he was, he was only a monster. "How did you get here without notice?"

"That doesn't matter, what does matter is that you kill me," she pleaded, her small soft hand grasped his calloused one. The tenderness of her gesture and the softness of her hands were like a volt of primal energy. His senses burned with the awareness of his sexuality as the touch of the opposite sex was so deprived of him, and he cursed himself for it. The last thing he wanted was to mirror King Saul's lust. It pitted him lower than his current physical servitude. He was not a slave to his desires as King Saul was. He did not worship Hedomas as Saul. Alvar secretly worshiped the God of the Light who called on men to be loving and respectful of women, to treat them as their equal.

Alvar withdrew his hands from hers, and everything inside him settled.

"I want to help you, but—" Alvar began.

"What are you doing?" Hyphus' voice sneered, interrupting their solitude. "A lovers' meeting? I thought the king forbade you to pursue women?"

"This isn't a lovers' meeting," Alvar growled.

"Then what is it?" Hyphus circled the two of them. His red hood covered his head once more and cast menacing shadows over his pale skin. "However, I am a generous, benevolent, priest," he drew out those last words as he put his hands on the girl's shoulders. "What is your name?"

"Triss," the girl whispered. The hope that had glimmered in her eyes at the prospects of being eaten was snuffed out like a candle after a prayer.

"Triss," Hyphus let the name slither out over his tongue. "Why did you come to see Scarbrow, Triss?"

"I want to be eaten by him," Triss replied.

"Eaten?" Hyphus laughed.

"She truly wanted to be my meal; she is afraid as the king desires her virginity tonight." Alvar couldn't take another minute of Hyphus' crass mockery. He felt the Cursed inside his body burning to emerge from its human shell.

"You're a virgin?" Hyphus' eyes glowed beneath his hood.

She nodded. "All he says is true."

"Now I know why the great Hedomas put us in this position! You are just the thing we need to take with us on our mission." Hyphus clasped his hands together with giddy delight.

Whether or not Hyphus held the key, Alvar wished to tear him to pieces right here and now. He could feel the claws waiting to burst from his fingers.

"When the king calls for you tonight, give him this message." Hyphus took a scroll from a pocket in his priest-gown and penned a short letter. He handed the scroll to Triss. "You need not fear to lose your virginity tonight, Triss, dearest."

The girl bowed her tawny head at Hyphus then hurried away from them.

Alvar sighed and reached for the handle of his cell door. He didn't know what Hyphus had planned for the girl, but it couldn't favor much over what the king intended for her. He needed to hide in his cell and seek out solitude so he could purge this exchange from his mind.

"Did I tell you that you could leave my presence?" Hyphus snarled.

"What is it?" Alvar turned to face Hyphus and glared at him.

"I will have that girl of yours for myself," Hyphus gloated.

"She's not mine," Alvar said with gritted teeth.

"From what I saw that wasn't the case." Hyphus withdrew the key from his pocket, "I don't intend to stop at just controlling you, Alvar, I want you to know how it feels to be helpless, just as I was for your misdeeds."

A puff of smoke rose in Alvar's throat, and he let it out in Hyphus' direction. "I told you long ago I had nothing to do with father's actions."

"You are wrong. You possessed all that power, and you did nothing to stop him!" Hyphus snapped.

137

The collar burned, and Alvar knew he'd lost all free will. As long as Hyphus clutched the key to his enchanted collar, he could make Alvar do whatever he wanted him to do.

Hyphus was right. Alvar did care about a slave girl he'd just met. And like everything else he cared about, her fate resided in darkness. He stepped down into the pit which was the hole he lived in when Saul hadn't any use for him and unleashed the Cursed. Letting his body stretch into the monster he indeed was and always would be.

Hyphus watched him transform, watched as the pain of it seared through Alvar's flesh, the wings erupting from his back.

"You will attend the ritual as I spill her virtue blood on the altar of Hedomas. Isn't it wonderful, Alvar? I will always have everything you can't."

*

"Lucy," Alvar's voice echoes in my head and the scene I'm witnessing is misting over again. *"Let go of the amulet, Lucy!"*

FIFTEEN

I'm suffocating in the mist. Everything turns black. I grasp at the nothing around me as reality continues to evade. The sensation is similar to the dreams where you wake up because you're falling.

"Lucy!" Alvar's voice whirrs in my head.

I open my eyes and gasp for air. I'm in Alvar's arms; he has his ear to my chest, the scarred side of his face in my sightline.

"Wha-what just happened?" I manage the words although I'm drowning in the experience.

"You silly girl," Alvar shakes his head and places the red pendant back on the vanity. "What were you trying to do? Kill yourself?"

"What - I saw..." I struggle to keep myself in reality. My head throbs painfully, like my skull is clamped upon by metal.

"What you saw were memories, Lucy," Alvar says, his gaze is far away. "*My* memories."

"But how?" I blink.

"This is a Mystar amulet," Alvar explains. "It takes your memories and stores them for you in case you need to recall something that happened later in life. I do not understand why the amulet let you see *my* memories." He pauses for a moment and purses his lips in confused thought, then, "The only explanation would be my Cursed blood you possess. Perhaps the amulet thought you were me."

"What do you mean, *thought*?" A shiver goes up my spine. I look at the seemingly ordinary pendant. So innocent to the sight.

"An essence lives inside it, a magical essence," Alvar says. "Similar to the kind of essence that lives inside my blood and makes me one of the Cursed."

"An essence?" I know my face betrays my fear, but needless to say, I'm glad Alvar has put it back on the vanity and *away* from me.

"Don't worry," Alvar chuckles, "The essence is unable to leave the garnet, it's permanently imprisoned there."

I'd just witnessed some of Alvar's memories. The heavy weight of such revelations weighs on me hard. I try to balance them without making too many guesses, but those memories give me clues into this mysterious man.

"Is there anything you want, Lucy? *Why* are you here?" Alvar asks his face darkens. He dips his head down toward me so I can feel the feathery warmth of his breath. He smells like burnt earth. His eyes darken to red.

I know the smell, from his memory. I know what the voice in his head sounds like, *his thought voice.*

"I'm afraid," I whisper. I'm like a rabbit, unable to move, hypnotized by the snake and his red eyes.

"You should be," Alvar says calmly; he closes his eyes, his expression pained.

"I'm afraid of this world." I shudder. What kind of world was this *before* Alvar took over? Dark and insane, with a ruler who abused women, enslaving everyone to his whims.

"What did you see?" Alvar asks, he's calm; he doesn't miss anything.

"I saw Fletch, Triss, Saul, Hyphus... It was horrible. How you met Fletch, Triss was serving Saul, and you were going on a search for a—"

"Memori. I know," Alvar whispers back to me. "I was there."

"This place... Axus... Underland... Ferar...was so... it was terrible. I'm so sorry. How did - how did you and Triss even end up together? Did Hyphus get his way? Did Saul? What happened? How did the tables turn?"

"Lucy, it would be best for you to forget what you just saw, those were my memories," Alvar growls suddenly. "And those particular ones are painful."

"I'm sorry," I murmur, but part of me wants to see more. Horrific as it is, my curiosity is immensely piqued, and I'm sure it'll kill me if I don't know more.

"Lucy," Alvar states my name somberly, his entire expression wrought with a sudden inn tension, he grips my upper arm in urgency, "You should go!"

"What?!" I jolt. Adrenaline buzzes through my limbs and my heart races.

"Tomorrow, we'll go to Remora's to present you to the gobli as my queen, but now you need to leave." Alvar turns his gaze from me, but his eyes emit a red glow, I can see it in the darkness of his chambers.

"Alvar, what is happening to you?" I ask. "Don't make me leave you. I can stay. You don't have to be alone." Being in his memories has changed me. What this person in front of me endured... it's too much for any one person to bear. My heart longs to reach out. To comfort, to protect, to... *love* on him?

He pushes me away and rises, clutching his sides as if in pain. "Go!" He roars, his voice deepened. "By Arlite, woman! Turn your gaze!"

I realize he's about to transform. I've stressed him. Maybe even angered and shamed him.

Tears well under my eyes. I nod vigorously and bite my lip, covering my gaze with both hands as I turn to leave.

He doesn't want me to see *it*.

*

Sleep evades me all night long. By the time morning arrives my eyes are sore, under the lids swollen, yet every time I close them I see Alvar.

I've seen the world he'd lived in once.

I've only scratched the surface of who this man, my husband, is, and it's a brutal dark place.

Were any of his memories happy?

Then I think about me.

My life is a muddle. I'm pretty sure I've never felt this confused on Earth. My heart is torn between the desire to despise him for making choices - major choices-for me, and to rule willingly by his side in a world he preserved despite everything against him. But how can I even play my part convincingly? I'm timid and not brave; I've always hidden away. I'm the type of person whose friends *speak* for her.

"Your Highness, I'm here to get you ready for the presentation in Ferar," Leeza's voice calls through my bedroom door. "May I come in?"

"Yes," I say, glad to be distracted from my warring thoughts.

SIXTEEN

Titan is provided to me in the courtyard when I join the others. Leeza saw that I wear a beautiful white dress made of spider silk and draped with strings of white crystals.

I'm relieved to find Emily sitting astride a brown mytonir beside Titan; it's nice to have someone familiar amid all the strange to accompany me.

"You're coming with?" I ask.

"Yes," Emily says, she pats her mytonir's neck. "These things are incredible. Smoother than any horse I've ridden."

"I know." I run a hand over Titan's silky side before a stablehand helps me up into his saddle.

Grey mounts a mytonir beside me, and another guard rides one on the other side.

"If you need anything, your majesty, let me know," Grey informs me.

"Grey's so hot," Emily whispers at me. "Do you think he's single?"

I try to brush aside Emily's remark. I'm too stressed to worry about whether my guard would be open to Emily's conquests. Which, while in the past I'd maintained a non-judgmental stance, are becoming annoying here in Underland as we have no idea of customs and culture of these people, she can't act like she's on Earth in the United States. I glance around at the party accompanying us: Fletch, Alvar, Leeza, Emily, Guards.

"Emily, where's my mom?" I ask.

"She refused to come with, said she wasn't feeling well or something," Emily rolls her eyes. "I think it's 'cause I'm here."

"Oh." I'd hoped to converse with her, see if she knew any details about how Alvar had found out about her having a dying baby.

We start riding down the cobblestone path outside the gates of the palace.

"I don't really want to come with, honestly," Emily says curtly.

"Why?" I turn to look at her.

"We're going back to Ferar," Emily grumbles. "I've seen enough of the Gobli, thank you very much. You ever have inbred scum tell you they're going to pull you apart limb by limb on some torture device?"

"That must have been awful," I say, "They thought you were me, and when they learned you weren't, they didn't have a use for you. If I hadn't married Alvar, they'd have done the same to all Earth humans in an invasion."

"Yeah, and why weren't they imprisoned for kidnapping me yet?" Emily accuses, staring coldly at the front of our procession where Alvar rides.

"I don't know, Em, I'm still trying to figure out this place," I say, I won't let her make me feel stupid. I look to the man I know Emily blames for the lack of action. Emily doesn't understand the politics behind everything, but I'm beginning to.

Alvar looks over his shoulder as if sensing my eyes on his back. Our eyes connect for a moment, and he smiles at me. His eyes crinkle up at the corners. I'm captivated by it and can't help but smile back. I catch myself lingering and quickly put my attention back on Emily.

"I could talk to Alvar about it, if you wish," I tell Emily. "Ask him why he hasn't made an arrest."

"So he *listens* when you speak to him?" Emily quips sarcastically. "I thought he made all the decisions in your relationship."

"Emily, you don't know what you're talking about," I surprise myself by defending him. *Oh no, Em is not going to go for that.*

Emily intently studies my face and then her eyes widen with a type of dread as if she's discovered her boyfriend cheating on her. "Oh my gosh, I can't believe it. You are falling in love with Alvar, Lucy!"

"What?" I blink in utter shock. Her words send icy shivers through my body. No, I'm not in love with him, but I'm growing to respect him. He's a man with a past as distorted and twisted as a crown of thorns.

"You just defended him!" Emily states, crossing her arms. "You don't defend someone who has kidnapped you and forced you to marry him unless you've succumbed to some Stockholm syndrome."

"He didn't force me to do anything, Emily," I state. "I *chose* to marry him. I saved your life by marrying him."

"There! See what I mean? Defending him again," Emily shakes her head and places her palm against my cheek, her eyes filled with sympathy. "Honey, remember Mike? He's decent, worth your love. Alvar, although I'll admit is hot as hell, is the definition of a bad guy, and not in a good way."

"I don't know about that." Tears start to swell, and I bite my lip. "I don't think he's bad, Emily. He's... you don't know him like I do!"

"Oh my gosh! You're admitting to it! And that is the same excuse every abusive relationship woman gives," Emily snaps, shaking her head in sympathy.

I recognize the look. It's the same look Em gave me when I'd first told her of my mom's stories.

"We need to go back home. Get you back to *Mike*," Emily says. "That's why I'm coming with you. To convince you and his royal highness over there it's for the best!"

"I've never loved Mike romantically, Em," I say, my cheeks flushing with shame over it.

"I know that," Emily frowns and sighs.

"Then why do you think it was okay for me to marry him?" I snap. Suddenly I'm infuriated with her. How dare she psychoanalyze me?

Like she's done almost our entire relationship, I remind myself.

"Instead you want me to divorce the person I can't get enough of?" *Huh? Had I just said I couldn't get enough of Alvar? But...* My image of Emily is transforming at that moment, from someone who was there for me my entire life to someone who has manipulated and controlled my lost and pliable soul since the beginning of our relationship.

"Get in a lay then with Alvar if you have to get it out of your system, then let's go back home. Back home to Earth! You don't belong here and you know you'll do a terrible job as a queen," Emily commands. "I know you better than anyone else, and I know that you're far too shy and paranoid to deal with all the crap here. You have trust issues."

"We're done talking now," my tone cold toward her. "I'm going to ask Alvar how long till we reach the Sky Wave."

I ride ahead of her and sidle myself in pace with Alvar.

"Lucy," Alvar says my name. He takes a sideways glance at me. "You're upset about something?"

"I'll be fine," I grit my teeth. We're in the center of the city. I'd seen it before at night, but in the daylight, it is gorgeous. Lush green trees are planted near the pristine white houses and the gold cobblestone glints in the sunlight. Exotic birds sing from the trees, and the air smells of spice.

I study Alvar a moment; he's wearing smart riding clothes with black leather gloves and boots, along with a slate grey cape, white shirt, and navy trousers. Around his neck is the Mystar amulet I know to be filled with his memories. Without thinking, I reach over from Titan's saddle and place my hand on Alvar's.

"You'll walk me through everything with these visits, right?" I ask.

"Of course," Alvar gives me a reassuring smile and takes my hand in his own and squeezes it. "But you'll do fine. Lucy, I believe you're much braver than you think you are."

SEVENTEEN

Underland is beautiful.

I can't help thinking this as we travel together in our royal company.

After exiting the city, we're surrounded by jungle, mountains, lush plains, and rivers. The air, however, is humid and makes my clothes stick and hair curl. I realize there must be a sort of air conditioning in the palace, for I don't feel such heat there.

We follow a white brick path, which snakes alongside a river. A white tower-like building appears on the horizon, attached to its side is a white waterwheel.

"The Sky Wave is just up ahead," Alvar informs me. I've ridden alongside him the entire way. I dare not go back to Emily. Still, I wish we could send her back to Earth. It's not right to keep her here if she doesn't want to stay. I hope Alvar will allow this exception for me.

"How do you travel on the Sky Wave?" I ask him, focusing back on our current venture.

"Well, it's powered by water and Arlite. It's too complicated to explain, but I'll say it's a way of teleporting."

Guards of Underland stand watch over the Sky Wave. They greet Alvar and his men warmly.

"My king, it's an honor," the man, I presume is in charge, steps forward, he wears blue unlike the white uniforms of the other guards.

"Is the Wave prepared for us, Rust?" Alvar asks, dismounting Shasti and taking off his riding gloves.

"Of course." Rust bows with his arm outstretched toward the entrance to the Sky Wave building, an ornately carved red door.

"Good." Alvar nods with approval.

Suddenly I realize we haven't packed anything to take with us. Hmm.

Alvar approaches me and places a hand on mine. "May I help you off the mytonir, my queen?"

"Uh-yes," I smile, and his hands grip my waist as he swings me down.

The touch is more intimate than I realized it would be. Once down, his hands still rest on the small of my waist, and we're close, face to face. I tilt my chin to look up at him. "Thank you."

"My pleasure," Alvar says, his voice gruff as if he senses it too.

Out of the corner of my eye, I notice Emily roll her eyes, and it takes all the good feelings away. I step back and smile politely at him and begin down the path to the red door of the Sky Wave building.

Alvar doesn't seem phased and follows after me. Our party comes in after us.

Upon entry, I'm shocked with blinding light. *Whoa.* I shade my eyes. The source of the light is coming from a blue shard of Arlite, so large it's the size of Titan.

"This shard is the pride of Underland," Alvar whispers to me. "Without it, teleportation wouldn't be possible."

He rests a hand on my shoulder and guides me to an extended bench, facing the magnificent gem.

Rust enters after everyone is seated on the bench and clears his throat. "Your Majesties, I am going to review the safety precautions of using the Sky Wave."

Safety precautions? I swallow. I wish I'd grown up here. It's frustrating to be in the dark about all the things used in this world that everyone else views as usual. Mother hadn't taken the time to inform me about their technologies, curses, and magical items. *Like the Mystar amulet...* I note the stone on Alvar's neck once more.

"You must all join hands," Rust begins. "Then look forward at the Arlite. Do not at any time let go of the hand or hands of those next to you or you may be dropped from the teleport."

I grip Alvar and Grey's hands. Emily is next to Grey and holding his and Leeza's hands.

"Everyone ready?" Rust asks, he checks to make sure we're all secure.

Rust nods at a guard behind him who pulls a lever. The Arlite gets brighter, and sparks fly, or is it *water*?

"Good travels to you." Rust bows his head.

The Arlite glows, and a buzzing sound vibrates around us. It amplifies until white encases us and there is nothing but the glow, the buzz, and the feeling of Alvar and Grey's hands filling my senses.

In mere minutes, the glow dims as does the sound, and as my eyes adjust, I realize we're somewhere else entirely. The sky is grey above us instead of the vibrant blue Underland's sky held. Brown muddy terrain is underneath our feet, and a mist shrouds the land.

"We're here," Alvar says. "Ferar."

I recognize this place, from his memories. Unlike Underland in his memories, it hasn't changed much.

The crunch of four-legged footsteps approaches and figures appear like shadows in the mist. They're riding creatures that resemble a hybrid of rat and rhino.

One. Two. Three. Four. Six. Ten... how many are here to greet us? My heart is suddenly pounding in my chest. An aura of foreboding fills this place.

"King Alvar," A female voice greets us from the group. "How wonderful to be blessed with your esteemed presence and that of your new bride."

"Remora," Alvar grunts. "Where is that fool Maggort?"

"Maggort?" The female figure rides up to us, and I view the gobli queen for the first time.

The gobli queen is not as warty as I'd expected, seeing as the male gobli are covered in them. She has the same grey skin and beady eyes but is feminine in countenance and body. She's tall. Taller than all of her gobli males. Her hair is black and slicked back on her scalp. Her ears are pointed like an elf's not bat-like as her male counterparts. Her facial features are soft and almost human, save a large hooked nose.

"The henchmen who kidnapped my bride, the queen's, friend," Alvar says.

"Oh, that idiot. He fled," Remora scoffs. She smiles at us, her teeth pointy behind her lips. "Come, my guests, you must be seen to your rooms to prepare for the feast I have tonight."

EIGHTEEN

Emily rushes to me and grasps my hand. "Lucy, I don't want to be here. Send me back to Underland. I don't know why I agreed."

I don't fight her and don't blame her. She had traumatizing experiences here, and it's understandable. "It's okay; no one will hurt you here. I think Alvar already wants to make sure those who brought you here are punished. Didn't you hear him speak of Maggort?"

"So, you going to do it with him tonight, then?" Emily asks, changing the subject to something entirely different. Something positively inappropriate.

"Um—" I blink.

"Lucy, I saw how you stuck with him the entire time we rode to the Sky Wave. Don't tell me you're not planning that tonight's the night," Emily says, crossing her arms over her chest.

"No way," I snap. "So just stop. It's none of your business anyway."

Remora and her gobli guards are leading us down a narrow tunnel into the earth. It's dark down here. My blood turns cold. Why can't I get rid of this suspicion that something terrible is about to happen? Like we're being dragged down into a pit of death.

'I am going to ask Alvar to get you back to Earth so you can resume a normal life and be with your family and those you know again," I tell her.

"Oh, you are; are you?" Emily snorts. "But you're not *coming back* are you? You know, Mike probably misses you."

"Yes, and I feel bad about that, but... I'm here to save our world, Emily."

"Save our world? Don't you think our militaries are strong enough to protect us? I don't know why I'm talking to you, *and* I don't know why I'm willingly here in Ferar again," Emily mutters. "Waste of my time, and you're a terrible friend."

She falls back in our group to batt eyes at Grey again.

"Has she always talked to you in this condescending way?"
Alvar asks me, motioning his head back at Emily.

"It hasn't always been so whiny, but it's understandable - her wanting to go back. I want to send her back so she can be with her family again," I say. "If you could do that for me, it would mean a lot."

Alvar considers me. "I will see if it can be arranged, but you know the dangers of it."

"You did plenty of travel to Earth the week that you went to claim me as your queen," I say aloud.

"Well, that was before I learned something." Alvar sighs.

Uh-oh. "Learned what?"

"I'll tell you tonight, in our bedchambers."

Oh. Are we sleeping in the same bed again?

"Lucy, there is something I've meant to ask you," Alvar says. We enter a hall lit by torches, and the sound of drums shakes the walls of the caverns.

"Yes?"

"Why did you decide to come to my chambers?"

"I wanted to talk. Ask you about a few things," I begin and shrug. "I'm afraid I'm just too curious."

"I don't think you're too curious; you're just the right amount of inquisitive." Alvar smiles, but then as if a thought strikes away the warmth, his smile disappears, and he grows serious, "Some doors are best left closed however."

"What do you mean by that?" I'm not going to let him stay mysterious. I want to know the truth about him. I'm becoming immersed in this new world, and for some reason, I want to embrace it and learn as much as I can about it and him—my husband. I focus on his scar. He'd said someone had given it to him at the age of seventeen because of his handsome appearance. What a terrible thing. Maybe... maybe he'll tell me more about it. Or maybe, I look to his Mystar, I can look into his past myself and see what happened.

"You keep eyeing the Mystar," Alvar says, his eyes narrowing and he grins. "You want another intimate look inside my head, my queen?"

I lower my gaze immediately. "I just... I can't wrap my head around what I saw, Alvar. I saw into your actual memories. It's something that never happens to anyone on Earth."

"Lucy, you would not like looking into the Mystar again. My memories are almost all... disturbing. The only good ones I have are of Triss and me, and as you may well imagine, it wouldn't be right for you to look at such things. Intimate times between my deceased wife and I should remain private and unseen by your eyes."

"Do you look at those memories ever?" I ask, and a pang of jealousy hits me as I imagine what sorts of things went on between him and Triss.

How would virgin, awkward me compare to his beautiful dead wife?

"I used to..." Alvar's voice trails and I know his mind travels to a time long past. "But I realized if I am to move on and begin a life with a new wife I can't drown myself in them. I miss my Triss, but I cannot bring her back. And no matter how many times I relive our memories, we'll never make new ones together. Someday, I hope to see her again in paradise, but even then, I doubt I'll make it in as I cannot die," He pauses, and his brow furrows with painful thought. "Besides, if I do die, after all I'm done, Elias, the God of light, will surely not grant me paradise," he adds in such a quiet voice I can barely hear it.

"You are a much better person than you give yourself credit for, I think," I whisper.

Our conversation is interrupted by Remora's booming voice, "Behold, the entrance to the city of Goblia."

We approach the edge of an enormous pit with ridges of staircases built along the inner sides of it leading down to the dimly lit city. All the buildings are made of rock and mud. A giant pool of water sits in the middle of the subterranean city. On further inspection, I realize there is not a single railing in sight, and if I were to slip on one of the narrow stairs carved out of the stone, I'd fall hundreds of feet to my death. I swallow and try to steady myself. I'm not good with heights. Not at all. I grip Alvar's arm.

"What's the matter?" Alvar asks.

"I think I'm going to faint," I whisper in his ear. "I'm terrible with heights."

"Oh, is that all?" Alvar chuckles.

"Excuse me?" I'm appalled. He finds my fear amusing, does he?

"I'm sorry, Lucy, but you're grasping hold of the arm of a man whom in a moment's notice could sprout enormous wings and fly you to safety," Alvar whispers back. He rests his hand on mine and pats it. "You have nothing to fear, my queen."

All the same, I let him take the outer edge of the path as we journey downward into Goblia.

NINETEEN

From what I can see limited by the darkness in the pit of Goblia, this place is like a nightmarish fantasy. The gobli here are not the most comely of creatures. I soon realize that Fletch is perhaps the most handsome of all gobli males I've met. Many of the males have humps on their backs and disturbing eyes the size of tennis balls popping from their skulls or no eyes at all. I cannot help but shirk away from time to time. I hope it doesn't insult them. Their bodies are covered with boils or warts, some are missing limbs, and others have more limbs than necessary.

When a rough hand tugs my hand, I jolt, only to look down and see Fletch.

"All those you see, inbred gobli. Remora is the mother of all," Fletch informs, his nose wrinkled. "There is only one female allowed to live in a gobli hive at a time. A barbaric old-ways custom."

"Oh, my gosh," I whisper, shuddering at the gremlins surrounding me. Inbreeding would explain it though. "Why?"

"Because the religion established in Goblia is one of the Great Matriarch goddess," Fletch mutters. "Most male drones have very short lives, do not live past infancy, and any female babies hatched are destroyed unless Remora sees fit to keep one as a princess to rule after she's gone. It's a terrible system, but Remora brought back the old ways after appointing herself the queen. She lays about ten eggs every week; those eggs are the future of the hive."

"How did she even start such a detrimental rule here?" I ask.

"Saul helped install her as queen and promoted these ways. If you ask me, he did this to weaken the last remaining organized gobli city. Remora is the only ruler left over from his reign," Fletch explains. "Our people were enslaved by Saul to work in his mines until Saul 'generously' appointed Remora our leader. As if that freed any gobli workers." Fletch snorts, "Goblia used to be a place of family clans, matriarchal, yes, but not to this extreme where there is only one female."

"I saw you were enslaved, that's terrible," I say, remembering my viewing of Fletch working in the mines in Alvar's memories.

"You know?" Fletch considers me. "How would you know? It was long before you were born that we served as slaves here."

"Sorry, I just meant, someone told me that," I cover.

"Oh," Fletch smiles vaguely and glances at Alvar's Mystar. "It's alright; you can keep secrets with me, Queen Lucy. I'm Alvar's oldest friend and know *all* of his secrets."

Our conversation comes to a forced halt when we approach Remora's palace carved out of the side of the pit.

"Come in, King Alvar *and* Queen Lucy," Remora cackles, batting her yellow eyes at my husband. "Our feast will be one to remember."

I shiver at her words and note Alvar's eyes turn red for a second. Hmm. Maybe he senses something is off... just like me.

We enter the palace and are surrounded by gobli guards on either side. They form a line up to a long dining table made of stone. Plates are set, and there are servers - inbred gobli much like those we saw in the city - waiting to deliver the meal to us. Remora walks to the head and motions for Alvar to sit beside her, and I am indicated to sit next to him. Fletch is on her other side.

Crap.

It is at this moment I realize I desperately need to pee.

"Alvar, I think I need to visit the restroom," I redden upon the words and hope he gets what I need. I'd never thought about what kind of words they use in Axus to refer to the bathroom. So far I hadn't needed to ask. My room had a gorgeous lavatory attached to it.

"Of course, Grey will stand guard if you wish," Alvar's tone is understanding.

Phew. He gets it.

Alvar motions with his head to Grey.

One of the gobli servers indicates for us to follow him. I leave my husband at the table and head down a side passage which ends at a single wood door, which only reaches the height of my chest.

"It's in here, Queen Lucy," the gobli server rasps, bowing to me and extending his scrawny arm toward the door.

"Thank you," I tell him, trying not to wrinkle my nose. He's particularly ugly, with boils covering his hide and no eyes. His ears droop on the sides of his head to the ground.

"I'll be waiting right here, your majesty," Grey assures, crossing his arms over his chest and standing straight. "If you need anything, call out."

"Will do," I say, and duck under the door and into the gobli bathroom. Once inside the carved out room, I find my senses assaulted with the smell of sewer.

Ew.

I hold my breath and realize it's a good thing I've been doing squats at my gym for the past three months as I'd rather not sit on anything this crude and disgusting place has to offer.

The room is dark; only a faint orange glow lights the black stone. I try not to dwell on how insanely creeped out I am. If this is supposed to be a palace lavatory, I don't even want to know what a common bathroom looks like!

I think back to what Fletch said.

No children, no women, no loving relationships, just the queen and her orders... I shudder. *What a world to live in! Poor Fletch. He must feel such an outcast to his people here **and** the humans and sylphs in Underland. I wonder if there are other gobli which exist anywhere in Ferar, gobli who aren't under Remora's rule.*

I walk toward a dripping water basin next to the door to rinse my hands. Suddenly, I feel a sharp sting on my shoulder, as if a biting bug has landed on me. On instinct, my hand swats at the spot, but instead of a bug, it's a dart I yank from my skin.

What the...?

I get a chance to scream before my head starts spinning and hear Grey pounding on the door as I fall back against something alive and substantial. I try to struggle against the drug, but I can't fight the drowsy effects. My world fades, and the last thing I see is the head of a sizeable ugly gobli looming over me and a familiar voice saying, "So you're the real bride of Alvar, huh?"

TWENTY

Thump. Thump. Thump.

Drums pound in my ears and a droning hum of voices shivers the ground as I open my eyes to darkness. Something is over my eyes, and it's wet and slick like leather. My hands are tied behind my back. My feet are free, but I realize getting up with the blindfold on and my hands tied behind my back would inevitably lead to falling or hitting myself into something.

Is this it?

The end of my life.

And like that, everything, all the turmoil of my youth, snaps through my memories. I wonder if Emily thought of the same memories when they'd mistaken her for me...

I thought of the first time I'd told Emily about being betrothed to Alvar.

Then the time when she'd sat me down in the coffee shop and explained to me why I needed to accept Mike's marriage proposal and get Mom psychiatric help.

"He'll close that door, Lucy," she'd insisted. "You need someone to keep you here. On Earth."

"Funny choice of words," I'd said dryly.

"You couldn't ask for better than Mike, he's the good kind of normal," she'd said, and we laughed together.

"Okay, but you'd better be my maid of honor."

"You know, Lucy... you need to get your mom some help, her outburst at the reference to the possibility of you having a boyfriend wasn't –um—healthy," Emily scolded as if it were my fault my mom acted the way she did.

"I know," I'd said, biting my lip and trying not to cry because I was ashamed.

My tears pool under my tight blindfold. Others have been raised with worse, and yet, I realize I'm miserable with the memories my life possesses at this point. I've never had control or a say in anything, and now I don't have power or a say in whether I live or die by the hand of Maggort.

Thump. Thump. Thump. Thump.

The drumming is getting louder. I open my mouth to say something, to ask what's going on, but I can't.

For all I know, someone is standing over me with a knife pointed at my breast about to sacrifice me in some religious ritual.

No. I'm not ready for death when I've just started letting myself live. Just when I found someone who understands me, I have to say goodbye.

God, whoever you are, anyone out there…? I know I've been whiny and pathetic and haven't done much with the time I've been given, but I promise if I live I'll find a way to make it right with myself, and be strong to stand up for myself.

"She's awake!" Maggort's voice cheers and is joined by a chorus of voices joining him as the humming stops. The beating of the drums continues.

"Alvar will retaliate," I quickly say. "He will be furious at you for killing me."

"Kill you?" Maggort snorts with laughter. I smell and feel rancid breath on my face. "Wouldn't dream of it," he whispers, then thankfully the smell and heat of his closeness leave me, and I hear him declare, "WE SEND THE EARTH QUEEN BACK NOW! Without her, there is no treaty, and we can take Earth."

So that's what this is about; they're sending me back to Earth?

"You might not make the journey though, the Bridge has been collapsing as of recent," Maggort whispers to me with a chuckle. "You know, the other bride was prettier than you?"

I have little time to process this insult because an incredible roar shakes the ground interrupting the "going away" party they're throwing me.

What now?

My heart can't take much more, nor can the level of adrenaline pulsing in my veins.

There are shrieks of terror from gobli, the sound of running feet on stone.

Another closer roar quakes the ground. Whatever it is, it's angry and of immense size.

I hear Maggort cry out and then, a *snap*. The sound of bones cracking as if they are candy.

I scream and huddle, bringing my knees to my chest and tucking my head down. I've never felt so alone. Unable to move. Unable to see. I am waiting for a horrific unforeseen beast to devour me.

Thud. Something drops next to me about the size of a body. I can tell by the sound. It's the squish of flesh against rocks.

I flinch. I can't stop trembling.

What sort of creature is out there?

"Untie her!" An incredibly loud and deep voice booms. The monster is speaking. "NOW."

Grimy gobli hands touch me, fumbling for my bonds.

"Don't touch me!" I scream at the creature, lashing out with what little will power I have left.

"Be still!" the monster voice commands. "All will be over soon."

I freeze when my eyes are assaulted by light as the blindfold is removed. To my surprise, we're not in the mines and caverns, but outside, on the mountains of Ferar. The moons are full and beaming down brightly upon us, illuminating the rocky landscape and the bloody scene before me.

As I'd suspected, just feet from me is the crushed body of a gobli.

I quickly avert my gaze from the disturbing image of the mangled corpse but find myself instead looking up upon a horrific dragon-like creature.

A creature flown in from nightmares.

Its sheer size is more significant than any living land creature back on Earth, save maybe a species of extinct sauropod dinosaur. Its immense jagged black wings are outstretched in aggression, and powerful jaws are wrinkled in a snarl with sharp white teeth glinting in the moonlight. Red eyes stare menacingly at the gobli undoing my shackles — a telling scar trails up the side of its serpent-like face.

I finally understand why his people fear his Cursed form.

This monster is my husband, and the paintings back in the halls of the Underland palace hadn't done the terror of his angry appearance justice.

TWENTY-ONE

The gobli who had untied me flees, but I approach the dragon-like creature who saved me.

"Alvar," I state his name, my eyes cannot leave him.

"Lucy," Alvar's monster form says my name with a voice deep and thunderous.

"How did you know?" I ask.

"When you didn't return after ten minutes," Alvar growls and snorts, an orange blaze escapes his nostrils during the act. "I knew something was off. Remora tried to distract us; she brought in human dancers and entertainers. She kept talking, but never about you nor asked why you hadn't come back."

"She was in on it?" I close my eyes to shut out his image. My skin crawls. Wow. I didn't expect to be this utterly frightened by his appearance, and I also didn't expect to hear what those powerful jaws of his could do. The *snap* of Maggort's body breaking stings my memory.

"Why d-did you kill him?" I finally say it, but my eyes are still closed, and I hold my breath.

"He's killed many others," Alvar snarls out the words.

"He could have stood trial, and—"

"Lucy, he was going to stab you," Alvar interrupts. "The second he saw me he pulled a knife. Don't believe me? Look to his corpse."

Oh, just as I'd feared initially, but I hadn't the ability to see during the attack so I couldn't have known.

Suddenly, I feel guilty. I don't need to look at Maggort's remains to know Alvar speaks the truth. From what I've seen of him, he wouldn't kill someone lightly.

A loud horn blares over the mountains. My eyes open. "What was that?"

Alvar's neck stretches high and surveys the landscape. "Get on my back."

"What?" My eyes widen.

His right wing extends down toward me, and he rests his chest on the ground, giving me less height to climb.

"Get on my back before they see us," he orders.

I swallow and run up to his extended wing and crawl up its length until I reach the center of his shoulders. I find at the base of his neck is a silver metal collar with red gems embedded in it.

"Hold on to the collar and don't let go," Alvar growls.

"The Fe collar?" I ask a part of me has no desire to touch the thing.

"Yes, the cloaking of it is not active when I'm in Cursed form," Alvar states.

I grasp the collar.

His wings move, shaking the bones in his shoulders and my body. Whoa. I steady myself.

He runs faster than I thought a creature of his size would be able to travel. He is snaking up the mountain until he comes to a cliff where there are hundreds of feet of space below.

Oh... he's going to jump off the cliff! I close my eyes as he leaps from the cliff. I grip his collar as tightly as I can, and my knees squeeze the sides of his shoulders.

We don't plummet to our deaths. Instead, we soar. My eyes open and I see the beauty of the mountains. Snowcaps on the tops of the black peaks. The wind is cold, but Alvar's body is hot underneath me. He's the temperature of a sauna and mist from his heat clouds the air around us, like when you place a hot piece of food in a freezer.

"Where are you taking me?" I ask him.

"Somewhere safe," Alvar answers me. "There is a secret gobli encampment just south of here. The gobli are of the same variety as Fletch. They desire peace, and freedom from the old oppressive ways. They desire a new ruler. This, what Remora did, is the perfect storm for me to help see them to a new ruler in Ferar. I do not want Ferar for the human race; it should be ruled by the gobli as it always has been. It belongs to them."

"What will you do though? You can't use your Cursed form to establish this," I think aloud.

"I have armies and allies among the gobli, and I also am too powerful for Remora to refuse. It would be an unwise move to go against me; she'll be lucky to get out of Goblia with her life after her attempt on my queen. Everyone else in Axus believes I'm the savior of our world," Alvar explains. "If

I were to rally the hidden gobli and return with accusations, I'd have enough to dethrone Remora. She was foolish in how she set up her people; her men are not as loyal to her as you may think. Many are her sons and are born deformed because of her. They are used and abused by her. Just as you saw in the memory of King Saul exploiting Triss, that is how many of her male gobli feel about her."

I shudder and nod, but I know he can't see me because I'm behind his head. There is a moment in our flight where silence falls between us, and I gaze down at the tiny trees and snaking rivers below.

"Lucy," Alvar interrupts me from my viewing.

"Yes, Alvar?" I ask.

"I'm sorry about what happened," Alvar apologizes. "And I'm sorry I couldn't realize the ruse sooner."

"It's alright, I'm okay," I assure.

Am I though? How can I be okay after being blindfolded and tied up?

I'm okay because I'm no longer the same Lucy who first arrived here.

I'm not the Lucy who did whatever my peers asked of her because I was too embarrassed about my upbringing.

I'm not the Lucy whose mother is crazy.

I'm Queen Lucy of Underland, a woman who knows what she wants: to live life on her terms, and being Alvar's wife… the idea is beginning to appeal to me.

I release a hand from the Fe collar and press my palm against Alvar's muscular scaly neck. "Thank you for finding me. You know, you're growing on me, dragon husband." I can't believe I managed a joke.

A sigh escapes him, and I can feel it as his chest rises and exhales. "I'll never be a normal human, Lucy. This is what I am. This beast lies inside me waiting for its next chance to surface. *You* don't deserve this, and my people don't deserve it. It would destroy them to see me like this. Maybe the plan needs to change."

"What do you mean?" I blink and don't like his tone. He's thinking about something dark and resolved.

"After everything is established... after Remora is overthrown making the last region of Axus stable, I may have to disappear... forever."

TWENTY-TWO

Maybe he's the one who doesn't like me. That's why he wants to leave because I'm just not good enough.

I find relief from my punishing thoughts as we enter a gobli encampment on the side of the mountain.

Alvar is hailed immediately by the gobli there with a cheerful welcome. The gobli rushing toward us with grins and applause are not as deformed as the ones in the depths of Goblia. They look similar to Fletch, warty, well-proportioned, and kindly. They all wear shaded spectacles to protect their eyes from the sun. How terrible for them to stay out here in the sun when they belong in the dark caves of their mountain. I realize I almost relate to them. I wonder if how they feel on the surface of Axus is similar to how I felt when first pulled into Axus from Earth. Completely out of their element.

"What news on the goblin queen, Remora?" The tallest of them asks.

"As of now, Remora has broken a critical treaty with me and all of Axus by insulting me with sending one of her henchmen to kidnap my bride," Alvar declares in a shout. "She intended to send Queen Lucy back to Earth. I will not stand for such actions; I shall dethrone her and help you all establish a new gobli ruler of Ferar!"

"AYA-ALVAR, AYA-ALVAR!" The group chanted, a chant I'm presuming means they are rallying behind him.

More gobli appear from their makeshift homes, and I notice a group of the deer-people emerging from the forests of the mountains into the crowds of celebrating gobli as well.

"Alvar," the largest stag among the deer people approaches, a magnificent set of antlers crowns his head. He is heavily tattooed and taller than any average human man. He wears a brown, leather kilt and brilliantly colored beads around his neck. "I shall go with you to help."

"You, Agnor?" Alvar asks. "Why do the stog take an interest in a gobli war or an alliance with me?"

"The stog have been hunted down and killed by Remora and her group. She claims we have no right to this mountain, but we have always resided on the surface of it while the gobli dwelled in the caverns and caves," the stag continues. "My son, Jahn, chief stag of his tribe in the north, will also be joining us to come with me. If you once and for all stop the genocide of my people, we will gladly ally with Underland."

I make a mental note. These are the stog people. They look like fauns from Greek myths, except their lower half has the appearance of a deer instead of a goat. The skin on their front and face is bare and white as snow. With eyes large and dark brown like a deer's, their backs are covered in red-brown fur down to their deer-like tails. Their bare chests are covered in red and white war paint.

"We will gladly accept your support," Alvar says, smiling vaguely. "We can always use more fighters. Remora will go down easier than thought; most of her warriors are at a disadvantage to us. The main thing will be getting through into Goblia. There is only one entrance, and it is heavily guarded."

"Aye, but what you don't realize, King Alvar, is that we've cut another hole into Goblia. A secret road into the city from the other side of the mountain. Some are spies for us in Goblia, and they've made it possible for us to have this advantage." The lead gobli drone of the encampment speaks once more.

"Then we shall trick them. Distract them, so all the gobli fighters are at the main entrance and storm them from behind. All we need to do is cut the head off the monster. We get Remora, and the head is severed," Agnor growls, he turns to a female warrior beside him. "Take a message to Jahn; let him know of these plans."

I don't know where I fit in all this, but I sense greatness at this moment as if a wonderful change is about to happen, and I'm somehow a part of it. Never in my life had I imagined to witness battle plans or ride the back of a dragon. Never had I imagined I'd start falling in love with Alvar of Underland. I know Alvar himself is in no danger with this plan as he cannot die, but I realize the sobering reality that some of those who stand before me, may not come out alive.

Conversations of the different groups drown out my ability to make out the rest of the plans. Alvar approaches me after they've finished meeting and presses his Mystar into my palm, closing my fingers over it.

"I dare not take you back to Goblia. You will be safe here. The gobli domesticates will look out for you in the big tent over there. Sleep with the Mystar on your forehead. You will see what you want to know about my memories and only that. I'll instruct the gobli domesticates to awake you when we've returned."

"And miss all the excitement?" I ask, rolling my eyes. "You're about to go to war, and you want me to take a nap?"

"There will be plenty of difficult things for you to experience in my memories, Lucy," Alvar warns. "I assure you that the loss of life in this battle will be minimal at the worst. We have the upper hand, and Remora already did us a favor by defeating her people."

"Who are these deer people... uh... the 'stog' I think they said?"

"The stog are people in hiding for many decades during Saul's reign. They are distrustful of the human race in general as Saul's religion demanded them as sacrifices for his god."

"Oh," I murmur and shudder. I understand why Saul is a person Alvar avidly acts to keep out of Axus. I wonder if, on Earth, Saul is doing horrible things to other people.

"Go, sleep. Dream of my life and tell me your decision," Alvar says. He presses his lips to my forehead and brushes a strand of hair from my eyes. "You're beautiful and smart, Lucy. I'd never give you up if I were a worthy man."

With those words, he leaves, following groups of gobli and stog away from the encampment.

I sigh and clutch the Mystar tightly. A tear forms without my willing it.

He doesn't want to leave me.

TWENTY-THREE

"That's six goats gone missing in a month," Father said, his arms crossed over his chest and brow drawn up in the expression Alvar, and his brother had come to recognize as the one they got before a licking. "Is there something you're not telling me, Alvar?"

Alvar cringed at his father's realization. Things were getting worse. His father suspected something was different about him; he just had no clue how *different*.

"Maybe Alvar has a secret girlfriend," Ashtar taunted, giddy over his older, more favored sibling getting in trouble instead of him. "And you realize if I were you, you'd already be getting a thrashing. But because you're father's firstborn and heir—"

"Enough!" Father snapped, smacking Ashtar across the face. "Let him explain himself first."

Ashtar whimpered and sulked out of the room.

Alvar didn't desire his younger brother to pay for his sins. It wasn't Ashtar's fault Alvar's affliction emerged and ate a goat whenever it did.

If I didn't have to hold it in and hide it, it wouldn't control me whenever I transformed, Alvar thought. *Maybe I need to tell Father. He will understand. He won't call me out to the people for fear of losing his family. I've hidden this for too long. The beast is restless and tired of hiding inside; it needs space to roam and to hunt for more food than normal men can stomach.*

Mother walked into the room at that moment. "Ashtar tells me you hit him," she said, glaring at Father.

"He deserved it; the stupid boy doesn't know when to shut up," Father snorted. "Alvar is his superior."

"I hear Alvar lost another goat," Mother said, looking at Alvar with annoyance. His mother was tall, with blue eyes and blonde hair, her grace and stature was that of a wealthy northern woman. Mother didn't like how Father had fallen from wealth during the economic depression, and she'd grown to resent him and how they'd turned to goat herding to survive. "You're too easy on him and too hard on Ashtar. Alvar is lazy with our precious resources, and yet you rebuke Ashtar."

"Father, Mother, I'm sorry about the goats," Alvar began, not sure how he would tell them. He opened his mouth; the words were on the tip of his tongue, yet they did not wish to fall. This revelation would change everything. They would hate him; he'd heard the stories. Stories his mother had told him since a child how the Cursed were the scourge of Axus.

Ashtar came back into the room, stomped up to Alvar, and punched him in the stomach, whispering in Alvar's ear. "I know you're secret, and now they will know, and Father will despise you and love me."

Alvar groaned and buckled over, closing his eyes tightly, but it was to no avail since he kept his Cursed locked inside. Deep inside him, let out a growl and a pain set into his joints. His eyes opened as he cried out in pain, trying to keep the beast within him.

"Red eyes, Father! He has red eyes!" Ashtar shouted.

"No!" Mother screamed, she drew a knife from a chopping block in the kitchen and approached Alvar, the blade glistening, "Get out of my house or I'll kill you! I'll kill you, and your Cursed demon!"

"Mother, please," Alvar groaned, kneeling on the floor, but the beast was angry with him for keeping it locked away, it let out a roar that exited his lips. A sound so vile he was sure it would strike fear in anyone's heart.

"Begone!" Father cried. "Begone, Cursed spawn!"

Alvar ran from them, away from his house, and took on his Cursed form so he could fly.

*

They burned his Mother for carrying Cursed blood on the Tuesday following his discovery. Although Alvar had fled his family after their discovery of him, he'd still caught wind of the news from the local villagers.

The priests were still chanting, when Alvar hurriedly approached the execution, ready to change forms to save her if need be. He covered himself with a priest's black hood he'd stolen from the temple clothesline. The fire blazed as tall as the rooftops by the time he was close enough to see all that was left of his Mother was a charcoal corpse.

No.

Alvar's heart sank into his gut. He had arrived too late for the burning. Too late to ever tell her he was sorry and didn't ever expect her to love him for what he was, but desired her freedom nonetheless.

Alvar reviewed the crowd and noted his father not present, but Ashtar stood, gazing at the still crackling flames without expression on his face. As twins, Alvar felt out of his body for a moment, what if the roles had been reversed? What if Ashtar had taken to the Curse and it was Alvar doing nothing while they'd tied Mother up to the searing hot metal pole to burn?

He would not have stood there.

That was the difference between Ashtar and Alvar. Ashtar never questioned any practice common to the people. He went with the group decisions as if they were always right.

"It's him, the Cursed!"

Alvar jumped in his skin, someone had recognized him! He noted that the one who knew him was an old friend in the village, Moly.

The reality that there were no friends now hit him like a slap in the face. No friends, no family, he was cut off from his race. What would he do? How could he hide this without hurting anyone?

"I'll kill you!" Ashtar shouted in Alvar's direction, "Isn't it bad enough that *you* killed our mother?"

"I didn't kill mother! You all killed mother!" Alvar shouted, shaking his head, but a knot in his gut formed. *I killed my mother.*

"Begone, Cursed scum!" Villagers started shouting, spitting, and throwing anything they could pick up at him.

The priests began their chanting, trying to drive him from their midst. "May the gods destroy you!" they said. "May your Curse die with you!"

There was no pity, no one reaching out to him; just anger, fear, and hate.

"Kill it before it becomes grown!"

"Burn it next to the devil that bore him!"

"I will not hurt any of you!" Alvar assured them, holding up his hands and practically begging. "You are my people!"

"How dare you say that!" Moly's mother shouted, clutching Moly by the arm. "You have never been human, nor will you ever! You are a great pretender! Leave us before you bring destruction upon us!"

Alvar had no choice, as villagers drew their swords, he took on his Cursed form, but instead of flying away, he dove into the pyre and grasped the corpse of his mother in his claws.

"I will bury her if you won't!" Alvar roared at the crowds.

"And I'll spit on her grave!" shouted Ashtar. The words were meant to save face most likely, to keep the villagers from burning him too.

Alvar flew from them. He'd make sure to bury her on a high mountain where none could spit or tread on her.

She didn't love me, but she was still the woman that carried and gave birth to me. I will honor her by providing a proper grave. Then I will leave this place. Go to the south, where none know my face or what I am.

*

182

"You'd better pay for that!" the bread seller growled. "I don't run a charity here. Things are bad enough in this economy without filthy street boy thieves pinching the wares."

"I'm sorry, sir," Alvar rushed, thinking on his feet. "I'm afraid I don't have any money. I'll work for food. I'll—"

"There is no need," a voice interrupted him, and Alvar watched as a tall, handsome black-haired man approached them. "I will pay for the boy's lunch." The man dressed in white and red, vibrant, and clean colors. This man wasn't an insignificant person. A lord, perhaps, and he was helping Alvar.

Alvar thought of objecting, but his empty stomach ached, and an empty stomach promoted an inevitable shift into his accursed form, which would eat something *for* him if he neglected to eat. "Thank you –?"

"Lord Saul," the man said with a smile at him. He extended a hand. "And your name is?"

"Alvar," Alvar said, meeting Saul's warm handshake. "I'm most grateful for—"

"No need to grovel, Alvar," Saul chuckled. "I'm glad to help you." He motioned for Alvar to follow him. "Come with me, boy. You look starved. I have more than bread for a poor orphan like you. 'Tis a shame Axus is plagued by an epidemic of fatherlessness in every city."

I'm not an orphan, but perhaps he should think that, Alvar thought.

"After we eat with you, I'll have my servants prepare you a bath and some clean clothes," Saul said as they entered a gate into a large courtyard of a grand house.

"We?" Alvar asked.

"My wife and I," Saul informed him.

Alvar paused in the doorway of the house. "Yes, but may I ask you something, sir?"

"Of course," Saul cocked his head but didn't stop his pleasant attitude at Alvar's suspicious tone.

"Why would you take in a street boy thief?"

"Because someone needs to make a difference," Saul said, placing a hand on Alvar's shoulder. "If I'd been born in your circumstances, I'd be stealing and dirty just like you."

"You are very kind, aren't you?" Alvar found himself smiling for the first time in a year.

"Come, Alvar, I'll see you looking like a young lord yet, I promise," Saul said, nodding his head inside the door.

*

Alvar sank into the warmth of the tub and let out a long breath. He'd never been in such a wondrous room or felt the exquisite feeling of warm water soothing his aching muscles. The home, large as a small palace, held artwork, architecture, and trimmings that cost fortunes. Saul was successful beyond the normal men in Underland.

Underland. The southernmost country of men in Axus. Underland was made up of jungle, rivers, and brilliant beaches on a warm ocean. So different than the northern country he'd fled. He loved the country. Of all the sights he'd seen traveling southward, this place had attached itself to him above all the rest. What made it even better was that no one knew of him here.

He closed his eyes and remembered the dinner they'd had—roast venison.

The meat *melted* in his mouth.

Saul had told him of his young years as a knight for the king of Underland, Umar.

"Umar gave me a title and enough coin to keep me fed the rest of my life."

"Why?" Alvar had asked.

"Because I saved his son in the battle against Ferar," Saul stated proudly. *"The boy (his son) was nothing but talk, and when a gobli sentry charged him, he froze with fear. He'd never seen a gobli before. I don't know if you've ever seen a gobli?"*

"No, sir."

"I'd be surprised, they rarely come above ground," Saul continued. *"But they are vile looking creatures. I lopped off the head of the sentry before it took the prince's head."*

Saul's wife had been an oddity. A beautiful, quiet woman who wore pendants and amulets on her neck. Her hair, a deep red, had bones braided into it. She hadn't spoken a single word the entire meal, but after it was over, she'd smiled at him and said, "I believe you have a good heart. A better heart than any lord I've met." Then she'd left them.

Saul had invited Alvar to stay the night in their guest house.

Although he wished to stay in the quietness of the tub forever, Alvar rose from the bathtub and dressed in the Underland robes provided. Underland clothes were much looser fitting than the trousers and wool sweaters he'd worn as a goatherd in the north. He left the bathing room and found Saul sitting in the courtyard.

"Is that you, Alvar?" Saul asked. "I hardly recognize you! My, my! Are all lads from the north so devilishly handsome? I'll have to keep my wife locked inside her room for the rest of your stay."

Alvar couldn't help but grow uncomfortable, and yet, was flattered by the compliment. But his happiness took a dive when it dawned on him that Saul and his wife would despise him if they knew his affliction.

The Curse. It follows me wherever I go. That's why I shall make sure these good people never know of it.

TWENTY-FOUR

His arrow flew true into the chest of the jungle cat. Quite a feat, considering the creature was rushing at their hunting perch in a large jungle tree. The massive creature fell, taking its last breath soon after its collapse.

"Perfect, my boy!" Saul cheered, slapping Alvar on the back. "Your aim is steadier than any I've met. Not many can kill a jungle cat on their first shot."

"Thank you, sir," Alvar beamed. Never had his father spoken to him in this way. Even when he'd done things right or brought home a hunting kill to feed the family, there hadn't been a praising word said. After six weeks of staying in Saul's estate, Alvar found that Saul and his wife, Ysta, treated him more like family than anyone before. He didn't dare admit to Saul that the only reason he could accomplish such an aim was because of his unparalleled senses. Senses he possessed from the thing that had driven him away from his past life.

"No more, 'sir,' Alvar, I'm Saul," Saul corrected him with a wink. "You know, my wife has been watching you... She says you are not like other humans."

Alvar stiffened and held his breath, waiting for what Saul would say next.

Does he know what I am? If he does, he will surely drive me away!

"You have faster reflexes, and your senses are more acute than an average human being."

"You flatter me," Alvar hurriedly said, he jumped from their spot in the tree to pretend as if he were inspecting his kill.

"Your eyes turned red, son," Saul said. No fear inflected his tone.

Alvar's skin crawled, and he closed his eyes to hide the shameful giveaway of his affliction. He would shift into his beast form from the stress if he weren't careful.

Not this man who has grown to treat me as his own. I can't abide any more shame.

"You're Cursed," Saul stated gently, but his words cut to Alvar's heart.

Alvar stifled an animal growl of pain.

Never will be home. Never will be accepted.

"Alvar, look at me, son," Saul said.

Alvar couldn't. His eyes were red; his beast was close to the surface. He could practically sense his muscles vibrating with the beginning of a transformation.

"Alvar, you're a good lad who would never use it for evil," Saul's words were incredible to hear. "I think I can help you, or at least my wife can."

"What?" Alvar opened his eyes and turned his gaze up at Saul.

Is he suggesting that the Curse can be removed?

"My wife is a sorceress," Saul began. "She is very knowledgable about magical ailments, and yours is no different."

"A sorceress?" Alvar furrowed his brow. Sorceresses drew their power from the darkness of the world, and their energy was sourced from pain, anger, hatred, and chaos. At least, that is what his parents told him as a child. But his parents weren't perfect examples of human beings either, so he wasn't sure if their views on sorceresses were even right. "Does she know I'm a Cursed?"

"Yes," Saul admitted. "She's sensed it on you for a while now, but didn't tell me until earlier today."

"I can't believe it," Alvar shook his head, trying not to hope that there was a chance he'd lose his Cursed blood.

"She can walk you through a spell, she told me about it, we need to source all of the Curse into an artifact of silver you wear," Saul began. "It will keep your Cursed form from manifesting itself."

"Are you sure that's even possible?" Alvar asked, afraid to hope.

"My wife is very talented. She is the reason I am wealthy. Her abilities are beyond many sorceresses," Saul continued, almost sounding eager now. He jumped down and put a hand on Alvar's shoulder. "If we can remove the Curse from you, you can be your own man. Have your own life. And Alvar, I want to name you my heir, but I can't have a Cursed as my heir, there are laws about that."

"By the gods," Alvar whispered under his breath, heart pumping like a drum. Could he have a life with these people? They'd certainly proved themselves kinder than any he'd met.

And wouldn't the freedom of being without the Curse be worth a try?

"I'll do it, Saul," Alvar announced and smiled to himself, his life seemed filled with possibilities suddenly.

Without the Curse, he'd be able to belong finally.

The thought brought happy tears to his eyes. *No more hopelessness. A loving family. A bright future. Never looking back on his painful past.*

*

"Alvar, I must warn you, I'll need blood," Ysta said.

Alvar had been led beneath the manor house into a candlelit room with many white chalk drawings on the walls. Sorceress symbols. Some of the pictures had blood smeared across them. Alvar couldn't help his spine-tingling at the oddities kept in bottles and cages in this strange room. Eyeballs in a jar. Tongues in another. There were human parts, too, not just animal parts.

Maybe this isn't a good idea, Alvar thought, *if Ysta has known of my Curse for this long and not thrown me out, I can live with them and not have to inherit anything.*

"I will forge a silver collar for you, it will have gems embedded in it, rare magical gems, that will draw the Curse from you every time it tries to manifest itself, but first I need your blood, Alvar," Ysta ordered.

"My b-blood?" Alvar furrowed his brow. "Why do you need blood?"

"I have to pour some blood into the liquid silver, it will bind the object to you, it will do nothing for you unless your blood is part of its creation," Ysta explained.

Alvar held out a hand. "I must warn you that sometimes when I get hurt, I just--um—transform."

"It will only take a little prick on your finger," Ysta giggled. She approached him and took his hand in her own. She smiled at the contact. "You have such power inside of you. I can feel it when I touch you."

Alvar practically blushed. Was she flirting with him? "Uh—thanks."

Ysta bent her head down and ran her tongue on his wrist.

"Whoa, hey! What are you doing?" Alvar tugged his hand away from her, but she kept her grip tight.

"Oh, my dear, don't worry, I'm just finding the place to draw the blood from," Ysta assured, her dark eyes looking up at him with a primal spark.

Ysta drew a needle from a bag she'd tied at her waist, and she placed fire over the tip. "To sterilize," she said, then she punctured his wrist with a quick in-out motion. A blob of blood formed on the small wound. She squeezed his wrist until it was the size of a small berry, then used a syringe to collect it.

She was busy over her fire for a while, adding the blood to the silver. Then she started working on crafting. It was taking a long time. Alvar waited until she finished. He tried not to think about how wrong everything felt about Ysta's actions. Saul came down into the magic room, and Alvar couldn't help but feel as if he'd done something wrong by the man.

"Alvar, how goes it?" Saul asked.

"Ysta took some blood for the silver," Alvar said quickly.

"Wonderful." Saul patted him on the back reassuringly. "You'll love how it feels to have control over your own life again, son. I promise. Everything I have will be yours."

"I hope it works," Alvar murmured. They both watched Ysta as she worked until she finally finished her craft.

She approached them with a beautiful gem embedded silver collar and key.

"Are you ready?" Saul asked, a huge smile on his face.

Alvar considered the magical piece. "What if it doesn't work?"

"It will work," Ysta reinstated with a smug grin. "A simple trifle of a spell."

"Alright," Alvar said.

"You must put it on yourself," Ysta said, handing him the metalwork. The piece was cold in his hands. *So soon after being engulfed in flames.*

Alvar brought the cold metal up to his neck and clicked it into place. "Nothing. Nothing happened," he muttered, disappointment washed over him. It would have been better if he'd never hoped.

"Wait," Saul quickly said, taking the key from Ysta and handing it to Alvar. "Lock it in. It must know itself to be bound to you."

Alvar turned the key in the small latch. Suddenly he felt it, a burning sensation. Something different than he'd ever felt in his life as he was immune to flames. "Huh? Argh! Oh, no, what is happening to me?"

TWENTY-FIVE

"Why did you do this to me?" Alvar asked, his body wasn't his own anymore. Before he could control his actions, now he was a slave to Saul's will. He'd transformed twice, from man to Cursed, and Cursed to man again. Panic filled him at first, but now an icy terror crept into his soul.

"I just wanted to see how it worked," Saul sneered, and then added tauntingly, "You don't *mind*, do you?"

Ysta stood next to Saul. "You told me you'd pay me after I'd finished the Fe collar for you."

"Yes, Ysta, go ahead, take some more blood from our Cursed friend," Saul said.

Without his willing it, Alvar held his hand forward. He watched in horror as Ysta approached, opened her mouth and bit into the skin of his wrist, and sucked the blood. Her mouth, chin, and nose stained with the red of his blood. He couldn't even struggle away from her; his teeth clenched as he endured the pain.

Finally, she finished, looked up at him, wiped her mouth, and kissed his lips, pressing her tongue into his mouth so he could taste his blood. "There. That wasn't so bad now, was it?" Ysta patted his cheek with a bloodstained hand, then turned to Saul, "Thank you for the blood, Saul. I'll be leaving now." She gathered up her things and exited, leaving Saul alone with Alvar.

"She's not your wife," Alvar said. He was such an idiot! For the rest of his life, he was going to pay for trusting someone else and thinking he finally had a home.

"Of course not. I don't even know what her real name is. It was a ruse, my boy — a ruse to get you to become my weapon. Everyone knows you can't kill a Cursed unless you have the proper weaponry, and as far as we know, all such relics have been destroyed. With you, I can have whatever I want. You were quite foolish, you know, to care so much about not harming human beings to have your way. I wish I had your gifts. You're part of an ancient bloodline. A bloodline of people that used to be revered as the gods of Axus."

"You said—" Alvar began.

"I lied," Saul interrupted. "You now have no choices left. You were so desperate for acceptance—for a family—that it was almost too easy." Saul held up the silver key. "You will do whatever I want as long as you wear that collar. No one can take it off of you except me. My blood was in the forge with yours. I added it before you added yours. We're bound together now. Forever."

"Why did the Sorceress want to drink my blood?" Alvar clenched his fists and tried to stave off tears.

"Because, she's a sorceress and your blood is worth more to her than anything, although she won't tell me why," Saul stated, but then he shook his head and rolled his eyes laughing, "I'm done talking with you, you'll stay down here until I can come up with our first plan of attack."

"May the gods curse you," Alvar seethed at him, even though every fiber of his being wanted to he couldn't move to attack the man nor shift into his more dangerous form. The invisible force of Saul's will stopped him. "May Elias see you destroyed by fire!"

"There are no gods," Saul spat back at Alvar. "Just me. The new god of Axus."

*

Alvar couldn't get the taste of innocent blood from his tongue. Every man in this town dead except one.

"Do tell those in other villages about me," Saul told the man, "Tell them about the horrors you witnessed here and how if they want to avoid it, they'd best join me. Saul is my name. Repeat that to them. Tell them that if they submit, their lives shall be spared."

The man nodded vigorously and fled as quickly as possible. Alvar surveyed the damage. Homes burning and bodies lay strewn in a bath of blood in the streets.

I couldn't have done this, Alvar told himself.

A little girl dressed in a fluttery yellow dress stained in blood caught his eye among the corpses. She was clutching her dead papa to her and sobbing. With glistening, horrified eyes, she stared up at him.

"You did this, monster; you killed my papa," she wailed. "Why? What did he ever do to you!?"

You did this.

I'm so sorry, little one, Alvar begged forgiveness of her in his mind, for Saul had forbidden him to speak in his monster form, *I will never forget your face for as long as I live.*

"Shut that little brat up!" Saul growled while grabbing one of the living women and pulling her by her hair toward one of the empty houses. "You stay out here, Alvar, and keep watch for me. I'm going to have a chat with this lass," Saul cackled sadistically, the woman screamed.

Alvar turned from the scene and closed his eyes. Tears sprang forth when he knew Saul wasn't observing. There was nothing Alvar could do for anyone, even himself. All he could do was exist as the weapon that killed for a power-mad, cruel man.

If Saul has his way, there will be nothing left of Axus when I'm done.

*

"Arena," Saul spat, grasping Alvar by the Fe Collar. "I saw her looking at you. You lay with Arena, didn't you? You know her to be my favorite concubine!"

"Master, I didn't lie with her," Alvar stated, without any emotion as emotions had long fled him. Saul was prone to fits of irrationality and paranoia lately, which was because there was a rumor spreading that the sylphs of the Skylands had forged a Sword of Darkness, a weapon that could pierce Cursed flesh.

This bit of news came as a relief to Alvar; perhaps an ending was in sight to Saul's tyrant rule and his hellish life.

"You know you control me. You told me I am not to lie with anyone," Alvar said blandly.

"You're stealthy, Alvar, you've learned from me and are becoming more like me," Saul growled, slapping Alvar across the cheek. "I don't believe you. You've grown too handsome. Look at you. You've grown into a man now. You're supposed to be a disgusting nightmare, not a woman's wet dream!"

"Master, I have no idea why you're so angry with me," Alvar said, bowing his head toward Saul. "She looked at me. *That's it.* I didn't even make eye contact with her."

"I'm going to make sure everyone can see how evil you are," Saul said. He drew a dagger. "Stand still. The Sorceress made this dagger. She gave it to me in case I needed to end you. But I can use it to mark you if I want so you can be as ugly on the outside as you are on the inside."

Alvar, of course, couldn't do anything but stand still while Saul pressed the tip of the dagger to just above his eyebrow. He painfully and *slowly* carved out a deep cut in Alvar's face. Running from above his eyebrow and circling it out around his cheek to the corner of his mouth.

Haven't you degraded me enough? Alvar thought, his skin seared with pain, it burned, unlike other weapons he'd felt used against him. He hated how he couldn't help crying out from the pain because he knew Saul loved to hurt him. The more he reacted, the more inspired Saul was to torture him.

"Scarbrow, that's what we'll call you," Saul declared with a wicked grin. "I like that, might make some of these peasants respect me a bit more. Alvar isn't exactly a name that exudes fear."

*

Alvar stood in the doorway of the room and waited.

Time: Something of which you always wish you had more. Or wish others had more.

The physician finally approached him, his expression grim. "I'm sorry, my King. It appears as if there is nothing to be done for her. It's not a—um—normal thing that is happening to her. I know of many different difficulties with pregnancies, but this is a magical problem. Something brought on by a dark Curse."

What? No! The physician might as well be sticking a dagger through his heart. Alvar wished at that moment that he had the blade which had marred his face so he could put an end to his suffering. *I'm a scourge to everyone I love. There is nothing good inside me. I'm killing the one person who let me in, despite my Curse and my past, to love them.*

He entered the room he and Triss shared. He recalled their first night in here, and how Triss had accepted and wanted his love.

"The news isn't good, is it?" Triss asked, looking up from her forlorn little place on their bed. Her once vibrant features were sallow and drained of life. The baby he had made with her was eating away at her system. The Curse didn't take kindly to an average human host.

"I promise," Alvar swore, "I will find a way for you to live."

"It's okay, Alvar," Triss said, her eyes crinkling at the corners as she smiled feebly at him. "Don't blame yourself. The Light knows you carry too much guilt already."

"Don't give up, my love," Alvar said, kneeling next to the bed and grasping her cold little hands in his. "I'll save you yet."

"Don't you see?" Triss said, her eyes shining with tears. "You already did."

*

"Queen Remora plans to attack Earth, the Bridge has been discovered by the gobli people and they have sent spies to evaluate the defenses of that world," Fletch told Alvar, his expression grim. "If she does that, we both know who could return once his prison sentence is finished."

They were meeting in the conference room of Underland palace.

Alvar ran a hand through his dark hair.

The hope he once held, the triumph of banishing Saul in the first place, it had all disappeared and now he longed to die, but he could not be killed, the knowledge of that was driving him mad. The dagger that had scarred his face was likely in the hands of the evasive Sorceress.

How many days will I wish for a death I will never have? How long will I rule a people who will always despise me? When will I finally go mad as the Cursed before me who go on to live their lives like feral dragons for eternity?

He recalled a story Father Ryland had told him of a Cursed living on the highest peak in Ferar, guarding the mural of a woman once beloved to him through the ages.

Was that the only fate of a Cursed? To never find peace?

"I summoned Sola, she should arrive any minute, she will tell us what we must do to see that Saul never returns," Fletch says, walking over to sit at the conference table. When Alvar didn't follow him to sit, Fletch furrowed his warty eyebrows. "Are you alright, my king?"

"I destroy everything, Fletch," Alvar stated, walking over to the window and looking down on Underland City. "Am I truly the right king for Underland? I will not grow old. They will notice eventually."

"You will have heirs, with a woman from Earth, Hannah Delaney, expects a child," Sola's voice interrupted the two of them. "You must go over the Bridge while it is still open. A woman carries a child that is dying within her. Infuse Cursed blood while the babe is within her and use healing magic to save her baby. Father Ryland knows how, I have let him know he will accompany you."

Remarry? Impossible.

Alvar was determined not to endanger another woman. "I cannot have children without the possibility of killing their mother."

"Not if the bride possesses Cursed blood," Sola said. "You must leave within the hour. I've provided all the details I saw in my visions on this scroll." She trotted over to the king and closed his hand over a scroll. "Hannah Delaney, Alvar. Your bride will be born to her."

"I do not wish to remarry, Sola," Alvar said, his fist tightening on the scroll. "I will not bring pain to another."

"You will experience joy again, my king," Sola told him, her expression reassuring. She placed a hand on his shoulder. "And one day, you will find the peace you long for too."

*

I wake up in my bed cold, so cold I'm shivering.

I can't watch it anymore.

I can't know anymore.

Not now, at least.

I still have questions, but it's unbearable for me at this point. This past was his living nightmare, and the Mystar has turned it too real for me.

I've felt his horror and anguish. The pain he's endured is unbearable. Mental, physical, and emotional abuse is the world he's known. He has a genuinely good heart, but a heart that has been distorted by the most disturbing of realities.

These things happened to him. I blink and can't cry even though I want to. *My husband, Alvar, I wish I could heal your spirit from what happened.*

TWENTY-SIX

As I pull myself from my slumber, my mind scrambles to grasp the present.

Who am I?

I'm Lucy from Earth, not Alvar from Axus, but I know what it feels like to *be* Alvar.

"Lucy!" Emily calling my name surprises me. She rushes into my tent, arms extended. "We made it out just in time before the caverns collapsed."

"The caverns? What do you mean?" I blink. Did that mean all of Goblia was buried in the collapse? Were there any survivors? "Is Alvar alright?"

"Of course he's alright! He rescued as many as he could before the caverns collapsed, it seems Remora committed mass suicide with explosives."

"Holy crap!" I gasp and cover my mouth. "Are Leeza, Grey, and Fletch okay?"

"Yes," Emily said, "We're lucky to be out of there with our lives."

"What of the Stog?"

"The what?" Emily cocked her head, obviously confused.

"The deer people?" I ask.

"Oh, them. Strange," she shudders. "But everyone here is strange. Lucy, why can't you understand why everything is wrong for us Earth people? Why can't we go back? It's dangerous here."

"I'm sorry, Em, I'm not going back, I don't want to," I say. Guilt over my anger toward her washes over me. Yes, I know she's controlled me, manipulated me, and dominated my life at times, and yet, she's been there for me. Emily didn't leave when everyone else thought I was crazy. For that, I sincerely appreciate her. I remember the times we went to coffee while cramming for exams and talking about boys together. We giggled over naughty romance novels, and she taught me how to act "normal" when my entire childhood and teenage years had been abnormal because of my mother. I wish Emily the best, even if I realize our close relationship is becoming strained. She's not happy here, and I'm to blame for her being here in the first place.

"Did you get a chance to talk to his high-and-mightiness about me going back?" Emily asked glancing outside.

Alvar was out there? Outside my tent right now? A shiver went through me, and I have the urge to dash from the shelter and embrace him. Maybe I'll do it. I stand up. "I think I may have convinced him to let you go back," I murmur, before rushing from the tent to meet him. There are many outside: dozens of gobli, some from Goblia. However, most of them are from the encampment where I'm staying. The Stog leader is talking to Alvar in the center of the group.

Alvar catches sight of me, and we exchange a knowing look between us. His stance is rigid and cold as he speaks with the Stog leader.

"Lucy, are we going back to Underland?" Emily asks quietly from behind me so as not to disturb whatever conversation is taking place.

"I am sure we'll head back there soon," I whisper back to her.

"Lucy, I've meant to ask you this for a while, but how did we get here even?"

"Huh?" I'm not quite following her.

"Well, how did we travel from Earth to Axus?"

"Arlite," I tell her, "A special kind of it."

"Really? What kind?" Emily prods me for more information.

I see where she's going, and it dawns on me that maybe I've already given her too much information.

"Emily, don't think of using it by yourself; it's much too dangerous," I warn. "I remember Alvar told me that once lost in the Bridge, you're lost forever."

"Well, if a gobli can make it across the Bridge, then why couldn't I?" Emily laughs. "They are much simpler creatures than we are. Especially the inbred ones."

"I'm serious, don't try to use Arlite to get across the Bridge by yourself. Anyway, I think Alvar would want to have someone take you, so he doesn't leave any of it behind on Earth," I begin, but when I turn to look at her, I notice Emily is gone back into the tent.

I sigh.

If only I could tell Emily what Alvar told me, it would make her understand the situation so much better! But I can't betray his trust like that, and if his people knew *he* was the Cursed who had killed so many of them through Saul, it would send this entire world into chaos and fear again.

"I assume you know much more than when I left you," Alvar's deep voice makes me jump.

I find myself staring up at him. His body is close to mine, his voice secretive.

"Yes," I answer, and without thinking, I touch his hand with my own. "I told you I'd make my decision after seeing everything, and now I believe I've made mine."

"What did you see?" Alvar asks, he takes my hand and leads me to a bench, far from the tents and the crowds.

"I saw how Saul persuaded you to wear the Fe collar and also how you got the scar on your face."

"And?" Alvar prompted, a pained expression on his face.

"You buried your mother."

"And?"

"Nothing more." I let go of his hand and look ahead of us to the mountains of Ferar. I think of Goblia and Remora, what a selfish act. "Why did she kill herself and all of her people?"

"Because it is more honorable for her to die at her own hands and bring her people with her into the afterlife than it is to be vanquished by a foe," Alvar says softly. "It's unfortunate, but not surprising. She knew she was outnumbered and overpowered."

"Are you going to send Emily back?" I ask.

Alvar nods. "Will you stay and rule Underland on your own or..?" He trails off. He doesn't even want to say, "*or stay with me and rule by my side.*"

I bite my lip; I study my husband, a broken person with terrible secrets and the darkest of pasts. "You have a strong heart," I state, and tentatively my hand reaches for his face, where his scar is. "Anyone else would have gone insane."

"Be careful, and I'm not sure I haven't," Alvar laughs bitterly.

My hand travels down to his neck. I feel his neck, and something cold and metal is beneath my fingers, although I cannot see it. As Alvar said, the collar was made invisible. I move my hand over the instrument of his complete slavery to Saul. The gems embedded in it bump my fingers, and then I come upon the keyhole.

Alvar grips my wrist suddenly, and I gasp at the touch. "You don't have to stay here, Lucy. Their own hands destroy Goblia. No one wants Earth anymore. You can go home with Emily if you wish."

"What about children?" I argue, although I'm not sure why I'm trying to talk him into having children with me. "What about heirs to your throne?" I flush upon realizing what I'd just implied.

"You want to make children with me?" Alvar's eyes turn red, and his breathing becomes husky. "Lucy, I can name a successor that isn't my own. It won't be customary, and my people may question why I never produced any offspring, but I will somehow find a way. I want you to be free."

"How are you going to keep people from going to Earth if there is no treaty?" I don't know why, but my throat is tightening, and I'm starting to cry.

"Lucy, I—I just want your happiness. I don't want to ruin you like I've been ruined," Alvar closes his eyes. "I'm not good. And I'll never be good enough for someone like you. I thought this would be a business arrangement, not, not this."

"A business arrangement?" I'm incredulous. A business arraignment! How dare he say that? Marriage, having children together, and ruling side by side, was a business arrangement to him?

"You didn't see all of the things Saul did to me," Alvar growls. "I'm nothing but a Cursed shell of a human being."

"Well, what else did he do?" I can't imagine anything worse, and I'm still a little annoyed at him for his "business arrangement" comment.

"He made me do things that I'd never do of my own free will," Alvar says, he casts his eyes downward, shame in them, "Sexual things."

My heart drops. Holy shit. I don't even want to know. Had Saul made Alvar rape others? Or had he--

"Saul used me," Alvar reveals, his brow pinched in pain at the thought, "you wouldn't see those memories because I erased them from the Mystar. I never wanted to see them again. I can't learn anything from them. The aftermath of many of the memories in which I'd done evil by Saul's will I kept to punish myself for being naive and to never let anyone in again, but *those* memories," he closed his eyes. "I couldn't keep the memories of him degrading me like *that*."

"What I am is too distorted ever to be loved — Saul's... advances... the nail in the coffin. I know what you're thinking. Did I tell Triss about it? No. How could I tell her that? I wanted to give her the luxurious life of a queen after all that she'd experienced? Saul was obsessed with me, in a strange twisted way, he fetishized my suffering and my Curse. He wanted to make me unable to be psychologically intimate with others. He was such a jealous person, especially of me."

I can't say anything as my stomach is turning in circles and twisting in a horrid ball. I stave off the urge to vomit. What an abomination Saul was in every possible way!

"Lucy, I'll not make anyone a proper spouse, like the kind you read of in great love stories. I put up a great front. I can even play shallow love if I want, but with you, I can't play that. Though I did with Triss, I can't for you," Alvar says. "I should never have done what I did, arranging for you to marry me, even if it saved our worlds. It still destroyed *your* world, and *your* world, Lucy, matters to me. Just say the word, and you and Emily can go home. I'll take you myself so as not to risk Saul coming back."

"Alvar," I start, and I can't get anything else out. I wrap my arms around him in a tight embrace. He's shocked by it. I can tell by how his body stiffens, and I sob for him. I don't think anyone ever has done this because the look on his face as I release him is one of bewilderment.

"What are you doing?" he asks helplessly, and my heart breaks for him.

"I don't ever want you playing any part with me. *Ever.* And I'm not ready to go back to Earth. I want to see the place that you've made Axus be through your desire for peace and restoration here. Damn that Curse, damn Saul. They don't get to make you what you are," I state with conviction.

"Lucy," Alvar's face is as stone, I can't read it. "Didn't you hear me? I'm not capable of—"

"Of what? Of having compassion? Or showing mercy? Or doing good? Everyone here—*everyone* is crazy about you and your heroics! You're a legend! You've changed Axus. Changed it from even the sad state it was in *before* Saul took over and made it worse," I persist, "I saw what it looked like, I saw in your memories what you've done. The people and races here work in unity and are no longer warring."

"You weren't Saul. Saul made you do things for him like you were his object. A sword to swing around and slice things to bits with, but a sword is not responsible for its master's wrongdoings. A sword in the right hands can be productive and instill peace and responsible leadership. You took that sword from Saul's hands when you cast him over the Bridge to Earth. With that same sword, you've done more good than anyone I've heard of in the history of my world and the history of yours."

Alvar's solemn face crackled off, and his eyes dimmed back to blue, a glassy blue as if he were about to cry. "Lucy of Earth, are you even real?"

I smile, sniffling back a sob, and nod. That's when Alvar kisses me; really kisses me. Nothing playing about it. It's the most genuine kiss I've received in my life, and what's more, we're too busy enjoying it to even think of the past.

TWENTY-SEVEN

Alvar draws back from our heavenly kiss, brushing my hair from my eyes with his tender gaze on my lips. He rests his hand on my cheek, and I close my eyes, willing, moaning lightly.

Yes. This is the best. And yes, this is the first time a kiss has captured my senses with longing and happiness.

What is going on?

All I know is that I'm falling in *love* with Alvar. Should I be afraid of these feelings, developing so quickly for a man about whom I'm unsure?

"Lucy, I don't know if you understand how much I—" Alvar growls in my ear, and kisses the skin under my ear. "--I want you. Right now, if I could. The beast inside me roars at your touch." His hands move from my face and drop to my waist. Firm fingers grip me, and he pulls me closer until our clothed bodies are touching.

Oh, his words make me tingle with excitement down to the tips of my toes. I want him too!

"Teach me how to love you," my cheeks burn at the words, and my heart skips a beat. I gaze up into his eyes and see them transition from blue to purple to crimson.

His irises are darkening in arousal for me.

"You have no idea all the things I'd love to *teach* you," Alvar whispers in my ear, and his hands brush lower, his fingers curl into my skirt, grasping the fabric.

I can't believe my boldness, but I respond by swinging myself onto his lap to straddle him.

Alvar clasps both sides of my hips with my skirts bunched up in two fistfuls, his thumbs brush the skin of my thighs.

I dip my head and find his lips. I'm still wearing my undergarments, but I can feel him hard beneath the fabric. My hands press against his chest, the beat of his heart pounds beneath my palms.

"By Arlite, you tempt me, woman. But we shouldn't, not until we are back at the palace," Alvar growls darkly.

He pulls me in to kiss him once more. "We're too exposed out here. The Stog have people in this forest. The last thing we need is for them to see the king of Underland with the red eyes of a Cursed, passionately making love to his queen in the woods."

I smile and tingle with excitement at how scandalous that statement sounds. Mike never talked like that. He never talked sexy to me, period. Sex was always a topic tiptoed around awkwardly or talked about in cliche terms. I guess some women probably like that, women who don't enjoy blushing, but I don't believe I am one of those women. I've grown rather fond of all my blushing.

"Come, my queen," Alvar takes my hand and leads me back to the encampment. "I have matters of business to attend to." He tells me once he's taken me to the entrance of my tent. His tone so different than minutes ago, like a king.

"Of course," I say in a proper queenly way. "I'll let you get to them."

He kisses my hand and leaves. I travel back into my tent on a cloud of happiness, and my heart is still racing. I'm surprised at Emily's absence. Hmm, maybe she's getting some food and speaking of food, I'm hungry. I leave my tent and follow the scents of roasting meat. A group of gobli and stog looks to be celebrating. They are sharing drinks and eating the excellent smelling meat. Leeza is there too. She's dancing, her bright yellow wings are outstretched. What a strange and wonderful place Axus is. People of the air (sylphs), people of the mountains (gobli), people of the forests (stog), people of the water (nixies), and the people of the valleys and flatlands (humans). I wonder if there are any more I'll meet as a queen here.

Leeza notices me and immediately looks guilty. She hurries up to me. "I am so sorry, my queen! I completely forgot to attend to you." Her voice is a bit slurred.

"Leeza, have you been drinking?" I tease.

Her cheeks brighten to red. "Maybe a bit."

"It's okay," I assure her. "You should have some fun. It is the first time I've seen you having fun."

Leeza laughs. "I suppose I've gotten too caught up in my job to have fun."

"Do you know where Emily is?" I ask her.

"Wasn't she back in the tent with you?" Leeza asks before a stog male takes her hand and pulls her back into the dancing circle.

Hmm, so Emily isn't here. Where is she then? I take some food for myself and a cup of the alcoholic beverage and head back to my tent. *Maybe Emily has returned*, I reason. *Or maybe she's with Grey, I know she was interested in him.*

Grey is standing outside my tent when I arrive. "Grey, have you seen Emily?"

Did Grey just roll his eyes at the mention of Emily? I smile. *Oh, Emily.*

"She asked me if I wanted to go for a stroll with her in the woods, and I agreed," Grey says.

"And?"

"And then she tried to kiss me, but I told her I have a betrothed back home," Grey announces, "And I wasn't interested in being unfaithful to her. That didn't stop her from encouraging me to kiss her anyway. Then I stated that my betrothed and I are not interested in a poly marriage either."

"Ah." I raise my eyebrows at his omission. I wonder if poly marriages are legal here if Grey felt the need to state something about it? Hmm, there is still so much I have to learn about this place.

"She huffed off after that, I thought she'd come back here, but when I looked in your tent, it appears she didn't return," Grey finishes. "I'm sorry I lost track of her, my queen."

"It's okay, Grey," I assure him. "That does sound like Emily." I sigh. *Okay, so where is she then? I* wonder.

I leave the encampment, but do not travel far, as it is growing dark by now. "Emily!" I call into the now misting woods. "Emily!"

Nothing but the sounds of the night answer back.

"Emily!" I call again. Then I see a light, in the distance through some trees.

"I'm over here, Lucy!" Emily's voice shouts back at me.

I hurry toward the light, dodging under a tree branch and then looking behind me at the encampment to make sure I'm not heading too far out. When I turn my gaze back toward the light, I'm face to face with a familiar face, but it's not Emily's nor is its familiarity from my memories.

It is the Sorceress, Ysta.

"Ysta?" I say.

TWENTY-EIGHT

"You seem to know me by a name I've long given up, and yet I've never personally met you," the Sorceress says, her eyes glinting in the light of the eerie green lamp she carries.

"Where is Emily? I heard her here," I say, as calmly as I can muster, backing away from her, my skin prickling with the memories of what she is capable of.

"She was quite excited when I gave her a shard of Arlite and taught her how to use it to access the Bridge. Said she couldn't stand it here, needed to get back to *your* world. She said *you* belong there too."

"I'm not going back to Earth." I lift my chin. "My husband is Alvar."

"Ah, Alvar, the king of Underland and the salvation of Axus," the sorceress's words drip with mockery. "A Cursed who thinks he can masquerade as human."

I hold my breath, is she going to tell everyone in Underland about this?

"Oh, my dear, don't worry." The Sorceress chuckles. "I'm sure he's on my side more than any of the humans here, I'm not going to reveal him, but I am so tired of the lack of chaos in this world. There is nothing to feed off of now. My power grows weaker every day. When Remora fell, I knew I had few options left. Emily is my last hope of causing chaos, you see? The Dark Lord demands it."

"What do you mean, your last hope?" I'm still backing away, unsure of what to do.

216

"You don't have any need to fear me right now. I can't hurt a thing, not with my weakened state...but hasn't Alvar explained to you how sorceresses and all dark magical beings survive here in Axus? I am the last of the pure sorceresses. I live for the one who brought darkness. *We* feed off of chaos and pain, betrayal and malice, greed, and perversion. If those things wither in Axus, we do too. All those who have dark magic abilities do." But her brow furrows in thought as she adds, "well, perhaps not all of us."

"What?" I ask her.

She scares me, the way she talks. I can almost perceive the darkness she speaks of surrounding her like a cloud of nightmares.

No, it's not just surrounding her, it's *living* in her.

"Saul gave me the benefit of all those things," the Sorceress continues. "I was so close to being more powerful than any Cursed, and overthrowing Saul myself and giving this world to the darkness, but Alvar found the Bridge and sent Saul to Earth before that happened. Saul will enjoy meeting you, the lovely pure woman his slave fell in love with. Oh, I cannot wait for the tasty moment when Saul has his way with you while he makes Alvar watch--or better yet--has Alvar pin you in place for him. That kind of agony and perversion...Mmm...delicious," the Sorceress licks her lips.

My stomach twists at her words, horror building inside me till I'm sure it'll spill out. I've never felt more violated in my life than right now by this woman's words. There is no soul in this woman. No light in her eyes. Only a hunger for death and misery. A shiver runs down my spine—fear creeping inside me, the need to run from this person of evil. "Saul won't make it back. Even if Emily is on Earth right now with some Arlite, how on Earth would Saul know where to find it? Earth isn't a tiny place."

"Because I sent your friend to find him and give him a message for me in exchange for the Arlite," the Sorceress cackles. "Of course, your friend never questioned the kindness of this stranger. She promised me that she'd give him my message as Saul and I are two star-crossed lovers parted by worlds. It didn't take long to spin a lie for her. She was so desperate to get back home."

"No, no," I shake my head, and my throat tightens, dread rending through my heart like a knife. "Alvar!" I cry out. "Alvar! Grey! Anyone! Help!"

"You should have gone back with Emily, Lucy," the Sorceress is fading from my sight, the lamp she holds is dimming. "But instead, you'll get to watch as your love sends this world to hell again."

She disappears completely, and I turn and run back to the encampment. Alvar. I need to find Alvar and warn him. There has to be something we can do. How much time do we have? My heart pounds in my chest like a drum; I feel as if I cannot breathe. I've seen what Saul does while in power here. I know what awaits this world if what the sorceress says is true. *It can't happen again.*

"Alvar!" I scream. I'm suddenly sobbing. I trip in my rush into the damp Earth, but hurriedly I pick myself up again. Almost there. Almost to the encampment again. A warm hand grabs mine.

"Lucy!" Alvar's says my name and pulls me against him, holding me as I sob. "Lucy, what happened?"

"I saw her! The sorceress from your memories..." My voice trails. The adrenaline is making me dizzy.

"What?" Alvar grips me by my upper arms. "Where Lucy?!"

"Back in the forest, I went searching for Emily," I quickly explain. "She sent Emily over the Bridge back to Earth to find Saul. Gave her a shard of Arlite so she could go back home. Emily is going to give Saul the Arlite so he can return."

Alvar holds me close to him again, gripping me to his chest as if I would fall if he didn't. I can feel his heartbeat. It's building in pace to match mine. "No," the singular word holds an unspeakable amount of doom in it. "Say it isn't true, Lucy," he pleads this in a whisper, his lips inches from my ear. "Say it isn't true."

"What are we going to do?" I ask him; I'm shaking uncontrollably.

"Sola Brightfeather," Alvar states stonily. "We must find her."

"Who?" I blink.

"A sylph priestess who knows my story, we must head to the Skylands of the sylphs," Alvar says.

"But do we have enough time to do that?" I ask Alvar.

"Saul won't return until the next bridge opening. You cannot open it every single day, you have to wait for the correct cycle," Alvar explains. "I'd say we have at the least five days."

"Five days isn't much time," I state, but my heart is calming, Alvar seems so sure this Sola Brightfeather person will have answers of some kind. I hope he's right.

"Go to Leeza, have her pack your belongings," Alvar orders. "I'll tell Fletch what you told me. I must make sure the gobli are set with their new order so they can live in peace."

Alvar, holding to his responsibilities as if the impending horror was nonexistent. Still, as calmly as I can muster, I find Leeza still dancing at the feast and set out with her to pack my things.

TWENTY-NINE

As we head to Sylphvr, I try not to think of what Emily is going through.

Yes, I'm furious and hurt with her for doing what she did. But, she's going to meet Saul, and Saul is not the type of person anyone should ever have to encounter. I hope he just takes what he has to from her and leaves her alone. A part of me wonders if Emily will even find him for the sorceress. I mean, *out of sight, out of mind, right? Why would she follow through on a deal made with a woman from another world?*

I haven't time to enjoy the scenery, even though in my panicked state, I note a group of strange floating islands above a flat valley in the distance. The rocks are floating in a circle, and in the middle of the circle is a beautiful, crystal clear lake where a waterfall from each island is pooling into it. Directly under the floating islands, there is bare stony ground, I suppose with no sunlight vegetation would not grow. Still, the bare ground looks so desolate and sad.

"My homeland," Leeza says proudly, pointing upward at the islands as we approach on our mytonir.

"What keeps the islands floating in the air?" I ask Leeza.

"Magnetism." Leeza smiles at my question.

Alvar glances back at me from his place in our party, and I smile faintly at him in reassurance. When he turns to look ahead again, I sigh. It seems intimacy between us will have to wait. Still, if this truly is the end of the world coming, I wouldn't mind sharing at least one more kiss.

We halt our mytonir near the lake, and Alvar helps me dismount. Leeza surprises me by stripping herself from her dress and running straight toward the lake in her undergarments, wings outstretched. I watch as her taloned feet dash across the grass, each stride longer than the other, and then she's dancing over the lake before becoming completely airborne. Her yellow wings are magnificent in the sunlight, and she glides high above us, up toward the Skylands of Sylphvr.

I am in awe of such a sight.

So the sylphs fly.

"I can't wait for you to meet Sola," Alvar casually says as we wait. "She'll love to meet you. She and Yal are some of my dearest friends."

"They couldn't make the wedding?" I ask, not sure why that is the first question that pops in my head. Still, if they are his dearest friends, I wonder why they didn't make the wedding.

"No, it was too short of notice. Sylphvr is disconnected from the lands below. It is difficult to get messages across to them. Arlite only sends someone straight over a skywave, not upward."

"How are we going to get up there?" I ask, realizing no one has told me yet.

"Leeza will send some uldons down; otherwise, you have to follow a strict schedule," Alvar explains.

"What are the sylphs like?" I ask. "Are they like gobli? A matriarchy?"

"No, they are equal partnerships in a fiercely devoted relationship. Just like many species of birds, they are monogamous to the end. It is said if one mate dies, often the other dies of a broken heart," Alvar says with a solemn face. "I didn't believe those tales until I went to Sylphvr. I do believe they are true. Their relationships are quite solid, and you wouldn't hear of a sylph cheating on their spouse either. They are quite unashamed of their public displays of affection with their mates. Another thing about them that may take some getting used to is that they do not hold to the same standard of modesty as the humans of Axus or the gobli. Leeza dresses modestly because she lives in Underland, but many wear practically nothing. Most of them wear naught but a small loincloth and elaborate jewelry. Clothes hinder their ability to fly, and sylphs pride that ability above almost everything, including clothes."

"Oh." I blink. "Well, how did you meet Sola?"

"Sola was captured by Saul and put in a gilded cage for decoration in his gallery," Alvar began, "She met me and knew my plight almost immediately. All she wanted was to get back to Yal."

"Her mate?" I ask.

"Yes, her mate is Yal. Anyway, Sola possesses certain gifts, she can see into the future, and she told me that I'd reunite her and Yal. For the longest time, I dismissed it as the ravings of a crazy person. Every day as I passed her cage, even though her bright blue plumage dimmed and finally her feathers started falling out, she reminded me that I'd reunite her and Yal. She was right. When the bridge opened and Saul fell through, I freed her and reunited her with her mate."

"So is that why we're seeing Sola? To hear about the future?"

"Yes, and no." Alvar took my hand in his, and our fingers entwined. "She also may know how I can... end my life. She has studied into the Curse more than anyone else I trust."

"What!?" I wrench my hand from his grasp. "NO! You are not going to do that to yourself! Alvar, don't say that kind of stuff to me!" I am hyperventilating, my throat is tightening up, and I shake my head as if further to affirm my disapproval of such a tragic plan. "Why do you think that's the only option? Why can't we do something else? Why can't we go over the bridge together and live on Earth?"

"Lucy," Alvar says, taking back my hand, "Although I wanted it for years so I wouldn't have to be Saul's pawn anymore, I truly don't want to die now. I want to live an entire life with you, have children with you, and grow old with you and..."

"Then we have to find another way," I sniffle and tighten my grip on his hand. "You'd *better* find another way. I'll not give you up."

"And I won't see you destroyed by my hand through Saul's control," Alvar growls darkly, his eyes turning red momentarily.

Those words make me think of what that sorceress said. I shudder. *Is this going to be the conclusion of my love story? Like Romeo and Juliet or Antony and Cleopatra, we both die rather than be apart?*

"Ah, there comes our ride," Alvar interrupts me from my pondering. I look up to see a group of feathered lizard-bird creatures who look very much like the dinosaurs you'd see depicted in movies with vibrant blue and green scales. They are being led down by a male sylph with dark black wings, wearing a dark green kilt and black sandals.

They land in front of us, and the male sylph dressed in black bows. "Your majesties," he says. "We are honored with your visit. Sola told me she cannot wait to be introduced to Queen Lucy."

"It is good to see you, Yal," Alvar says, and then he smiles. He and Yal give one another a hearty handclasp embrace.

"How long do you think you'll be staying?" Yal asks as we mount the winged dinosaur creatures, the uldons Alvar mentioned.

"Unfortunately not long enough to enjoy the scenery," Alvar turns serious again. "There may be cause for great concern in all of Axus, but I feel like Sola will make that clear to us before we start a panic."

THIRTY

Our uldon mounts land on the top of the largest island. We come upon a beautiful city decorated with lush green grass and tall trees sporting dark purple and blue leaves. There are no streets.

The sylph homes are all made from dark purple and white bricks and end in gold curled turret roofs. However, the doors to these houses are not on the ground, but at the top of the building with an entry ledge.

Designed for people that fly, I muse, and a part of me forgets the imminent danger we're in, *no one on Earth would believe me if I told them about all of this being real.*

Yal motions for us to follow him, and we lead our uldons by their reins.

"Sola is in the sanctuary meditating," Yal says. "It's not far from here."

Leeza lands to join us. We approach a lake, and there is a large white cathedral building with a pointed roof on an island in the center of the lake. We remount our uldon and land on a ledge leading into the cathedral.

Quiet piano music plays in a beautiful melody of high notes as we walk down a spacious hallway. The sanctuary's roof is practically made entirely of glass, letting in the sunlight and causing the white stone's minerals to glitter continuously. The glass windows have ornate imagery in the black panes.

I reach for Alvar's hand and whisper to him, "This is so beautiful. I almost want to cry."

"Isn't it?" Alvar says, his tone is solemn. "I really shouldn't be in here."

"What do you mean?" I ask him in a whisper back.

We approach a large double door. Yal bows and extends an arm. "The king and his queen may join Sola."

"Lucy, we're about to enter the circle of truth," Alvar explains in a whisper, "You will see very soon, why I don't belong in this place."

Leeza and Yal open the doors for us and close them behind us. The room we enter is circular and has brilliant white marble floors with three circles of water, each one about three inches thick, and all fit inside each other. In the center ring, Sola stands with her arms and sapphire blue and white wings upraised. There are mirrors all around us, and I gasp.

There is something so different about the reflections I see than the one I'd see in a regular mirror.

My reflection is shrouded in a fog-like mist, and Alvar's is dripping dark with blood, especially around his mouth and hands. He is also wearing a black, red-gemmed collar with an eerie wraith-like chain that wraps around him in a painfully tight appearance.

"The mirrors see us for what we are. We can't hide in here." Sola speaks. Her voice is soothing and light. I search for her reflection and note a lovely blue and white glow coming from her reflection, but she has a broken wing in her reflection.

I ponder if the broken wing symbolizes her years spent in captivity.

I understand the blood on Alvar, but why do I have mist surrounding me.

"So I finally meet Lucy, queen of Underland," Sola says. "And the only one who loves my dear friend, Alvar, in a way he deserves."

Sola closes her wings and brings her arms down to her sides. She turns, and I'm greeted by two brilliant sapphire eyes staring right into my soul. Her tresses are raven black, and she wears a silky white dress that glitters in all the bright light shining from the windowed roof of the room.

"I apologize for the darkness I bring to this holy room," Alvar states respectfully and bows his head. "I would not intrude unless it was urgent."

"I know," Sola smiles warmly at him, embraces him, and kisses his cheeks, then she does the same to me. Suddenly her smile disappears. "You're time left in Axus is short, Lucy."

"What?" I blink and grasp Alvar's hand. *No. Does she mean I'm going to die?*

"Sola, do you mean Lucy is going to go back to earth?" Alvar asks. "We need to know what we are to do about Saul if anything. Will Emily bring Saul here?"

"Take my hand," Sola orders, but she winces when he takes her offered hand. She closes her eyes and furrows her brow as if in pain. "So much darkness. I can hardly see through all the wretched blood you are covered in...Wait...I *can* see something."

"What do you see?" I demand. "Please, there has to be a way to--for us to be okay." I don't know what it is, but I feel unworthy and intimidated by Sola's radiance.

"Saul *will* return to Axus," Sola says. "He's coming back. And he's determined to take everything you've accomplished since his absence and make it worse than before. But, I cannot say if he will accomplish his goal."

"How can we prevent him from getting back?" Alvar is the one who asks this; his eyes are bright red with fury and horrified anticipation.

"You will not be able to prevent him from returning, and there will be death in Saul's wake," Sola adds, "But I cannot see anymore. There is a fog in this room. It veils the future."

I wonder if she's talking about me. "Maybe I should leave," I offer. "You say there's a mist and, well, if you look at my reflection in those mirrors, I'm covered in mist."

"Your mist will stay in this room even if you leave this room right now, Lucy. I believe you are the deciding factor to what will playout for the future of Axus," Sola declares. She drops Alvar's hand and motions for us to follow her out the double doors. "Come, you both must be starved from your journey. Come and visit my home for the night, stay in one of my rooms together. Enjoy one another's love, and you can decide what to do in the morning. We have three days before Saul returns."

"Thank you, Sola, I pray your foretelling can somehow help us. And I cannot wait to show my wife a proper sylph feast. Your hospitality is unsurpassed," Alvar says, his facial expression is grim despite the easy conversation he makes.

I can't help but lag behind Sola and Alvar and look in the mirrors once more. Alvar, a blood-stained and darkened murderer, Sola, a beautiful sylph woman with a broken wing, and me.

My heartbeat quickens, and a chill goes up my spine.

You are the deciding factor.

THIRTY-ONE

By the time the feasting finishes, I feel as if my stomach has expanded to maximum capacity. But wow, that food had been delicious! On that positive note, I can't shake the devastation creeping into my soul.

Three days until Saul returns.

Three days left to spend with Alvar as himself.

We are seated next to each other at the table, and my hand covers his. He's almost cold to the touch, his skin is so pale, and there is no light in his eyes.

My heart breaks for him. I can't imagine what he's thinking and feeling.

Yal and Sola rise from their seats. "We shall retire to the nest," Yal says. "There is much to meditate on."

"But feel free to ask for anything of the staff. They will accommodate if you are still hungry or in need of a drink. You may stay the night here if you wish, but I understand if you decide to take care of other matters," Sola assures. Her expression is sympathetic. "We shall pray and hope for salvation from Saul and the other evil forces at work in Axus."

Alvar leans to whisper in my ear, "Lucy, let's get out of here."

"Huh?" I ask.

"There isn't much time left. I don't want to spend a minute of it away from you." He grips my hand in his. "Is there anything you wish to do?"

"Yes," I manage the words, but I am still numb, too much is happening at once. I can't focus on him. The fate of Axus is up to *me*. "My mom. I want to send her back to earth. Save her life."

"Of course," Alvar agrees and stands. "We shall go back to Underland, to our palace."

"Thank you," I mouth. And he whispers something to one of the staff.

"What was that about?" I ask him as we walk to the ledge of Sola and Yal's home. The night air is warm, and the moons glow in the sky, casting their light on us.

"I would like Leeza, Fletch, and Grey to go home to their families," Alvar answers. "If this truly is the end of a pleasant world, especially for those who live in Underland, first, they need to spend as much time with what matters to them as possible."

"Oh, Alvar," I murmur.

Alvar leaps from the ledge. I wonder what on earth he's doing, but I note he's shifting forms. Moments later, his Cursed form crawls upon the ledge. Its intimidating face is at my level. "Get on my back. I am faster than any uldon."

I didn't dare argue.

*

We soar just below the cloud line. The moons illuminate the landscape below us in white and purple light. The wind from his speed whips my hair, and at this altitude, it's cold. I lean low and embrace his broad neck. His body heated underneath me; the Cursed form has fire in its belly. The landscape changes, we leave the floating islands behind, and we're in Underland again, I can see the jungles beneath us. I ache with a longing that, up until recently, I'd been unfamiliar with it.

"Can we land?" I shout above the wind, taking matters into my own hands.

"Why?" Alvar asks.

"Do you know a place we can go to be alone?" Whoa, I surprise myself at my boldness, but I want something we can remember forever and draw strength from when our world ends.

"Lucy, time is short," Alvar's voice rumbles back as if he's scolding me.

"But, if it is short, then...You said you wanted to spend every minute of it with me. Let's make our last days together count. You are about to lose everything, your free will is about to be taken," I begin, and I stop myself from picturing what that means. "Where can we go?"

A silence falls between us, and my heart sinks. Perhaps I am foolish, and it is a terrible idea. After all, I'm the virgin over here.

"I know a place." Alvar breaks the silence.

Those simple words shiver through me, and I'm almost dizzy with the implications.

I forget that Saul is about to return and wreak devastation on everything we've dreamed about together. I am too nervous and aroused at the same time.

Alvar swoops downward to land. I can see the lights of Underland in the distance, as well as the outline of our palace to the east of us. We land in front of a small stone building, and Alvar stretches a wing down to the ground so I can climb off his back.

"Go inside the fisherman's cabin," he says, his beast voice gruff. "There should be a light inside. I will join you shortly."

"Okay," I manage to say.

As I step into the cabin, my nerves start bundling themselves into knots.

I turn on the light and note a cozy little one-room home with a bed, stove, sink, and small washroom in the corner. It's a quaint English-cottage feeling place. The bed looks comfortable, and there are fluffy pillows spread across the top.

I flush. Is this how it happens? You just decide you're going to do it? Emily had lost her virginity six years ago with some boy in high school whom (she'd reported) had lasted a total of a minute. I know the biology and what the act entails. But I've never done it, and now I wonder if I'll be any good at all, or if Alvar will be. And if he isn't good, would I pretend to like it?

"Lucy," Alvar's voice behind me is deep. I turn and see him standing in the doorway of the cabin. He's breathtakingly sexy, wearing a clean white undershirt and black pants, his dark hair tousled from the wind outside. His eyes are blood red.

"Oh." I gasp. *Screw those last thoughts, I'm overthinking all of this... just let it happen.*

"You're so beautiful." Alvar smiles tenderly at my dumbfounded look and approaches. My breath hitches when his hand presses the small of my back, and the other tilts my chin upward. "You're tense," he murmurs. "Are you sure you want this?"

I respond by claiming his lips and encircling my arms around his neck.

He responds hot and filled with need. My skin shivers as his hands rest on my shoulder and spread the sleeves of my loose-fitting dress until they slip down my arms over my softly-curved breasts.

My heart is beating like a drum. I've never been naked in front of a man before. I inhale sharply when one of his hands cups a bared breast, the other breast is exposed to the cold air.

He kisses my jaw, my throat, my collar bone, and—*oh*— he kisses my *breast*, his tongue rolls over its hardened center.

My body stirs to life by that simple action and I watch his eyes close in enjoyment of me.

This. Is. So. Hot.

Low noise in his throat sounds. The effect he's having on me is mirroring the impact I'm having on him.

I groan, and my hips press against his, and I can feel his need for me. I remove his shirt and press my palms against his statuesque chest.

He draws away, and our eyes meet. His eyes have cooled back to blue, but haven't lost their intensity.

"I love you," I whisper, my voice barely audible from panting. I'm falling off the edge of sanity. He affects me uncontrollably. My dress falls to the floor, and I'm bared to him, save my panties.

"You're perfect," he growls in appreciation, but instead of taking me right then and there, he kneels and takes my hand in his. "Do you really want me... as your husband in this way?"

A smile tugs at the corners of my lips, and I nod. "Yes, Alvar. I want you to be my husband."

He kisses my hand. "I've always been alone. I can't give you what a human man can. This Curse, my past..." He bows his head and presses my fingers to where his scar trails. What is he doing? He's breaking down.

I get down on my knees, so we're face to face again. "Look at me, Alvar."

His gaze rises to meet mine, and I note his eyes are glazed over, and the way his brow is lined with pain makes my heartbreak.

"We're equals," I whisper. "I want you and everything you are. I'm taking it all on alongside you. You don't have to be alone anymore." I take his hand and bring it to my cheek and kiss his fingertips. "Touch me. Touch me wherever you want."

Alvar moans softly, his eyes alight, alive once more. With his free hand, he reaches for my breast and sighs as he cups my softness.

I place the hand I'm holding onto my other breast and squeeze my fingers over his. "I *love* this. And I loved it when you kissed me here. I've never been kissed like that."

"Come here, Lucy," Alvar whispers, sliding his hands down my waist to my hips and pulling me to him so he can nuzzle and kiss my sexually awakened body. "I want to take my sweet time with you; cover your body in kisses, savor you all night long."

And my magnificent king makes good on that promise.

THIRTY-TWO

I have no idea of the time when Alvar and I finally lay beside each other sated and exhausted. My breath is husky, I'm sticky with sweat, and a bit sore, but my body remains euphorically high.

So this is what all the fuss is about? I muse with a half-smile on my face. I *think I'm an addict. How many times have we done it now?*

Alvar lies on his back, his chest rising and falling from our lengthy tryst.

My, my, don't you have quite the sexy afterglow? I appreciate. His dark hair is messed and damp, his eyes are closed, and the stubble on his cheeks only enhances his rugged appearance. The sight of his hard, muscular body that moments ago had utterly shattered me is enough to throw me back in the thralls of sweet memory.

My eyes mischievously travel downward. I *never realized how big it would look up-close.*

"Just keep staring," Alvar states as if he can sense my gaze as his eyes are still closed, but a sly grin spreads across his sensual mouth.

"I think he's my new best friend," I state with a silly returning smile.

"Glad the feeling is mutual between the two of you," he teases.

I answer by hitting him with a pillow.

*

"Oh, I don't think I can walk," I moan as I hobble away from the cabin.

"When we get back to the castle, I'll draw you a warm bath," Alvar promises with a sympathetic smile.

I look back at the cabin. And a thought strikes me. Oh, dear.

"Um, Alvar, whose cabin is this?"

"It's my cabin, Lucy," Alvar rolls his eyes and chuckles. "Did you think I'd have us trespass on some poor stranger's house and make love on their bed?"

"Oh, well, you never know," I giggle, embarrassed, but I don't care. I'm still floating.

Alvar grabs my wrist and pulls me into him. "You are so adorable," he purrs in my ear and kisses my neck. "I wish we could stay here, live in this simple cabin, and never see another dark day."

"Me too." The mood swings. I know we're both thinking about Saul and what his return will mean for us. As beautiful as it was, it isn't destined to last.

"Let's get your mother back to Earth," Alvar says solemnly. "Then we can decide what *you* are going to do."

"Sounds good," I agree, but I'm starting to choke up. *It is so perfect, and it's going to end as soon as it started.*

I watch as he stretches into his Cursed form, and my breath leaves me. Our reality is right before me in the form of a monstrous beast that will destroy Axus once again. Hopelessness like a dark ink spot expands inside my heart.

We fly back to Underland, and I grip the Fe collar tightly and realize I loathe the evil thing with all my being.

*

"No, I don't think *you* understand. I'm not going back to Earth. My home is here with you."

"Mom, you don't have a choice," I grumble at her. Why is she so difficult? Why can't she just trust me? *It is my childhood in a nutshell right here.*

"I command it," Alvar states, he hasn't left my side since our arrival. "It is a matter of your safety, and you are the queen's mother. You will not have your safety compromised. I cannot evacuate Axus inhabitants to Earth, but I can evacuate you. Emily has already left."

*Except you've left out the part that she's the reason **why** we have to evacuate,* I think dryly.

"You can't take my daughter from me!" Mom exclaims. "If there's danger here, I'm not leaving her."

"I can't go with you. I have to stay here to—" what do I say? Save the world cause I'm the "deciding factor"?

"I will protect your daughter to the best of my abilities. She is my wife, but she is also the key to saving Axus, and we can't send her back to earth," Alvar finishes for me. "If all goes well, and it is safe here, we will go back to get you."

"I promised you, my daughter, because I believed you, that the marriage would save both our worlds. Now—now I see you have no control over anything and that the marriage did nothing to prevent disaster," Mom seethes at Alvar.

Ouch. Harsh.

"You promised your daughter to a stranger," Alvar growls, "who claimed they could save the world. But do you know why I'd traveled to Earth and 'bumped' into you in the first place?"

Mom furrowed her brow but remained silent.

"Because I was making sure the tyrant king who once ruled here would never return. I had him arrested by *your* authorities. But I could only lock him up for so long. I knew I needed a fail-safe, to cut off Axus from Earth further. So I came up with a plan. Your girl baby was dying. There was no way to save her unless she received a transfusion of my blood. I knew the baby would become a grown woman by the time Saul's sentence was up. If I married that woman, I'd secure a treaty and Axus would be cut off from Earth, but now that same tyrant king, despite my actions, *is* returning and when he does, you'd better pray you aren't here to suffer under his rule. A very reliable oracle has deemed Lucy is the deciding factor for whether Saul will rule or not. So she needs to stay here, for the sake of my people."

Mom glares at Alvar, as if to object, then her face softens, and a sorrowful expression crosses her face. "Lucy, give me one last hug."

I sigh with relief and embrace her. She holds me tight, and it hits me that this may be the last time I see her. A ball forms in my throat. "I hope I see you again," I say.

"Please, let me come back to you," she whispers, and the words are enough to cause a sob to escape me as I nod in half-hearted reassurance.

THIRTY-THREE

I wish I could hang on to this moment forever. Bathing with Alvar is so surreal. I had no idea I'd ever experience this kind of love for someone.

The sensation of his strong, muscled arms around me from behind in the ornate tub in his room is heaven, and the warm water soothes my body.

Yet my anxious thoughts cannot be contained even by this bliss.

"What are we going to do?" I ask softly, taking Alvar's hand and pressing it to my lips. I am determined I want to do this every day for the rest of my life, which *may only last a few more days if we don't figure out something.*

"You are quite appetizing like this, all wet and slippery, I think we should see how good you taste," Alvar answers, and he kisses the back of my neck, his teeth lightly grazing my skin.

I smile at his compliment, but I can't erase the overwhelming shadow of doom I see over everything.

Even this sensual perfection.

"Am I just going to die?" I ask without looking at him.

"No, I forbid that from happening." Alvar tenses at my words and grips my upper arms from behind in a protective kind of way.

"How can you say you forbid that from happening? You will soon have no choices left. I love you more than anyone

I've ever loved, but I don't know how I can save this world. How can I do anything to stop Saul? I'm just a helpless woman from Earth." I finally get it off my chest.

"Lucy, I don't know the answer, but I do know you're not helpless. I pray it comes to you; but for now, I just want to be near you." He nuzzles into my hair, his breath lightly tickling my ear.

"I do, too," I whisper. I turn in his arms and press my breasts against his hard chest. "Kiss me."

His lips are on mine before I can say anything else.

"I'll do more than kiss you," he growls between our kisses and firmly grasps my hips in his hands to place me astride him so he can fill me with his heat.

A while later, we are both wrapped in each other and fur blankets on his floor by the fireplace. I am enjoying this simple moment until I notice his eyes turn red. He abruptly gets up and walks to the window, magnificently naked. I languidly watch him with appreciation and stretch against the soft furs with a low moan.

"What's going on, baby?" I ask him breathlessly.

"That word again. Baby." He laughs and turns his head to look at me with teasing skepticism. "You said it during our lovemaking."

"It's an Earth expression. You know, like 'hey, baby, you're so sexy.'" I try to defend but laugh with him. I guess such a word would sound strange to someone, never having heard it used that way.

"Still not making much sense to me," he says amusedly.

"How should I address you?" I ask, rolling my eyes dramatically.

"*My love* is fine," He says with a shrug, but then he gets a playful sparkle in his eyes, which have gone back to normal, "or my king."

"Alright then, your majesty, how may I serve *my king*?" I laugh and move my body, letting him get a clear view of my nakedness.

Alvar growls and pounces on me, pressing me against the furs, swiftly bringing me against him in a kiss and making me shiver with happiness. His hands are on my body, touching and exploring every part of me, making me squirm with desire.

My fingers curl against the muscles of his back. He lowers his head to my belly, running kisses along my side, tickling my skin, so I shudder. He presses his tongue over the curve of my breast, finding its sensitive center and making my back arch at the hot sensation. A moan escapes my lips.

His gaze rises to mine, and I realize his eyes have begun glowing red again.

Alvar draws back, taking the incredible heat of his body away from me, and closes his eyes, rubbing his temple. "In about five minutes, I'm going to belong to my Curse."

"Then go, I'll be here waiting for you," I say with an understanding smile.

"I'm going to tell them, Lucy," he says.

"Tell them what?" I call after him with a giggle at his abrupt change of subject.

"My people. All of Underland. They need to know the truth."

*

"I've called you all here today because I have been alerted to grave news that will affect all of you," Alvar announces. "The malevolent tyrant, Saul, is returning and will once again try to oppress you, my people. But I cannot save you from the monster he controls. I cannot protect your families as I've promised to."

There were terrified murmurs among the people, and a desire to run up and hold Alvar's hand is strong as I sit in the front bench of the chapel where he is declaring the imminent threat.

"The truth is, my good people, I am undeserving of being your king as what I am is a facade.

Many of you do not believe in magic, and I understand this sentiment, how can we believe in something that has no scientific grounds? But I do believe in magic and the supernatural, as I've witnessed, it's power in myself. There are forces at work in our world and in the worlds outside of our realm that cannot be explained by science or even our transient logic.

I'm deeply indebted to you for accepting me and allowing me to do what I can. But you have never been free of the monster Saul used to enslave you for I--" He stopped, and the entire room falls silent.

"I *am* that monster. Before you come at me with weapons drawn, let me first explain my story.

I was enslaved to Saul just as you all were. True, I was the instrument of his death-dealing, but I had no choice. My family threw me out of my home when I was but a young lad when they discovered I carried the Curse. Saul found me and saw me as a way to get what he wanted. He placed a Fe collar on me. For all of you who do not know, a Fe collar is a device of dark, evil magic. Whoever holds the key to the Fe collar can control the one who wears it. I never told you of my origins because I was afraid if I did, you would shun me and stop my mission to use my Curse to free Underland once again."

Some people rise from their seats, they start crying insults, but the rest remain hushed, and some even hold the angered ones back. I'm surprised at this.

"I want to give you the gift of preparation. It is the last gift I can give you. You must flee this palace as Saul shall return and again take me under his control and use me to destroy the good people here. I wish it weren't so. I would end my own life if I could, but as a Cursed, I am unable to do that. I beg you if you know of a way to kill a Cursed to begin preparations. I will not be able to stop myself once Saul has returned."

THIRTY-FOUR

Silence covers the room.

I hold my breath, and my eyes fix on Alvar. He's not alone. I want him to know he's not alone.

A human man dressed in expensive clothes stands. "Many of us have been suspicious of this from the beginning, your Majesty."

Alvar motions with his hand. "Come forward, Lord Calbir."

Lord Calbir rises and walks up the center aisle of the cathedral. His hand rests on the holster he wears, but once he stands before Alvar, he kneels and kisses Alvar's hand. There is a gasp that goes through the crowd of people.

"I know of the magic, it runs rampant in this world," Lord Calbir explains, loud enough for everyone to hear. "A Fe collar is a treacherous device. I remember the days when Saul reigned over us. He placed a Fe collar on my daughter. When I received her from his harem after he was banished, there was nothing left of her soul. She'd done things without choice or struggle that haunted and terrified her. She killed herself just three months after returning home. We couldn't bring her back."

Another man rose from the crowd, yet another human nobleman by the looks.

"I too have heard of this kind of magic, but that does not change the fact that King Alvar is a Cursed and has no right to rule," the nobleman objected. "The Cursed are named so because they are the descendants of vile humans who brought a curse upon themselves by for their corruption. They do not belong to themselves; they belong to fire and death. They are only produced by those who are despised by anything holy or good. If what King Alvar says is true, he has terrorized us since Saul's rule ended, by taking on his true form and flying in the skies above our city and leading us in this deception."

A few other people seconded what the man said, and there is much murmuring.

A sylph noble rises and shouts above it all, "If what he's saying is true, Alvar has given us the ability to flee by his information. We shouldn't waste one more second here in this cathedral!"

Lord Calbir speaks once more, this time to the people, "I shall lead you, we shall prepare for a battle." He speaks once again to Alvar, "Your Majesty, we must have permission to destroy you."

"With all my heart I grant it," Alvar says without flinching, he brings Lord Calbir to his feet and offers his weapon to Calbir. "Take this—a symbol of my passing of command to you. Lead my army against me. I cannot guarantee that you will succeed, but I hope because of Saul's stay on Earth, he will have lost some of his skills in using my body to kill others. Find a place of safety, do not tell me the location of it and prepare."

Lord Calbir takes his gun and nods his head solemnly. "Of course, your Majesty. Elias shine on you for the kindness you've shown in warning us. May He grant you passage to Paradise."

Lord Calbir turns and walks back down the aisle, and many of the people start to follow him toward the exit

"Kindness!" the angry nobleman, who had spoken against Alvar, shouts, and throws over a lamp stand. "Why not try to kill him now? Before Saul comes and controls him?"

"Have at me, Lord Vessin," Alvar states, he steps forward and removes his shirt.

My eyes widen. Whoa, what is he doing? Is he going to have his people take shots at him now?

Lord Vessin charges forward and fires his gun. The first shot hits Alvar's bared chest, a wound forms, and he writhes in the impact, but it heals almost immediately, and his eyes blaze a fiery red. Alvar is transforming in front of his people! He's making it clear to them just what they're going to be facing.

Screams ring out. Lord Vessin continues shooting. Alvar's beast form screeches in the pain of it's changing bones, the windows in the cathedral shatter, his body crushes the podium as it expands.

Lord Vessin's expression changes to one of fear. "He's going to kill us all right now!" There are screams from the remaining people.

"Silence!" Alvar roars. "I am not going to kill you. I'm just showing you what you're up against. Use every single weapon against me. See how powerless they are against a Cursed. Saul had a blade he enchanted that could harm me; a sorceress made it for him. If you can create such a weapon, you have the greatest chance of succeeding."

"Then let's kill that Earth queen of his, for all we know, she's pregnant with his Cursed child," Lord Vessin exclaims, and his eyes glare scorchingly at me. I shiver. He means it.

Alvar's great wretched wings raise, and he launches himself forward, so his great head is inches from Vessin's body. "Harm her, and you'll more than regret it. She has nothing to do with this, she did all she could and sacrificed much to take part in a plan I'd hoped would save you all, show respect to her!"

I don't know why, but I am blushing at these words. Even with the appearance of a monster, Alvar is my beloved, and this strikes my heart.

Lord Vessin snorts in disgust and stomps out of the cathedral. What looks to be his family and a few others follow close behind him.

Lord Calbir leaves with everyone else.

Once they've gone, Alvar collapses, his enormous body filling up most of the cathedral. He curls his wings against his back and rests his head down the center of the aisle. I get up from my seat and approach him. My hand runs over his rough scales until I've reached his face, my hand trails along the scar, and I touch that ugly twisted face of his Cursed form and stare into glassy crimson eyes. I press my face to his. A tear the size of my palm falls, wetting my cheek.

"Why are you doing this?" He asks, his voice a whisper, and yet it rattles the ground. "Why are you touching me like I'm--I'm not a monster?"

"I love you," I say and press my face harder, reaching my arms around and holding his face in my embrace. I startle when he changes shape beneath me, and suddenly, I find myself against the sturdy chest of my love.

"You are everything to me, Lucy," Alvar says and tightly holds me against him.

THIRTY-FIVE

After the last citizen leaves Underland, a knot of dread forms in my gut that I can't shake.

This is it.

Now we stand on his balcony, watching as the gates of Underland close for possibly the last time.

"You should leave, too," Alvar states somberly. "I will not have you die because of me. I love you."

"I can't leave," I say, turning to him, my eyes wide and pulse wild.

I don't want to leave you. Not now. Not ever.

"Lucy, we are no closer to knowing what to do when Saul comes back. At this point, I think it's safe to say you shouldn't stay with me," Alvar says, his gaze turns away from mine.

"Come here," I tell him, my voice dropping low. I fight my tears, extending my arms out to Alvar.

He doesn't wait for a further invitation. Swooping me into his grasp, he holds onto me tightly.

Our love is real and within our reach, but all we have left is this fleeting time left to savor it.

I remove his shirt as he removes the ties from my dress. With the last light of the sunset kissing our naked skin, we entangle into each other's embrace on his balcony. I trail my fingers over the scar on his face tenderly, intending to memorize every edge and plane of his body.

252

I'm determined never to forget the moments I've had with him.

His heartbeat beneath his broad, muscled chest pounds in rhythm with mine.

*I don't want this to stop. Together we are stronger. I believe in **us**.*

We make love till the moons are high in the sky, their sleepy glow covering the balcony.

I fall asleep, praying for an answer, nestled against my husband's chest.

*

My eyes flutter open, I remember the night vividly before, and I stretch, groaning in appreciation at the reminder of the way Alvar took me and shattered me.

I squint into bright sunlight, but I feel off. Something is different.

"Lucy! Lucy!"

Huh? That voice... it's familiar. It's a voice from another life, another world.

"Lucy! Oh, thank God!"

Hands are touching me, pulling me from my bed in an embrace, but not the embrace of Alvar, not the same muscular chest and fervent intensity I've come to crave. This person is less firm to the touch. He's treating me as if I were a flower that can be broken.

"I thought I'd never see you again! Oh, Lucy," the person is almost crying. "What happened, *where* have you been?"

My eyes focus, and I see the distressed face of Mike staring down at me.

Mike?

"Mike!" I cry out, my eyes wide. And I note to myself that I probably appear more upset to see him than I should. "Where's Alvar?"

"You're back," Mike says with teary eyes and holds me so tightly I wonder if I'll suffocate.

"Mike, where's Alvar?" My eyes are filling with tears, and I can't believe it. He's sent me back to Earth.

"Who is Alvar?" Mike blinks and won't let me go.

No. No. No. NO! My mind screams in a tantrum of fear, rage, and hurt.

"What happened, where am I?" I ask Mike directly, gripping him by his upper arms.

"I found you in my home," Mike says, "You were lying on the bed when I got back from work. Where have you been, Lucy?"

"What do you mean?" I feel violated; I had no choice. "How could he do this to me?"

To protect you, an inner voice whispers gloomily. *You know this is the best way to ensure nothing happens to you.*

"Lucy, I don't understand, you've been gone for months. We all thought you were kidnapped and being held captive by some pervert or dead even. I mean... you don't know all the things that have been going through my mind." Mike shakes his head. "We got a letter saying you'd gone to Underland and to not look for you. We thought it was some cruel letter sent by the sadistic bastard who took you."

A pang of guilt hits me hard, but my frightened and frustrated mind can't possibly process it. Still, "I'm sorry, Mike, but I'm not sure how to explain this."

"Take your time," Mike soothes.

"I wasn't kidnapped." *Well, not really.*

Mike stiffens, his body tense against mine. "So, you ran away? Why would you leave me like that? Without an explanation or a goodbye?"

"I don't know how to explain it," I say, I don't have time to feel bad for him when my husband's entire world is at risk.

"You said that already," Mike states, and he practically drops me. "What is this, some kind of sick joke? Don't you understand I've looked for you everywhere, made every inquiry, never gave up, and now you're telling me you weren't kidnapped?"

This is too much. It's too much. I burst into sobs. I can't control myself. "Just go away, Mike, please, just go away and leave me alone. I'm sorry, but you'd never believe me if I told you!"

"What do you mean, Lucy?" Mike won't stop persisting.

By now, I'm sure, Alvar is at the mercy of Saul, and all I can do is try to comfort my faithful fiancé who searched for me tirelessly while I went and married someone else. Do I feel terrible about this fact? Yes, any decent human being would, I imagine. But my mind isn't on Earth anymore, I belong in Axus, and I will return to save Alvar and all of Axus or die trying.

THIRTY-SIX

I am lost. Alvar has sent me away so I won't suffer, and yet, I'm suffering so much without him. To think of what is happening to him right now kills me. Doesn't he know how much pain this is causing me? His embrace is such a near memory, and now it's a world away. *This can't actually be happening,* I tell myself, and if it is, I'm sure years of therapy won't fix me.

"Lucy, you're scaring me," Mike shouts, his face twisted in real fear.

"I'm sorry, Mike, I really am," I apologize, and I want to cry more, but I can't. I have to think of how to get back. "But I don't know how I can explain this so you'll understand."

"I liked you, Lucy," Mike exclaims, "I liked you a lot. I was going to marry you. I liked you that much!"

I notice how he doesn't say "love" in that sentence and wonder.

"I know, Mike," I say, my voice monotone and soft.

"How can you be treating me like this?" Mike is incredulous, and I feel terrible, but I can't stop thinking of my last moments with Alvar. I should have known something was up, but we'd become so somber I hadn't read in between the lines. The way he'd kissed me so tenderly as if he'd never get to kiss me again. I close my eyes.

I'm growing dizzy. I can't imagine life without Alvar. I'd been preparing myself to die, not live on without him.

A door opens from outside.

"Mike, I got your call!" A female voice shouts. "What's going on? Are you okay?"

A woman enters the room. She's a cute, short brunette wearing a coat covered in snow.

It's snowing? Huh.

"Angie, I'm so glad you're here," Mike says, looking at me in the way I'd seen people look at my mother. The way one looks at a crazy person they are not sure if they should be afraid of or not.

"Oh my gosh, you weren't kidding." the brunette freezes as she catches a glimpse of me. Her brown eyes get buggy. "You're dead fiancé isn't dead."

"Who is this?" I ask, but my vision is turning to a haze.

"Lucy, this is Angie, my kinda girlfriend," Mike states.

"Kinda, huh?" Angie says dryly, shooting him a look that makes me wonder how such a small person can appear so threatening.

I blink. The world won't stop spinning.

"I need to get back to Axus." I walk to the door his girlfriend just came through.

Mike grabs my hand. "Lucy, you need help. Something obviously happened to you."

Yes, something has happened to me. Alvar happened to me. I'm not the same person I was before stepping through the "looking-glass" and entering Wonderland. Alice has gone mad.

"Lucy, look at me," Mike says. "Look at me and try to remember what happened. Breathe."

"Have you seen Emily?" I suddenly think of Emily and how she'd returned.

"Emily is dead, Lucy, that's why we thought you were dead too because you went missing at the same time. Her body was found about a week ago."

Oh, Em. Why couldn't you have seen sense! Why couldn't you have listened? This is all my fault. Everything is my fault. I try to breathe, but my lungs are tightening inside my rib cage.

Mike catches me as I fall, and my world blacks for a moment. I'm so defenseless.

"What is this?" Angie asks the question, but it doesn't make sense, and her words are fuzzy to my ears as I fight for stability.

"It looks like some kind of necklace," Mike states, "she was wearing it when I found her, but I took it off her because she was clutching it so tightly. I was afraid..."

This is the first hint of good news I've heard since arriving as I knew the necklace held Arlite.

"What happened to Emily, do they know why she died?" I ask, it will hurt to know, but I need to know. I want to hear if it was painless. *Please, let it be painless how she died.*

"She was found beaten in a basement. She died of internal bleeding. She wrote something addressed to you in blood on the wall."

"What did the note say?" I swallow hard, and my body starts trembling.

"She'd wrote it in her blood, it said, 'Lucy, your blood is the key.'" Mike's face is somber, and my own heart wrenches from my chest, *to know she'd died in that way.*

"Give me the necklace," I say. Emily's death wasn't going to be for nothing. None of what had happened was going to be for nothing. The note she'd left behind was cryptic, but I suddenly understood. I needed to test my theory. "Turn on your stove, Mike."

"Shit, Lucy, what is wrong with you?" Mike shook his head at me, and his hand goes to his scalp, stroking his hair back. He thought I'd gone bonkers. "What have they done to you? Did they torture you too?"

"No, the man who killed Emily hasn't gotten a chance to meet me...yet," I murmur, my fist closing over the necklace as I snatch it from Angie. "But it won't be long until I send him to hell."

"What are you talking about?" Mike shouts, "Will you just hear yourself! My Lucy never talked like this."

I see Angie cringe at the reference, but I ignore it. I wasn't his Lucy anymore. I'm not the Lucy, who let people tell her what to do - doormat Lucy with the crazy mother.

"Turn a damn stove burner on!" I command, my eyes blazing as I glare at him. I feel a little guilty for cursing at

Mike like that, but it gets me the result because he stomps to the kitchen.

"Fine!" Mike yells back as he flicks the burner. The tiny flames leap from the grate.

I can't believe I'm about to do this. Before Mike can stop me, I force my left hand into the heat. It's hot, but it doesn't burn me. In fact, it's not even painful.

THIRTY-SEVEN

"Thanks, Emily," I murmur to myself, tears falling as I watch the flames dance around my fingers.

Poor, poor, Em.

I have enough self-worth to realize that maybe she wasn't the best friend I'd wanted her to be for me, but all she'd wanted to do was go home.

I'm immune to fire.

I've never noticed this ability in the past, but why would I if I'd safely avoided it like most humans are told to do?

It makes sense. How was I supposed to know my reactions to heat in the past hadn't been normal? I suddenly remember when Mike had stared, open-mouthed after I'd touched the pizza pan fresh out of the oven without burning myself.

How strange, I've practically known it all along?

I'm the answer to rescuing Alvar and saving Axus if I play my cards right. Sola hadn't lied when she'd said I was the only one. Now I need to get back to Axus before any more lives are lost. Still...I can't take the key from Saul that controlled Alvar through his Fe collar. I need to come up with a plan.

"Lucy, holy crap. You're not burning," Mike states the obvious, his eyes huge. "Why are you not burning?"

"Mike, do you own a gun?" I ask, my mind working quickly. Time is of the essence.

"How are you even doing that?" Mike asks, his eyes still on my flame engulfed hand.

"It will take way too much time to explain," I snap. "Do you have a gun?"

"My brother does," Angie says, her own eyes mesmerized by my supernatural ability. "Why are you asking?"

I'd forgotten Angie was even here. "I need one. I can stop other people from dying." I look at her.

"Lucy, what is going on with your eyes?" Mike suddenly asks.

I blink hard. What does Mike mean? Are they red like Alvar's? Can I be a Cursed too?

"Did they turn red?" I ask.

"They're more like an orange," Angie says, her gaze snapping up. "I can get you the gun."

"You believe her?" Mike stops staring at me and gapes at Angie instead. "Are you serious?"

"Something is going on here, Mike," Angie shrugs, "I believe in the supernatural. You know that about me. And something supernatural is happening here. Emily already died, and apparently, Lucy knows who killed her and can get the bastard."

"Angie, it's illegal to take the law into our own hands," Mike objects, "Why don't you tell the authorities, Lucy, if you know who this guy is—"

"He's not of this world, and our law enforcement wouldn't do anything anyway, he has a..." my voice trails. How do I explain this without sounding crazier? "A dragon that breathes fire and can't be killed."

"Lucy, stop!" Mike covers his ears.

"Look at my hand, Mike," I yell at him, "Does that look normal to you? I am the only one who can save the lives of a ton of people from that world. You need to trust me. Mike, if you ever really cared about me, you need to trust me on this."

Mike shakes his head, and his brows furrow in a kind of pain. I care and regret that I made him suffer in mourning from my absence, and that I didn't get to properly part ways with him. I care about Mike, just in a companionship kind of way. I always have.

"Mike," I say his name more quietly, and I take my hand from the fire and put it against his cheek. "I'm sorry for everything. And I know this is really hard to believe. But I promise, if I get out of this alive, I'll come back to you if that's what you want." I can't believe I'm saying it. I don't want to go back to Mike. But I'd go back to him to save Axus and Alvar.

He closes his eyes and takes the hand that's on his cheek in his and lets it drop from him. "Angie, do you know how we can get your brother's gun?"

"He lives like half an hour from here... He may not give it to us, but maybe he will. Do you know how to fire a gun, Lucy?" Angie asks.

"Yeah," Mike and I both say in unison.

"We went to the firing range together a couple of times," I explain.

"Okay," Angie says, "let's go."

I can't believe my luck that Angie, this person I hardly know, is willing just to drop all logical thinking and help. I don't know if it means she's a bit crazy herself or just a good person. I don't care, and thank God, whom I believe must be helping too, because I can't think of any other explanation.

*

Angie's brother probably will never get his gun back, but I don't have time to feel guilty about stealing it. I can't just walk up to Saul and take the key away. Since I'm fireproof and Alvar is his weapon of choice, there's not much he can do to me unless he is also armed with a gun. I'll just have to count on him being surprised by my reappearance and shoot him first.

"So this is it then?" Mike asks as I holster the gun. "How do you even get back to Alvar?"

That's a good question. I'm not even sure if the Bridge is still open. I'm just going to have to hope my luck keeps holding out, and somehow I can get back to Underland. And then, when I go over the Bridge, that I don't get lost.

I lift the Arlite and close my eyes. I picture Axus and Underland. I wish to be there. Nothing happens. Crap.

THIRTY-EIGHT

Mike stares at me, shaking his head, and Angie furrows her brow sympathetically.

Here I am looking out of my head, holding a necklace, and closing my eyes with belief while nothing happens.

I blush, trying to remember how Alvar used it when we'd first gone to Axus together. He'd taken me in his arms before the spark had ignited, and we'd gone over the Bridge. But before *that,* he'd touched my forehead with the crystal.

I know I'll look even crazier to Mike and Angie if it doesn't work, but I lift the crystal to my forehead.

The crystal starts to glow.

Mike and Angie's expressions both change.

"You don't have to come back, Lucy," Mike says. I can tell he's relieved my story isn't the ravings of a madwoman. He takes Angie's hand in his. "I understand."

"You do?" I ask.

Mike nods. "You belong with whomever it was got you so passionate. You never were like that with me, and that— that's okay. I'm happy you found someone you're passionate about, Lucy."

"Thank you, Mike," I say, astounded by his compassion and understanding.

266

No wonder I was comfortable with marrying him.

My eyes well with tears. This is the goodbye I've wished for with all my heart. "Goodbye."

"Goodbye, Lucy."

I hug the crystal to me tightly and think of home, and in a flash of white light, I cross over the Bridge.

*

I find myself in a soft patch of grass, much like when I'd first traveled with Alvar for the first time. I'm dressed like a woman from Earth, and I once again don't fit in here in this magical world. But I'm magical, I've always been magical. Like Dorothy from the Wizard of Oz realized the power was with her all along, I realized the same thing. Alvar hadn't needed to send me away to save me. I could have saved him right away.

I know I'm in the same field we'd landed the first time we'd crossed, but I also don't think I'll get the speed of Mytonir to get me to Underland this time.

I breathe in the air, how I'd missed Axus air, but something is different. Smoke. I can smell smoke. I sit up in the grass and notice over the horizon an amber glow in the distance. Saul is already using Alvar. I rise to my feet and run in the direction of the fires, not knowing what else to do. I find the road, so I'm not running through fields or jungle.

Once on the road, I notice a small wagon in the distance, as I get closer, I see a large jungle cat is pulling it. I freeze and pull out my gun.

"Ah, I see you've returned," the voice speaking out from the wagon could be likened to that of a snake.

I know who it is—the Sorceress.

The Sorceress rises from her seat in the wagon and glances at my weapon dismissively. "You should have stayed where he left you on Earth. But it will be quite delicious to have you here. The pain and suffering you will endure under Saul. I can't wait to taste it."

"Tell me where Alvar is." I spit at her feet. "Or I *will* shoot you."

"I'm not afraid of your Earth weapon, Lucy," the Sorceress says and rolls her eyes at me. "But since you're so eager to see about your doom, I'll tell you where you can find him. Still, are you sure? Have you forgotten how he kidnapped you and brought you into this mess in the first place? If you don't remember now, you will later as you writhe and shriek in agony to Saul's whims."

I try not to let her words take ahold of me, but there is something drug-like to them. My mind grows hazy, listening to her. A fog surrounds us.

I'm so in over my head, and yet my love for Alvar urges me to continue, even in this strange world of magic, even with this darkness, I can *feel*.

"If I were you, I'd use your Arlite to go home. Right now." Her eyes glow amber, and in a creepily self-satisfied way, she smiles. She knows she's making me overthink.

I close my eyes. I remember Alvar and everything he's gone through to keep Axus safe; how he'd tried to keep Axus free of our world and Saul's return by marrying me.

If I hadn't married Alvar, Remora would have gotten into Earth. And instead of just Axus being in jeopardy, Earth would join her with a gobli invasion.

"I'm tired of your games," I say, as calmly as I can muster. "Tell me where Alvar is."

"He's down this very road a little way," the Sorceress whispers in my ear, and I jolt. How did she get that close so fast? "Do you want to hear what Saul did to him when he returned?"

I shake my head. "I don't need to hear it."

"Saul will destroy what's left of Alvar's soul," the Sorceress says, "If he hasn't already. You might as well give up now. It is best if you went back home."

"I don't know what made you like this! But I'm never going to give up on Alvar," I state, my cheeks burning with anger as I step toward her aggressively and hold the gun to her head. I'm taller than her. Huh. I hadn't realized that. "Now get out of my way!"

"Your husband is a wise man," the Sorceress murmurs, stepping back from me, and her eyes flicker with intrigue. "He married a creature immune to my powers of persuasion; most would have followed my command completely. Which means, the Cursed blood has affected you. You are the only one who can help defeat the darkness of Axus. For now." She shrivels from a magnificent beauty into a decrepit, emaciated old woman, and gets back into her wagon. "Goodbye, love, I guess I will have to find a way to torment Axus another day."

She pulls out a whip and hits the jungle cat with it, "Git up, beast! Get me out of here!"

I shudder at her words, but can't ponder on them for long. I'm not looking forward to meeting Saul, but hopefully, I can kill him before we have a chance to exchange any words between us.

THIRTY-NINE

The Sorceress hadn't been lying about how far I was from them. Finally, after a half-hour of scrambling along the road, I find myself in a haze of smoke. The smell of freshly burned wood hangs in the air.

As predicted, the fire and smoke leave my lungs unharmed. I'm immune to it, but that still doesn't make it pleasant. The burning village is not far from the central city of Underland. I am hesitant at first as I notice the blazing inferno I'm about to enter.

That is a lot more fire than a gas stove.

My hands curl into fists, and I hold my breath, stepping into the flames.

It's hot, but pleasantly so—nothing I can't handle with ease.

I have superpowers and never knew.

I squint my eyes, searching through the thick shroud of smoke created by the inferno before me.

Alvar must be at the center of this. He's the source.

Movement catches my eye as I travel along the scorched alleyways. A large creature moves in the flames with scales as black as the charred wood on the buildings.

Alvar. He's here. Now I just have to find Saul and not let Alvar see me before then. I reach for the gun and realize my clothes are on fire and I hadn't even noticed. Crap! The holster is made of leather, and leather isn't fireproof and the gun itself...oh shit! I'm so stupid. The bullets haven't gotten hot enough yet, but I need to get out of the fire.

I hurry outside the flames and practically fall into a sturdy person I hadn't seen until too late through the smoke.

"Well, what have I here?" A dark male voice asks. "A little mouse falling right into my trap? Did your home happen to catch fire, little one?"

I'm face to face with Saul. He's lost weight from the time I saw him as ruler of Underland, and he's taller than I thought he'd be, but maybe that's because I'd seen him through Alvar's memories and Alvar is taller than me.

Saul takes my gun before I can think to put it to his chest.

"No need for that anymore," Saul whispers and grabs my wrist, bringing me up against him, he buries a nose in my hair. He's much stronger than me. I shriek, and he shoves his soot-covered hand over my mouth. "Hush, mouse! What a lovely thing you are! You're quite warm to the touch, do you know that? Why aren't you completely singed, mouse?"

Is he just going to keep asking questions and expect me not to answer him? I bite down on his fingers. I'm not a complete loss yet. I'd rather die than go through the nasty stuff I know this guy can dish out.

"Little bitch!" He shouts and slaps me across the face. "Don't do that!"

My jaw stings, and blood heats my face as it races to the abused area.

"You've got a lot of spirit. Have you not heard of me?"

He removes his hand, and I say his name as if it belonged to the Devil, "You're Saul. The enemy of Underland that King Alvar defeated."

"Wrong, my dear, your beloved King never defeated me. He only gave me a short holiday to another world," Saul chuckled, and he bent his arm around my neck so that it was like a steel trap, cutting into my throat.

I grasp his forearm and dig my nails into his skin as hard as I can.

"Stop that!" He growls and tightens his arm around me, so I am gasping for air. "I'm not going to kill you yet. If I just keep you like this eventually, you'll pass out. I wouldn't expect you to understand, but I've had quite the hiatus from a woman's touch here in Axus, and since it seems most people have been smart enough to evacuate before my return, you're my first taste of Axus wench to enjoy." The wetness of his tongue against my cheek makes me wince.

"*Mmm*," he moans. "I'll save you for later after your little town is burned, mouse."

I struggle against him, fighting the effect of his chokehold, but a flash of optimism comes upon me when I realize Saul doesn't know who I am and how that's a good thing. He'll underestimate me if he has no idea I'm Lucy, the one immune to Cursed fire. As my world fades away to black from his constricting the blood flow to my head, I'm unrealistically and illogically hopeful.

*

I wake up, and I don't know where I am until I notice the decor of the room. I'm in Alvar's room.

Unlike in the beautiful memories I share with Alvar in here, the room is dark. The windows are closed and the lights are turned low. My wrists and ankles are bound together, so I can't move.

My situation is bleak at best, but I won't stop fighting. Won't stop until I'm dead.

"What are you doing here?" Alvar's voice says in a harsh whisper. "I made you safe. Why would you come back?"

I strain in my vision to figure out where his voice is coming from. He's in the corner of his room, near the bathing pool.

"I'm going to get that collar off you," I state.

"That's impossible!" Alvar growls and his eyes flash red. He walks over to me. "Saul has the key on him at all times."

"I'll just have to get close to him," I say.

"That's exactly what I don't want to happen!" Alvar snaps, "You were supposed to be somewhere he couldn't find you."

"He doesn't know who I am," I snap back at him, "You have to trust me. I'll figure out a way."

"What do you mean?" Alvar asks.

"I can't be burned, Alvar," I whisper in his ear. "If you wanted to burn off these ropes, I wouldn't burn."

"I can't do that. Saul has me locked in as a human right now," Alvar says, and kneels next to me. "I love you, Lucy. I thought Saul had done the worst things to me already, but if he hurts you..." His voice trails off, and he chokes up, his hands fist in my hair as he kisses me madly.

I kiss him back, melting into his touch like I always do. He reaches for my bindings, and I shake my head, pulling away from his kiss.

"No, I must look like you don't know me. What if Saul comes back and finds you like this with me?"

"He's eating right now, he has another captive he found, and you were still out. Since he likes his victims awake for his pleasures, he left you up here with me," Alvar says. His voice is gruff with arousal from our kiss. "Before he returns I must have you, Lucy."

Whoa, slow down, honey. Let's escape first!

"You realize this is the most inappropriate thing you've ever done?" I blink at him, shocked at his lack of sobriety in our current situation.

"More inappropriate than when I asked you if I could kiss you in that grocery store back on Earth?" Alvar challenges and grins before kissing me again.

"Alvar, you're being stupid," I say, trying not to be caught up in his words. "It's not that I don't want you too, it's just... we're on the precipice of disaster and need to keep clear heads."

"I want you, Lucy, right now," Alvar murmurs against my ear and bites lightly into my neck, prickling to life so much desire that I'm doing all I can to stop him.

And then it dawns on me: My worst fear is being realized.

Saul knows who I am. I don't know how he does, but this isn't how Alvar would act were he in his right mind.

As much as Alvar loves me, he wouldn't compromise our escape like this.

Saul's game has begun.

FORTY

I decide I need to act like I don't know what's happening. My lips claim Alvar's as I lean in to kiss him.

This man is my husband, and if I die, I want to savor this for as long as this blissful moment lasts.

His eyes betray the illusion Saul is creating through him, but I know Saul can't see through Alvar's eyes, and when I draw away, I mouth the word, "I know," to Alvar.

His expression brightens for a second, and then he grasps my wrists painfully tight. It isn't Alvar's will, he always used a firm grip while making love, but I know what Saul is doing now. He's going to have Alvar hurt me to crush Alvar's soul once and for all.

"That hurts," I state bluntly and bite my lip.

"Lucy," Alvar states, his voice wooden, robotic, it's not him. "I like hurting you." He rips the fabric of my sleeve roughly off. My clothes are already burned and frail. He easily rips the other sleeve off.

I notice Saul sitting in the darkest corner of the room quietly, watching us.

"Then hurt me," I whisper in his ear, "I'll always love you, Alvar."

Alvar growls an animal sound, his eyes are deep red, and I can tell he wants to resist whatever Saul is ordering him to do.

There is the sound of footsteps next to my head. Saul has gotten up from his place, and he's come to play and relish in his sadistic triumphant return.

"Look at you, Earth Human, so helpless. You came back here to save your love, but now your love is going to destroy you in every way possible. I love how easy it is to terrify Earth humans. Your friend, Emily? She was incredibly easy to manipulate into telling me what I wanted to hear. I know your story, know how you've fallen in love with a Cursed—as if it were even possible. Did Alvar tell you about us? Did he tell you about all the people he killed for me? Or he did tell you of the times he pleasured me with the very mouth he just kissed you with?" Saul leans down, so his face is next to mine, and the heat of Saul's breath is against my cheek. He pinches my cheeks painfully and forces my head to face him.

I close my eyes, not wanting to give Saul the pleasure of my troubled, fearful gaze.

What an evil monster. Saul's words cut like a knife, but not for the reasons he wants. I know it's Alvar he's trying to hurt. Not me. *My beautiful, noble husband, made to do such horrible things by this vile, cruel man.*

"I'm a bit jealous," Saul continues, an evil grin spreading across his face, "I hear Alvar is in love with you. I don't like my pet being in love with someone else. Alvar is mine, Lucy. Long after you're gone, he'll be mine. I learned he killed Triss, and now he'll kill you." Saul pauses and gazes down at Alvar thoughtfully, taunting, "How it must feel to kill the ones you love."

Suddenly Alvar grasps my bound together wrists and yanks them over my head. I know this is Saul's doing. I wince and cry out in surprise. With his other hand, Alvar rips the rest of my shirt off, so the only thing covering my breasts is my bra.

Saul lets go of my face. In my prone position, he runs his fingers from my throat in a straight line between my breasts down to my navel.

"Do you like to watch me touch her?" Saul asks.

"Yes, Master," Alvar answers, the words are so wooden I know they are not Alvar's.

I'm shaking, the place where Saul's finger traced feels dirty. I hold back a relieved exhale when Saul steps away from me and walks back to his seat.

"Proceed," Saul says, waving a dismissive hand at us.

Alvar bows his head into my chest, every exhale from his nose sends a rush of hot air against my breasts.

It's hopeless. I don't know what Saul will do next, but I close my eyes and roll my head back. A gasp escapes me as Alvar nuzzles against me tenderly.

Saul can't have all the victories.

"You're so beautiful; I can't be a luckier man," Alvar whispers in my skin, his voice choked up. "I love you."

"You're not supposed to say that," Saul's voice interrupts, coming from the dark corner he inhabits again. "Tell her, you find her disgusting and never loved her. That she can't compare to Triss, your wife, who was trained in my palace on how to pleasure a man properly."

"Go to hell," Alvar hisses at Saul. "You can't make me hurt her." Alvar pulls off my bindings from my wrists and drops my raised hands so he can embrace me protectively, but Alvar's body is changing forms. I can feel the skin on his face harden and contort against my bared skin.

"Lucy, you can't love him into breaking that binding," Saul growls, he pulls his key from a pendant he has around his neck and holds it toward Alvar. "Obey me."

Alvar's words come out jumbled together as he fights Saul's command.

"Obey me," Saul repeats. Alvar begins shaking violently, and he lets go of me. He falls back on the floor, writhing and crying out in pain as his body changes forms, and he tries to resist the spell binding him.

Finally, he fully transforms into his Cursed form, expanding in the space and destroying the room as he does so.

"Yes! Look at that ugly monster you're in love with, bitch," Saul shouts at me, and he yanks me up by my hair, sending tendrils of pain through my scalp and down my neck.

I scream. My ankles are still tied together, and they painfully twist as I try to balance myself so I can ease the discomfort of Saul pulling my hair.

Alvar, entirely a monster now, snorts and roars at me. I notice smoke seep through his jaws.

I take Saul's distraction as my chance. I whip my head and yank myself away from him while at the same point grabbing the key from Saul's hand and using all my body weight as I fall to break the chain holding the key around Saul's neck.

I notice a shard of broken glass on the floor from when Alvar transformed, and I remember the blood exchange I'd seen in Alvar's memories and how they'd bound their blood to the key and collar. I take the shard and slice open my palm up to my wrist, deep, covering the key to the Fe collar with my blood.

"Alvar, fire!" I shout. "Fill this place with your fire!" I'm not sure if my crazy plan will work, but I scream out the word again, "Fire!"

Saul has but a moment to stare in disbelief at me before Alvar's flames engulf him.

Blood is pouring from the wound. I've cut myself too deep. The flames are hot around us and I hear Saul's cries as the fire streams out around us. What was left of Alvar's bedroom is destroyed by it. The ropes around my ankles burn off as does the rest of my clothes. I rise to my feet and run to Alvar and wrap my arms around the trunk of his thick monster neck. I force the key I'd stolen into the lock of the collar and twist it.

Alvar groans, the sound so deep and loud it shakes the room. The collar falls to the ground, and I watch as it melts into a pool of blood-like substance.

The flames vanish as if by magic, and Alvar's form wraps into itself until he's but a man again. A man I'm leaning up against now. For a moment, he holds me to him, but then he shudders and collapses.

"Alvar!" I shout, reaching to catch him as he falls, but I'm so weak that I collapse on the floor with him. My blood is all over both of us, pouring from the slit I'd made and draining my life away. I need to stop bleeding!

"Is he dead?" Alvar chokes out the words, his eyes closed and his chest rising and falling as if he'd run a marathon.

I survey the damaged room and see the burnt remains of a body. "Saul's dead."

"Good." A smile hints at the corners of his mouth. "Good."

"It's over," I say, "forever."

"Forever." Alvar opens his eyes, and he notices my bleeding, he rushes to sit up. "Lucy! What happened to you?"

He must not have seen how I'd spilled my blood all over the key to bind my blood so I could command him.

"Lucy!" his voice becomes a faint echo as I slip away from reality with a smile on my face. *It is over.*

FORTY-ONE

I open my eyes and am greeted by a bright light.

I'm alive? Huh?

An overwhelming amount of bittersweet pleasantness surrounds me.

I can't bring Emily back and just thinking about her tears me apart, but I do know Saul won't hurt anyone ever again, and that brings an overwhelming peace of mind.

"My queen!" I hear Leeza somewhere to the left of me. "You're awake."

I'm relieved that Leeza is here. I missed that sylph.

My head hurts. Everything hurts. A strangled groan escapes my lips as I try to sit up. I ache down to my bones, and my body screams at me as I move.

"Where is Alvar?" I ask through gritted teeth.

"Lucy, I was so worried," Mom's voice is near, "If it weren't for Alvar giving you his Cursed blood again, you wouldn't be here."

Alvar gave me his blood?

Just as he gave me his blood long ago when I was dying in my mother's womb, and it healed me.

"Mom, where is Alvar?" I ask, my eyes are starting to adjust to the light. I'm in my room at the palace.

"The people of Underland are returning now that the threat is gone," Mom says, refusing to answer the urgency of my question. "They are here to celebrate you. Their queen and the savior of Axus."

"They think I *saved* Axus?" My voice almost squeaks.

Damn. It is going to be incredibly difficult. I'm not the type of person who is comfortable with hero worship.

"Without you, Underland and Axus would be lost," Leeza says as if she's read the embarrassment in my face. "You may not feel it, but you are the hero of our world, and the hero of Earth too." Leeza chuckles. "How does that make you feel?"

"Terrified," I mutter, "now, where is my husband?" my eyes search the room.

"Lucy, there's something you need to know," Mom says, her face twisted in a cringe of sorts as if she doesn't want to talk about this, "Alvar is leaving."

"What?" I scramble out of the warmth and softness of my bed and realize I'm wearing only a silky nightdress, but I don't care. Let them think their queen has gone mad, running down the halls in her nightdress. I need to get to my husband!

"Lucy, stop." Mom grabs my hand. "He's a monster," Mom says, "many of his people don't want him to be king anymore. Don't you see it? I don't want you to be with him either!"

So she's learned she sold her daughter off to be married to a beast instead of a man and is uncomfortable with it? How silly that only after that knowledge she doesn't want me to be with Alvar?

"Had I known—" Mom begins, trying to place her arms around me.

I pull myself away from her, my body rigid and cold. How dare she?

"He's a hero," I state, glaring at her. "He saved his world and ours too."

"A world that wouldn't have been in jeopardy if he didn't exist," Mom mutters, and she narrows her eyes at me suspiciously. "You're not in love with him, are you?"

"Mom, I *am* in love with that man. If he's leaving, *I'm* leaving." How can she be upset at me about my being in love with the man *she* set me up with to marry?

Mom rolls her eyes. "Lucy, think sensibly. You don't have to lower yourself like that. You're talking crazy!"

I'm the one who is crazy now? How ironic life is!

"I'll do what I please; I'm the queen after all. You ensured that fact," I say to her.

"A queen whose best interest politically is to remove herself from her *Cursed* husband," Leeza objects, her feathers are ruffled with annoyance.

My jaw could drop to the ground. I can't believe both Leeza and Mom agree on this. It makes sense, though. I remember when Leeza first told me about the Cursed and how much she'd feared him.

"Where is the *king*?" I demand.

"In the ruins that were his chambers," Leeza says, her voice short. "But, you should think long and hard about what I just said."

I dismiss her curtness and hurry from my quarters, brushing past Grey as I do so.

"Your Majesty, where are you going?" Grey calls out after me, but I can't stop.

Fletch is outside the door of Alvar's quarters. He's wearing a traveling pack over his shoulder. He must be going with Alvar.

"How are you, Queen Lucy?" he asks me warmly.

"Is Alvar inside?" I ask.

"Why, yes, he is, but, my queen, I don't think you should go in." Fletch stares at the ground suddenly.

"What do you mean?"

"He's not dressed," Fletch states.

"I'm his *wife* and don't care if he's stark naked in there! I'm going in!" I say, stomping my foot and giving an ironic laugh, probably sounding like a crazy person and looking like one too. There is a rage burning in me over how these people who had been loyal to Alvar for years suddenly aren't because he is a Cursed.

I push past Fletch and throw open the door. Instead of a man, I'm in the presence of Alvar's beast form.

"Alvar, you can't be serious about leaving." My words are an accusation more than a request, but I don't care. He's going to stay with me, or I'm going with him. It's that simple.

Grey, who is still behind me, catches sight of Alvar's beast and evacuates the room. *Fletch had meant those words more for Grey's benefit than mine,* I realize. *Even Grey is afraid of him.*

"Lucy," his voice is dark and deep as a beast. He turns his magnificent head to face me, and he lays it down near me. "It is pleasing to see you're awake, my love."

"Yes, and I was expecting you to be there when I woke up," I say, "What are you doing here in this form?"

Alvar changes back into his human self, but keeps his distance from me, and this makes me scared. What's going on?

"I'm sorry, it's taking more and more effort to remain human," he admits.

"What does that mean?" I ask, and a knot forms in my gut. Does he mean what I think he means?

"Lucy, you're going to make a wonderful queen," Alvar says with a pained smile. "All you need to do is distance yourself from me. You are Queen Lucy, the Fireblood, slayer of the tyrant, and rescuer of Axus. That's what your people are saying about you."

"I'm tired of people not answering my questions like I don't have the emotional ability to take it," I say, ignoring the silly title. Still, then I pause for a moment thoughtfully before saying, "And maybe I will cry when I hear the truth, but that damned sure doesn't mean you need put off telling it to me.

I'm ready to be hurt. So tell me the truth. What is going to happen to you? Are you giving up?"

Alvar eyes glow dark red, and he closes them as if keeping his monster at bay. I know when he is stressed, it is harder to stay human, and that is what is happening.

"You're all I have, Lucy," Alvar says, "There are those in the kingdom willing to forgive me and understand, but most do not have that kind of compassion... and it's understandable."

"Alvar, I—I can't rule this place without—without you," I stammer, and fight back the tears. I bite my lip and shake my head at him. "You can't leave me alone here. You're my husband. You *deserve* to be the king. You can *protect* Underland. You're the only one I know who has that power. I don't have anywhere near the power you have."

"I won't ever leave you, Lucy, I'll fight for you when you need me to," Alvar says. "But I can't reign as king. I'm a Cursed, and I can't live here with you. I've done too much. Killed too many people..."

I can't stop myself anymore. Alvar's standing there ravaged in guilt and self-loathing, and I want to empower him with my passion and love. I rush to him and wrap myself about him, kissing his neck, his strong jaw, and then the scar on his face before reaching his lips.

"I'm your wife, don't you dare leave me," I whisper between my kisses on his perfect lips. "Don't you dare!"

He gathers me up against the warmth of his hard chest and welcomes me in. "You drive me mad, woman!"

"Get used to it, because I'm not letting you go anywhere," I say dryly, before slipping off my dress. "And you better stay human, because I'm still mad at you for sending me over the Bridge without asking my permission, and we're not going to make things right unless we make love."

"Let's make things right then," Alvar growls with approval, effortlessly grasping me by the hips and pulling me up so I can wrap my legs around his waist.

FORTY-TWO

We are lying in a state of undress on the ledge that used to be his bedroom balcony looking out at sunset. With my head nestled against his chest and his arms around my waist, I ask the question burning in my mind, "What are we going to do, Alvar?"

"I don't want to leave you, Lucy," Alvar's voice is husky from the aftermath of our lovemaking. Tingles of pleasured appreciation shiver through me.

"Then *don't*," I murmur into his skin and inhale his scent.

I will never get enough of him—my husband.

"What about the people of Underland?" Alvar asks, gazing tenderly down at me. "You are still so new to this place, but there is a whole line of corrupt people waiting to take it now that it's vulnerable. Right now, all the people love you because you defeated Saul."

"I don't know the first thing about ruling by myself," I state. "And you helped defeat Saul too."

"Well, you wouldn't have to rule by yourself, Underland isn't a dictatorship. There is a group of leaders already set to help you. These are good men and women I appointed myself while I was ruling and bringing about peace here."

"Will they accept a ruler married to a Cursed?" I ask.

"Probably not, but that doesn't mean you, and I can't stay husband and wife—" He pauses, then finally says what I know he's thinking: "Secretly."

I laugh and sit up from where I was snuggling. "Are you serious? What about providing a successor? I'm not marrying someone else."

"Yes, there is that to think about," Alvar says, laughing with me, but then he stops and tilts my chin up to look at his face. "Look into my eyes. See the effect you have on me?"

I smile as I gaze up at the beautiful blue eyes of the man I love. "Feeling more and more human?"

"Thankfully," Alvar says and kisses my forehead. "You bring out the best in me."

"Why can't we find a way for you to stay? Why can't we prove to these people that the very best thing is to have a Cursed as their king? Only, they should call what you are something different. The term 'Cursed' is so demeaning."

"Lucy, I don't know if we can change them so radically," Alvar admits, a bemused smile crossing his face at my relentless defense of him, "they'd have to decide to change all the prejudice of the past to accept me. That's not going to be easy."

"But what if they did change what they thought of someone with your condition? What if they took it as a sign of power rather than as an abomination? Saul ruled almost all of Axus because of you. Why not convince Underland that they have nothing to fear with a king who has your abilities on their throne?" It makes sense to me, but I know it's crazy to believe that could happen so fast.

Heck, even Leeza is caught up in the fear, and she always struck me as a humanitarian type of person.

"How will we do that?" Alvar asks hopelessly, "it's not as if I haven't already made a public announcement. Remember the uproar from some of the most powerful members in Underland?"

"I think they are threatened. They may believe that a person of your ability has too much power and that it will eventually turn into a dictatorship, just like what Saul did when he was controlling you. Prove them wrong. Those who don't want to be a part of Underland can leave," I snort, "But Underland will become strong under your leadership. We can start from the ground up. Restructure everything toward the people's safety, so a disaster like Saul or the Sorceress can't happen here again."

"Easier said than done," Alvar says with a sigh.

"Just hear me out. We'll make another public appearance together. We'll explain how a Fe collar works and why it could never happen again," I continue, "We need to educate the people on the dangers of not having a weapon like you in their holster too."

Alvar laughs and gives me a comically, surprised face. "You're going to make a better queen than you think. I love watching your determination, my dear."

"Shut-up," I say, giving him a shove.

"No, I'm serious, you're a strong woman who will make Underland an amazing queen. You also have the knowledge from another world backing you up. Maybe there are things you can teach us from your world," Alvar says.

"I should hope so! For starters, this whole betrothed thing you've got going on here is very backward."

"Well, it did save our worlds," Alvar mutters to my roll of eyes. We both laugh together.

FORTY-THREE

"Lucy, stop!" Mom runs after me down the hall as I hurry to the great dining room. "Let's talk some sense into you. You can't stay married to *him*."

Her words astound me. *After everything...*

I whirl around and face her. "Mom, if you're not interested in seeing where this story ends, go *back* to Earth. I can get you there because you're originally from there, but if you're willing to trust my judgment, then stay."

"I'm worried about you. Have you any idea what that *thing* which is your husband did while Saul was the ruler? How many lives he took?" Mom shouts, her face is livid. "I'm afraid of *him*."

"Who told you?" I ask.

"Leeza explained it to me," she shudders and closes her eyes. "Horrible."

"I saw into his memories, Mom. Believe me, I know what he's done," I say, and I take her hand in mine, my heart softening at her concern for me. In the past, I'd wondered how much she was willing to put me through. But it's nice to see her a little protective. "You don't understand magic as I do. Alvar didn't do it because he wanted to. He did it because someone else was controlling him. And I think you've underestimated how dangerous this world is if you think Alvar is the one you should fear at this point. He's the one who can protect us. There is another creature out there in the world of Axus who would see us all suffer here. Who feeds and lives off of pain and chaos."

294

I find myself wondering what the Sorceress is doing right now, and it sends chills through me.

"Lucy, what are you talking about?" Mom shakes her head at me in sympathy.

I've always been the one who is crazy to her. Some things never really change, do they?

"Maybe you should go back to Earth, Mom, it would be safer for you. Our world is protected from here now thanks to the marriage you arranged for me before I was born," I assure her, "And I could maybe even visit you there. But I have to stay here and make sure Earth and Axus stay separate."

Mom shakes her head. "I won't leave you. I can't. I've already put you through too much to have you go on alone as the only other being from Earth here."

"Thank you, Mom." I throw my arms around her, even if I'm unsure how her semi-apology is hitting me. "I hope I can convince the leaders of Underland to accept Alvar as their king." I don't have time to let her unsettle me. I'm a queen now with a husband to fight for.

"I'll stay and support you, but I'm afraid of him, Lucy, he's done horrible things," Mom admits.

"Good," I say, "You should be." And I enjoy one moment of seeing the shock on her face at my words before entering the great dining room where the leaders have gathered. Alvar is absent from the table, but I didn't expect him to be there.

This dinner is about my witness of who Alvar is. *Whatever that counts for.*

Everyone gets up from their seats when I enter as a sign of respect.

I try not to rush myself. I nod my head in approval the way Leeza instructed me is custom, and say, "Please be seated."

Fletch sits next to me, and I'm grateful to have him there as a bit of moral support. I notice Lord Vessin and Lord Calbir among those gathered, and my nerves start to get to me. I know among those two, Lord Vessin is the one who needs the convincing. I decide it is best to let us eat before discussing the future of Underland lest our hunger creates animosity.

After everyone is served and has had their fill, I rise and tap my goblet.

"I want to first thank you for coming to my table and sharing in a meal," I begin, I'm shaking with nervousness.

Maybe I'm not cut out to be queen after all.

I glance down at Fletch, who gives me an encouraging smile.

I take a deep breath and continue, "I don't know all your names yet, but I do know what Underland has been through. I can't imagine some of the horrible things that have happened to you and your families through difficult times. But I ask you to think of what happened after Alvar banished Saul, how peace settled on this land. How homes and towns were rebuilt, and how you'd picked yourselves up and built an even better country than before Saul conquered your lands. Some think Alvar is the root of all evil, that he is a Cursed and thus cannot rule." I pause, hoping I'm not saying everything too fast.

I notice Lord Vessin roll his eyes.

I ignore him, "I'm not here to convince you to change your beliefs. I—I'm here to convince you that what we need right now, more than anything, is someone powerful to protect us here in Underland. We need someone who intimidates our enemies and can liberate the oppressed people of Axus. Alvar is a good person and wants what is best, forgetting his interests in favor of yours. Saul may have been the enemy for a long time to Axus, but there are others out there who will never stop trying to destroy the peace. I cannot stress enough that even if Alvar isn't the ruler, he will protect you."

I stop there and notice a few people murmuring to themselves, so I raise my voice a bit as I state, *"But* if he is the ruler, he knows better than *anyone* how to keep evil away and what must be done to avoid corruption in our cities. Did he not lead you into victory against the tyrant queen, Remora, without using his Cursed form to command your respect? Did he not help you rebuild your homes and claim back the lives Saul stole from you? Did he not make peace with the other peoples of this world and restore order and freedom to live your own lives again? He appointed you all as leaders because he believed you are good people. He believed you had the same vision of making Underland into the best nation in this world."

Lord Calbir stands and places his arm across his chest and bows to me. "I've always loved my king, Alvar, and I will continue serving him if he were to continue on his throne."

"Thank you, Lord Calbir," I say, bowing back at him respectfully.

"What of your children?" Lord Vessin speaks up. "If we were to let this *noble* monster continue his rule, we cannot let our heirs be as he is! A Cursed is unpredictable and easily corrupted by their abilities."

"Then a non-Cursed heir will take the throne after Alvar and Lucy's rule," a voice says from behind me. I recognize it, but only until I turn around do I realize it came from Sola. She stands beside me in the doorway of the great dining room.

I bow to her respectfully. "I did not think you'd be able to come. It's such a great distance."

"Thank you, Queen Lucy," Sola says, raising her wings in greeting and bowing back at me. "I am glad you called me to this meeting. As ruler of the Skylands and your friend, I pledge my allegiance to you and Alvar as the respected rulers of Underland. You will have two children. One will be like you, Queen Lucy, and the other like King Alvar, one with his red eyes."

My spine tingles, and I flush. Sola's telling me the truth. I know how her gifts work.

Alvar and I will have children.

"Once your heir comes to the age of twenty-five, as is tradition, they will be judged by the council here whether they are worthy to succeed you," Sola explains to me, her wings fold back, and she walks over toward where Lord Vessin sits. "Lord Vessin, Alvar has ruled these lands for years without your objection. He has never used his Cursed state to take advantage of any of you, though he could have. And I will tell you this, from what I can see in the future, there is nothing to worry about in taking Alvar as your king once again and letting him resume his duties in serving you. In fact, it would be better to have him than to send him away."

I'm beaming with appreciation at Sola. To have her, a well-respected leader behind Alvar and me, is building my confidence and giving me peace of mind. Beautiful to know a morally inclined person that can see the future thinks we're going to make great rulers. I'm trying not to let it get to my head.

"We must forge a weapon that can kill a Cursed," Lord Vessin states, although I can tell his expression is softer as he rises from his seat. "We must not be defenseless again."

"To do what you ask is not going to be easy, and may even be impossible," Sola says, she closes her eyes and focuses as if deep in thought, "But I understand that desire and I am in favor of it. I'm sure Alvar will be in favor of it as well."

"Who is in favor of taking Alvar and Lucy as our king and queen once again?" Lord Calbir asks.

"I may not like it, but I admit Sola has always spoken the truth, if she says they will produce a child without ill effects," Lord Vessin shoots me a look as he says this, "Then they shall. And I shall expect such a child to come into this world soon."

I try not to look annoyed, but I am, and I flip my gaze to the ground to hide it.

"That is the queen you are speaking to," Lord Calbir snaps, "Show some decorum."

"I'm sorry, your *majesty*," Lord Vessin mutters at me with a glint in his dark eyes that makes my skin crawl. "I spoke out of place."

The meeting finishes, with miraculously only a few dissenters.

I know I have to tell Alvar, so after it seems polite, I take my exit.

As I walk to report the good news to my husband, I get a strange feeling, as if something isn't right.

It's because I'm alone in the hallway walking toward Alvar's quarters, and I realize Grey hasn't been watching out for me since the incident in Alvar's bedroom.

Someone's hand wraps around my wrist from behind right before I reach Alvar's door and yanks me down to the floor.

"Hush, my queen, hush," a man's voice hisses at me as I struggle and scream against the hand stuffed in my mouth, "You won't have to worry about Sola's prophecy coming true when it's my baby you'll be carrying."

FORTY-FOUR

"What is it that this Cursed sees in you? Anyone can see he's obsessed with you," my captor grumbles.

It's Lord Vessin, and he has me pinned facedown to the tile floor.

I struggle against him, but it hurts; the floor is cold and hard. I hit one of my elbows painfully and bump my chin.

Besides our fight, the halls are too quiet. No one wants to go near Alvar's room. The corridors are unlit also. The lighting in this area is still out because of the fire from when Alvar killed Saul.

Oh, where are the guards?

Lord Vessin tears my gown from my shoulders. "Such finery doesn't belong on such an ordinary Earth woman," he taunts me.

I bite his hand. Hard.

He yelps and pulls it from my mouth, and I take that chance to scream, but only for a second as he stuffs something made of cloth in my mouth to quiet me.

"Bitch," he spits out the word, "Are the women from Earth as dull in bed as they look?"

I'm not giving up. I fight hard, kicking, thrashing, and shoving away from him. Lord Vessin is stronger and bigger than me, but he's nuts to think I'll let him take me without using every ounce of my energy to stop him.

"You think that because you married Alvar, that gives you the right to be the queen of Underland? That gives you power over someone like me? You'll have my child, and my child will be on the throne instead of his. A child that didn't come from Cursed seed."

I gaze longingly at Alvar's door.

So close, and yet so far away...

"Ah, I see you're thinking the Cursed husband you whore yourself out to is going to come and help you," Vessin mocks. "No, he's flying about in his monster form. He won't be back in time to save you." Vessin's breath is hot against my neck as he whispers in my ear, "Shush, my queen, don't worry, I won't take long. And once I'm finished, you won't tell anyone this happened because they will all see it as weakness, and we can't have weakness as the representative of our queen. And you won't want Alvar to find out either. We all know he's obsessed with you because you're pure, unlike him."

"I'll have you as many times as I want because I have access and power. Do you think it's a surprise your guard isn't with you? I bribed him. I was born here and have fought to have a place in this nation, unlike you. I don't want to do this, but it must be done to ensure an Underland *human* succeeds the throne."

My heart is pounding in my head as I try to think my way out of this.

My hands are held behind my back by both his hands. But he switches to using one hand to undo his belt, and I take that as my opportunity. Using all my strength, I thrust my hands from his grasp, place them underneath me, and although he's sitting on my thighs to keep me down, I push up, so I buck him off of me. I scramble to my feet, knowing I'm bloodied and bruised at this point from hitting the tile, but I somehow run in the direction of my quarters, praying someone will be there.

I tear the cloth from my mouth and scream, but just as I see lights at the end of the hall indicating I'm near the lights of the gallery, one of Vessin's legs kick the back of my knee, forcing me to fall, hard and painfully on the tile floor.

I see Grey out of the corner of my eye.

"Grey, help me!" I cry.

"You know this needs to happen, Grey." Vessin overpowers me and holds my wrists to the floor while using his body weight to keep me down. "She won't stop fighting, but she needs to see reason. Help me hold her."

"Grey!" I scream.

"You'll have to do it yourself, Vessin," Grey tells him, and then he looks me in the eye. "You married a Cursed, Lucy. We can't have a Cursed heir, go with him," he somberly says.

What is wrong with these people?

I'm suddenly filled with the desire to go back to Earth, where people don't want to rape or kill me because I'm the wife of Alvar. After my perceived victory in the great dining room, I am shattered by those whom I thought I could trust, those who were entrusted with keeping me safe.

"You won't get away with this, Grey," I seethe at him, "You're despicable."

"Lucy," Grey says, turning his gaze from me. "I'm sorry. It's the best way. We can't risk a Cursed on the throne again. Alvar killed my parents while Saul ruled." I watch horrified as he walks away, letting Vessin drag me by my hair into a darkened room of the palace and throw me to the floor.

Something cracks in my arm, and pain sears into my shoulder.

"What are you doing?" A female voice shouts as he's shutting the door behind him.

"None of your concern," Vessin says, "it's business of state, sylph." He slams the door in her face and bolts it.

"Queen Lucy!" It's Leeza, and I hear her pounding on the door as Vessin looms over me.

"Leeza, get Alvar!" I scream to her. "He's going to hurt me!"

Vessin glares at me, his hair is disheveled, and clothes are torn. On his face is a crazed expression. Eyes bulging from his skull, face red, mouth twisted in a wicked grin. "I guess I underestimated Earth women."

"Just let me go," I choke out the words, pretty sure with the sharp pang in every breath that one of my ribs is cracked.

"I can't do that. I have to finish what I started," Vessin laughs. "You've got me too excited not to finish. Now I do want you. Going to find out what that Cursed enjoys about you so much."

I'm going to throw up. I know I am since this man disgusts me to my core, much like how Saul disgusted me.

"Elias sees your evil," I state, not sure exactly what I am talking about here.

"Shut up, bitch, you know nothing of our faith."

"I know enough to know that Elias sees your evil," I repeat it. Not sure what I'm doing, but realize I need to get under his skin somehow and gain some time. This Deity, Elias, I'd heard sounds compassionate and kind, at least from the viewpoint of Lord Calbir.

"Don't you understand? I'm not religious. I call on the name of Elias to gain support from those of faith, not because I believe any of that crap," Vessin snarls. "Now, rollover, so I don't have to look at your ugly bruised face."

I glare up at him, not moving an inch, challenging him, and letting him know that while my body may be broken, my spirit isn't nor will it ever be.

I want to go home, a small voice says inside me, even though I'm showing defiance. *I want to be safe again.*

The door is broken open, letting light stream in the room. Vessin turns and finds himself face to face with Alvar standing in the doorway.

"Scum of Axus," Alvar growls, his skin is contorting and changing, "You shall know what it is to die at the hands of a Cursed!"

Vessin shrieks in terror. "No! Don't kill me, foul demon!"

"Alvar, no!" I shout. I have to stop him from killing my attacker, even though I don't want to. "Don't kill him."

Alvar has Vessin by the neck, the unnatural strength from his Cursed blood apparent as he holds the man a foot off the ground with one hand.

"Don't kill him. Use him as an example. He must have a trial. You must not use your Cursed abilities to kill a leader." I can't believe I'm thinking like a diplomat in a moment like this.

"He deserves to die," Alvar hisses out the words, glaring at Vessin as if on the verge of transforming into his more terrifying form.

"He wasn't going to kill me," I state, although I felt like he was going to kill me.

"Fine, a trial," Alvar says through clenched teeth, blood irises never leaving Vessin's anguished face. "Leeza, get me the guards."

"Grey was a part of it," I hurriedly added.

"What?" Alvar's eyes widen and face pales. He sets down a choking Vessin.

"Vessin paid him off so Vessin could produce a human blood heir through me," I explain. *How am I doing this so calmly and rationally?* My body is numb. I can't even feel the pain anymore.

"Did he—?" Alvar asks, his brows drawing together in a knot of rage and fear for me.

"No, he didn't rape me," I say, the words dropping like a weight.

But that doesn't mean I don't feel violated by him.

Some guards appear, and they show Vessin to, I don't know, a dungeon? But I don't care.

At least Alvar is here with me, I'm safe, and Vessin is gone.

Alvar approaches my crumpled form and kneels next to me. "You need my blood." He bites into his wrist and draws some blood, smearing it over my wounds.

"Alvar, I want to go home."

"You *are* home," Alvar soothes, and I flinch as he caresses my cheek. He withdraws quickly. "My poor sweet girl."

"I'm *not wanted* here," I sob.

FORTY-FIVE

"Lucy, I'm here," Alvar says, lifting me and carrying me to my room. His strong arms wrapped tenderly around me are comforting and help me fight the remainder of my panic off. "You're safe now. You're safe."

I'm safe with him. Breathe, Lucy.

"I'll stay with you as long as you need me to, love. I promise he'll never hurt you again," he soothes, his voice husky and cracked in quiet rage at Vessin's attack.

"I can't stay here, Alvar, no one wants me here. I'm going to--to *fail,"* I murmur, I'm not sleepy, but the adrenaline and injury have exhausted me. My body is healing because of Alvar's blood.

"I can't keep you here if you don't want to stay. I can send you back to Earth. But, Lucy, *I* want you here, I want you here to stay with me," Alvar says, his voice choking up. "I promise I will protect you. You didn't fail, Lucy, you changed Underland forever! When I think of what almost happened... It's my fault! I was so wrapped up in the stress of all this that I didn't think about—"

"Don't blame yourself!" I start to cry. "Alvar, I—I'm not innocent the way you wanted me to be anymore. Why are you taking care of me?"

"By Arlite, girl, you're an angel! Did you leave me when you found out about Saul and his treatment of me?" Alvar asks quietly.

"No, I'd never leave you for that!"

"So, why would I leave you for this?" Alvar asks, his expression pained, "If you want to leave, I won't blame you. You shouldn't have to feel unsafe. If we can't keep the queen safe in her own house... We're going to have to change the staff. I was an idiot for not thinking this through. I forgot how many still have a prejudice against the Cursed. It's obvious we need to find guards we can trust. This example of Lord Vessin will be important to change things. You told me to stay, so I'm staying. I heard you convinced a room full of our leaders to keep me as their king. Others may fail, but you, Queen Lucy, despite everything thrown at you in life, you prevail." He pauses and sets me down on my bed, tucking me in as if I were a child. "Leeza was the one who found me. She flew out of the window as soon as she saw what was happening. If it wasn't for her--I--I don't want to think about it." Alvar shakes his head and shudders.

How lucky I am that Leeza was willing to put aside her prejudice to help. I can just picture her, flying headlong toward the thing she feared most just to save me.

Bless her.

Guilt sits on my shoulders when I think how I had been so angry with her on being judgmental of Alvar. I squeeze my eyes shut. *Oh, Leeza, thank you!*

"Lucy, I'll be staying by your side at all times until we get a good security staff," Alvar promises. "Unless you still want to go home?"

It's as if what happened with Vessin is a bad dream now, but as I close my eyes, I see Vessin's evil leering gaze at me. I sit up and grab hold of Alvar's arm and whimper, "Please. Stay with me."

"Always, love," Alvar assures me, getting into the bed fully clothed and holding me close to him. Alvar's warmth and the sound of his breathing lull me to sleep.

*

I don't do much the next week. I stay in my room. I take lots of baths. The only people I let see me are Leeza and Alvar. I don't know why, but I don't want to face my mother yet. She wanted me to leave Alvar, and if I had listened to her, none of the crap with Vessin would have happened.

Alvar enters the room, and I stay under the bubbles as I take another bath. There is concern written on his features. He notices me, and I can tell he also sees I'm naked, but doesn't want to say anything because of what happened with Lord Vessin. We haven't had sex since the incident, and I know Alvar is just giving me time, but I'm starting to be afraid it's something more.

"We're leaving for the ocean," Alvar announces to me, "It could bring you some healing."

"I'm fine," I hurriedly say, wrapping my arms around my knees and hugging them to my chest while in the bath. I don't know why, but the water soothes me and keeps the frightening memories at bay. I've been through a lot. I know I have, but I want to be resilient. "Is his trial soon?" I ask.

"You don't need to worry about that. There were enough witnesses. Grey also is standing trial."

I cast my gaze downward at the water.

"He was technically an accomplice to your assault, Lucy, I will not have him go unpunished."

"Your physical injuries may have healed, but that's not what I'm worried about," Alvar says, walking over to my bath and leaning over the ledge. "Let's get you a change of scenery. It hasn't just been Lord Vessin that has shaken you up. It was what you went through with Saul and everything you've experienced since coming here. It's understandable if you want to go back to Earth."

"I can't go back to Earth because you're not there," I say, shaking my head. "I love you, Alvar. I can't go back to Earth because I love Axus and Underland and want to see it prosper. I can't go back because I want to have your babies."

Alvar raises his eyebrows. "You do?"

"Yes," I whisper, my eyes glassy as I gaze at him. My husband. "So take me to the ocean, Alvar."

"I'll arrange to have the SkyWave take us tomorrow," he says, his face brightened, and he turns to leave me.

"Alvar," his name leaves my lips a bit louder than I'd wanted it to be.

He stops and turns. "Yes?"

"Want to join me?" I uncurl myself, letting him see my body. I'm not sure if I'm crazy to be feeling this after such an attack, but I want my husband's arms surrounding me once again. I long for it.

"If you're sure you want to?" Alvar says, unbuttoning his shirt and shrugging it off his muscular shoulders.

"Yes, I love you," I murmur, why does he always have to be so freaking amazing? "Are you sure *you* want to?" I toss back at him.

"I love you," he says with an adorable grin. "More than anything in the world, Lucy."

"What about in my world?" I say, unable to help a giggle.

"I love you *beyond* worlds," Alvar says.

Yes, this is home. It will always be home because I'm with Alvar.

EPILOGUE

The first sight of an ocean in Axus is breathtaking. The south sea is a shimmering blue-violet, and the sand shines in the sun white as snow. An emerald, tropical paradise stretches on the other side of the sand seemingly to infinity.

"I like you especially well on a beach," I tell Alvar, kissing his cheek with a grin.

Alvar and I walk hand in hand on the shore listening to the gentle waves and seabirds. After all that we've been through, our tranquility here is surreal to me.

"This world is still perilous, Lucy," Alvar tells me. "I cannot promise what the future will bring us here. There are still many prejudices to overcome. I can't change my past, and there are those who would wish me dead after all I've done. Entire countries in Axus are sure to be enraged by the fact that it is general knowledge I'm a Cursed."

"Let's not talk of the future, my love, let's just be here. Right now," I say, wrapping my arms around his mighty torso. We stop, gazing out at the horizon of the ocean, and I breathe in the salty air and smile. "Right now. It is pretty amazing."

*

Like Alvar had said, our trip to the ocean was a healing experience, and I had plenty of time to be alone with my husband there.

My husband.

I shiver with happiness every time I think about Alvar being my husband.

313

No longer is our marriage one of duty or cause. It's one of love.

A love that I thought I would never experience for myself.

In a way, we found ourselves on a real honeymoon at the ocean.

Alvar had us stay in his beautiful ocean-side castle, and it's like stepping into a real fairy tale. This castle has peaked turrets, whimsical staircases, and charming tropical gardens with colorful exotic birds flying overhead. I'm in love with it.

Alvar agrees with me that we shall stay at that ocean abode as often as possible.

Despite my more than shaky introduction to this place, I am comfortable with my decision to stay in Axus. There is more danger here, yes, but after Lord Vessin's and Grey's imprisonment, it was quite clear that Vessin acted on a personal vendetta rather than a group one. Grey apologized ardently, but Vessin refused to speak. Grey was sentenced to serve time in prison for his betrayal, and exiled from the palace forever. Vessin committed suicide before his sentencing. He left a note saying he'd rather die than serve a Cursed household.

My new personal guard is a stog male who stands seven feet tall with an immense crown of antlers coming from his skull. He has broad shoulders and black and red fur. He's the strong silent kind of person. However, I like him even though his intimidating appearance makes me jump if he enters the room unexpectedly. Alvar trusts him and has assigned me five more guards to accompany me wherever I go, so I feel safe.

Leeza still serves me faithfully, and we have become great friends. I trust her decisions with my wardrobe and personal needs completely. She's taught me a lot about Underland and Axus, too (like the fact that wearing bright purple in front of a gobli queen is a sign of disrespect, go figure).

As for my mother, I know we'll never have the ideal mother/daughter relationship I've always wanted. But, we're starting to figure out how to agree to disagree on some of our personal choices, and she's allowed herself to be happy.

Sometimes I miss Earth and miss those I've lost and left behind. But life has a way of finding you and sending you to places you never imagined, and I don't think that's a bad thing.

Alvar and I spend each day together. Although we have our points of difference or frustrations like any couple, we are in love, and our love and bond grow stronger every day. I know I have a lot to learn about Underland and Axus, but I'm determined that I can help make this beautiful and fantastical world a better place for its people.

I don't know what will happen in the future except that Alvar and I will have two children, which sometimes makes me nervous as I'm not sure when, if ever, I'll be ready for that. However, what I do know is that already Alvar and I have made a difference for our people.

As for our future...Our future is exciting and filled with possibilities, and for the first time ever we both <u>belong</u>.

READ BOOK 2 OF THE REDEMPTION SAGA,
DAUGHTER OF ALVAR

Like my father, King Alvar, I was born a Cursed... the first female Cursed in the history of my world.

That means my care-free twin brother, Kalvar, is destined to be the next heir to Underland's throne. Kalvar is celebrated and loved by the people, while I live as my people's shame, the freak with dragon wings, avoided by most... including any suitors.

However, with the kingdom weakened by my father's sudden disappearance, it becomes apparent that an old enemy has been waiting in the shadows for the perfect moment to strike.

Could it be a Cursed princess like me may be the only person capable of protecting the peace my father and mother risked everything to establish?

Excerpt from **Daughter of Alvar**

I lick my lips clean of blood and a deep purr settles in my throat. The beast is satisfied.

I've settled down on a hill overlooking the palace. The view is breathtaking, and a filmy mist has settled on the valley the palace in Underland City rests in.

I could paint a pretty picture from here, I muse, *but first, I need to go back to the party and see if I can't have my first dance with a partner who isn't doing it out of obligation my title.*

I spread my wings and return to the party, swooping back into the courtyard and shrinking into my human form as I do so. I pull up my underwear, and then pick up my dress, taking some time to smooth out the wrinkles from the hasty way I'd thrown it aside. I'd better hurry to get it on. It had been not very smart to have taken it off in such a public place.

"I was wondering where you'd wandered off to," a familiar voice says from behind me.

With a scream, I whirl around crossing my arms over my chest to cover my breasts. I know my eyes are glowing red from the scare, and likely my face is the same shade from embarrassment.

Here I am, naked, save the underwear I'd managed to pull on, and the handsome Rift is in the courtyard with me.

*Great, one chance I get to dance with a guy, and fate deals me **this** hand.*

"I like your wings," Rift says, "you shouldn't hide them under your clothes."

"You—you do?" my voice squeaks, and something inside me dances at those words

Rift turns around, "Go ahead and put your dress back on, I'm sorry for walking in on you."

"Thanks," I murmur, and hurriedly pull my dress up over my head and tuck my wings tight against my back so they don't show in the dress. "Okay, I'm decent now."

Rift turns around and smiles, he approaches me and squints at something on my face. "You've got blood on your chin."

Oh!

I gasp. I've never been more mortified.

Could this night get any more embarrassing?

My fingers go to my chin and rapidly swipe.

"Did I get it?" I ask, hopefully.

"I've got it," Rift says, his eyes flickering with playfulness. He licks his thumb and presses it over my chin, swiping over it a couple of times. The action feels more intimate than it should, and our eyes lock for a moment. His touch is gentle and I kick myself for being a little turned on by it.

"Do you always eat your meat raw?" Rift asks, having finished clearing my face of blood.

"Is that gross?" I ask, furrowing my brow in confused concern. I'm not sure if he's teasing me or disgusted.

"I still want to dance with you, does that answer your question?" Rift says with a nonchalant shrug, and extends a hand to me.

"We can't hear the music out here," I say.

"Do you want to go back into the great hall?" he asks.

"Who are you?" I ask, unable to help a giggle. Okay, this guy is handsome, charming, and non-judgmental. Is he even real?

"I told you already. My name is Rift," he says, cocking an eyebrow and grinning in mischievous challenge.

I resist the urge to give him a shove at his stubbornness. "I mean, where are you from, and why haven't I met you before?"

"I'm from Erlund, the son of a lord," Rift explains, "this is my first time in the southern lands. We were invited because your brother is marrying our princess."

"Ah," I say, "well, Lord Rift, shall we dance then?"

"Of course," Rift says, "It would be my pleasure."

I flush and take Rift's hand in my own, letting him lead me back inside the great hall. Once inside, we sneak in amidst the dancers. Rift settles a hand on my waist, and I rest my hand on his shoulder.

Good thing I've taken dancing lessons since forever, because I'm finally doing something right in front of this man! Rift appears to have had some schooling in the art of dance as well, because we swing and sway perfectly in rhythm to the lovely traditional Underland melody the musicians are playing.

As we dance I'm almost afraid to look up at my handsome dancing partner. It's unfortunate this is a one time thing. Rift will most likely need to return to the north after tonight, and all I'll have is this memory. A moment I had something romantic, albeit an embarrassing romantic something, with a handsome man.

"What are you thinking, Princess?" Rift asks me, his voice soft and thoughtful.

"I was thinking how much I wish you hadn't caught me half-naked in the courtyard. I'm embarrassed," I admit.

"Really? Because I was thinking how glad I am that I caught you half-naked in the courtyard," Rift whispers into my ear.

I laugh and gape a moment at him. "Sir, you make me question your morals!"

"Good," Rift says with a self-satisfied smile.

A shiver runs through me, this stranger intrigues me, and the act of flirting is a new things for me. I look up to study his features trying to decipher if he's serious or not.

Rift laughs, "Don't worry, Princess. I'm a gentleman. I shall take your secret to the grave."

"Well, that's good!" I say with a nervous laugh, "The last thing I need is rumors circulating of me naked in the courtyard while alone with a man."

The music ends and Rift takes me to the table with drinks and has a server pour us some wine. "Why aren't the men lining up to dance with you?" Rift asks. "They're a bunch of idiots."

"A bunch of cowards," I mutter, taking a sip of wine. "In case you didn't know, Rift, I'm a Cursed."

"Really? No!" Sarcasm oozes from his voice. "I'd have never guessed. I thought a pair of delightful dragon wings decorated all human women."

I give him a shove while also blushing. "You're messed up."

"You have no idea." Rift smiles another secret kind of smile and takes a sip of his wine. He gazes out at the partygoers, and his light-hearted face dissipates when something catches his eye. He turns to me and kisses my hand. "I'm sorry to leave you, Princess, but I'm sure we shall see one another again."

"Well, if that is the case, next time you can call me Kyla," I say, "All this 'princess' stuff is making me uncomfortable."

"I'll be sure to, Princess," Rift says, kissing my hand and giving me an impish grin. He bows to me and walks into the group.

I sigh as I watch him stride out of sight into the crowd, and my stomach is full of butterflies. I do hope I see him again.

I really do.

"Handsome devil, isn't he?" Elle interrupts my fanciful thoughts. "Who is he anyway?"

My sister-in-law stands next to me.

"Rift of Erlund. He's the son of a lord visiting because of Kal's marriage to Sylvia," I explain.

"That's weird," Elle says.

"What do you mean?"

"No one from Erlund is supposed to arrive until next week."

ABOUT THE AUTHOR

Silver Reins is a mother of two, writer, artist, and musician. She lives with her family and pets in Florida.

Author Website: www.silverreins.com

Follow her on Wattpad:
https://www.wattpad.com/SilverReins